REFLECTION
OF
FIRE

SACRED STONES BOOK ONE
REFLECTION OF FIRE

ANNALISE AZEVEDO

Reflection of Fire
The Sacred Stone Book One

Published by Ouroborus Book Services
www.ouroborusbooks.com

Cover Design by Sabrina RG Raven
www.sabrinargraven.com

Cover photo by Matheus Bertelli
instagram.com/bertellifotografia

CHAPTER 1

Laria Alfero was not a daydreamer by nature. But even while she remained seated on a hard chair, her chestnut eyes occasionally slipped out to the window, recognising the clouded sky was threatening rain. Her mind was preoccupied by the strangest sensation in her stomach – the same feeling she got when she was in the presence of fire.

She had only been a child when she discovered that she was afraid of fire. It wasn't like a natural fear that children possessed, but a phobia that sent fear shooting through her veins. As soon as she saw any sign of fire, her body locked up and terror crawled its way to her heart.

It was mystery to Laria what caused the fear. Sometimes she wondered if it had to do with her late father and that it was the way she coped.

She barely knew the man. He'd died when she was an infant – a time that Laria could never remember.

However, as her history teacher continued to explain the records of their small town, Golden Cliff, Wyoming, Laria leaned on the palm of her hand to consider his words. The strands of her dark brown hair brushed her tanned cheeks when the winds came through the screens.

Anyone who grew up in their town knew about the infamous massacre that resembled the Salem witch trials. The massacre was decades ago. People had been so afraid that they slaughtered each other.

Then, apparently, one woman changed everything.

Changing her focus back to the teacher, Laria shook her head and forced the fatigue to the back of her mind. While her history teacher, David Embers, did not care if she spaced out, it was Laria's responsibility to possess the knowledge for any exam.

'It was true that town founders were, in fact, Native Americans that migrated from Utah.' David was popular with his dishevelled, dirty blonde hair and stormy, grey eyes. His easy-going personality made an excellent impression on the school girls, but much to their despair he was happily married with a child. The man merely scratched his scruffy beard as he met eyes with Laria. 'We all know who they are, right?'

The history teacher was a decent guy; far closer to a friend than a mentor, but Laria knew that he liked to tease people; her especially for some odd reason. Everyone knew that her ancestors were a part of this town's foundation.

With a smirk, David turned to write the four names on the board. "Rosa", "Laurence", "Forte" and "Alfero" imprinted in the back of Laria's mind. They were the most common surnames in Golden Cliff, yet aside from Laria's mother and brother, she had never met another Alfero.

It was claimed that the Alfero family were considered "extinct" due to the brutal massacre. There was a possibility that some were out there, however Laria didn't care. She was nothing more than a cynical but dedicated teenager in a small town.

Her eyes narrowed into a sceptical glare, yet she wasn't surprised when she spotted her current neighbour lift her manicured hand. It was something that one of her friends would do in order to learn about the mysteries that were buried in the town.

'Mister Embers,' said the blonde with a charming smile on

her glossed lips. 'If the founders were Native American, then why were they given European names?'

Jenna Sommers was Laria's friend since first grade. Growing up in a small town, it was impossible to break the ties of friendship. It was clear that Jenna didn't fall in line with the stereotypical blonde girl. Her charm mostly came from her sweet personality and intelligence.

With innocent, chocolate coloured eyes, perky personality and intelligent outlook, it wasn't hard for the hormonal boys to fall for her. If it had been a story, Jenna would've been the perfect example of a Mary Sue appearance wise, however Laria knew better. Jenna had her flaws and made mistakes.

David moved his hand from his face and crossed his arms with a pensive expression. He considered it wisely. 'Golden Cliff was founded in a not so accepting time, so of course many Native Americans were forced to take European names in order to be accepted into society – except that didn't give much improvement. However, there could be a whole other reason to their decisions.'

The shriek of the school bell halted David's explanation and he raised a curious eyebrow towards his phone. His harsh stare towards his it was only for a moment, as he immediately glanced back at the class with a smile.

'That's enough for today class – I will see you tomorrow.' He dismissed his class and went through his files as Laria returned her books to her bag. She didn't realise Jenna had already finished her packing until the blonde started prattling about their plans after school.

It was the day to celebrate their friends' victory in basketball. It was their first week back and their friends were working hard for finals. For a normal person, anyone would've been nervous, but they were the two most confident people that Laria knew. While there were other sports they still played in, basketball was the town's favourite and sponsored the team known as the Sabres.

'You don't even know that they've won,' Laria said when she lifted her bag to her shoulder. Together they left the room after waving farewell to David and headed to their lockers. 'Besides I thought you were into football because of the vegetable quarterback.'

A scowl came from the other girl's pretty face. 'Laria.' It was a warning tone, however the brunette brushed off the scolding. 'Taro isn't as bad as you think. It's Sara that is the bad person – he just doesn't see it yet.'

And this was what Laria meant by flaws. 'Jenna, Taro Launten is a jerk full stop.' Out of all the people Jenna wanted to go out with, it was the popular school quarterback who was dating the school president. 'He's been a moron since second grade and he only got worse when we were freshmen. Sara just happened to get in the way and I'm not going to keep explaining how much I hate him.'

'You don't have to,' Jenna responded with a light huff. 'You and Maya just have to accept that I like him. Look – I wouldn't be mean to the guy you liked.' Unlike Jenna, Maya was a tomboy and outspoken. She played in the dirt without a care in the world and she was far more rebellious than the rest of Laria's small group of friends.

'Of course you wouldn't,' Laria muttered flatly. 'That's because Maya and I are horrible at the dating stuff. I still remember when you set me up with your cousin and I said that he had a decent sized forehead.'

'How could I ever forget? No normal girl comments on a boy's forehead in general!' Jenna exaggerated and raised a hand dramatically to her own forehead. 'I remember him telling me never to set him up with you guys again.' She sighed, her shoulders sagging. 'I suppose it would be for the best, he has a weird thing going on.'

Before Laria could respond, she flinched when a hand pressed on her shoulder from behind. 'Oh boy,' said a gruff voice and Laria grinned in recognition with anger forgotten. She tilted her head to the side, recognising the curly mop of cinnamon coloured hair and hazel eyes. 'Is Jenna talking about the human vegetable again?'

While Laria laughed, Jenna's cheeks went bright red in anger. 'Brodie Forte!'

He laughed and scratched the back of his head. 'Sorry Jen, I can't help myself teasing you. Anything that makes you blush is worth it.' He turned to Laria and flashed the boyish smile that she couldn't help but return. 'I see that you awoke the dating dragon.'

Brodie Forte had been Laria's friend since they were in diapers. Apparently, his father Leon worked with her father before they were born. However, it was through her mother Lesley that they managed to keep close.

His face glistened with sweat from the humid air and Laria recognised his black jersey with a red logo of a sabre tooth tiger. His shorts were replaced by regular sweats however, as if he was uncomfortable walking around in pants that didn't reach his knees.

'I see that you're back alive,' Laria replied before squinting her eyes and leaned towards his face. 'No bruises, so it's safe to say that Maya didn't peg the ball at you in frustration. So you won.'

The smirk twitched on Brodie's face. 'Yep – she's absolutely terrifying when it comes down to motivation.'

Jenna squealed and raised her hands to her mouth. 'That's amazing Brodie! So where did Maya run off to anyways?' While both Maya and Brodie played basketball, it was Brodie who represented the team. Maya managed to remain as the coach's aid – mostly succeeding when it came down to yelling.

'She said she wanted to meet us there,' Brodie replied with a light shrug. 'I'm guessing that she wanted to meet up with Seth.'

Laria's smile dropped at the thought of the boy. Seth Laurence. While Laria didn't hate him like she did with Taro, it was hard to connect with Seth. He gave off a vibe to everyone that he didn't want to be disturbed. But it was hard to understand Seth, especially since the most that Laria knew about him was that he was a friend of Maya's and that he wanted nothing to do with society.

Laria shook the thoughts of Seth away and replaced her frown with a determined grin. It wasn't about Seth, but at the end of the day he was still friends with one of hers. 'Alright – now that school's over we should head to the Silver Roots. Heather said that she had to go on ahead for something.'

'Okay,' Brodie agreed before looking at his jersey. He stopped the girls with an unsure mutter. 'But maybe I should get changed first – I'll probably get kicked out if I walk in like this.'

After waiting for Brodie to finish changing clothes, the trio settled in Jenna's old car with a satisfied sigh that they beat the storm. While the Silver Roots bar and grill wasn't far, rain had a habit of pelting heavily during the summer time.

Silver Roots was a common hangout for high schoolers and lone adults. It wasn't Laria's favourite place as she preferred less people, but it was good company for her friends when they needed to hang out.

Laria entered in first, with her pair of friends following her after their attempts at avoiding the rain. How they didn't slip and slide on the wooden floor was a mystery to her. She peered through the crowd, spotting a familiar face and smiled.

'Heather!'

The single brunette peeked her head up with a tender smile before shying back into her soda. Heather Verdas was a simple girl; with wavy, light brown hair that reached her shoulders, olive skin and hazel coloured eyes. She was gifted with her studies, attaining the top ranking of her class.

'Congratulations on your win Brodie,' Heather said softly. Despite her high-level intelligence, Heather was soft spoken and quiet. It was sometimes hard to understand what she was saying when crowds were busy.

'Yeah, I know,' Brodie responded with a boyish grin. 'But what we need is some drinks.' And Laria knew that he was going to turn to her. On cue, Brodie patted Laria's shoulder as she placed her bag on the table. 'Could you get me a drink Lil Ria?'

Great. That was back. 'I will if you don't call me that disgusting nickname.' It was a nickname that Brodie picked up after her older brother Chris had said it. Laria liked her name, but she hated it when people purposely mispronounced it.

'I'm sorry,' Brodie said despite not sounding apologetic.

It felt like an eternity when Laria turned away, giving a thumbs-up when Jenna asked for whatever Brodie was having. Laria headed to the bar after taking a mental note. She didn't fail to notice the woman with a black hoodie sitting by herself.

Laria avoided gazing at the stranger. Sometimes Laria saw her sitting alone, drinking her troubles away. Despite going to this place for as long as she could remember, nothing was known about the hooded woman.

A cheer for Maya echoed in Laria's ears and she turned briefly to spot the raven-haired female being hugged against her will by Jenna. Standing with them was a brunette male that Laria instantly identified as Seth.

Laria made a sharp turn towards the bar, however she felt her body hit something hard and she stumbled back. The wet floor made her feet slip and gravity didn't give her a chance to regain her balance, thankfully managing to catch herself on her hands and knees to prevent any twisted ankles.

In the background, Laria heard the bartender freaking out in fear of being sued.

Laria dismissed the voices and looked to see that she hadn't been the only one that fell. It wasn't a face that she recognised instantly, but there was something about it that gave her a sense of déjà vu. The male looked roughly her age, with dark, curly hair and blue eyes.

It took him a moment to compose himself before realising the situation. He had a mixture of panic and distress flashing in his facial features.

'I'm so sorry,' he said with a familiar voice and Laria shook her head to dismiss it. It wasn't right – she'd never met this stranger. 'Are you hurt?' By now, more people were looking at them, even Laria's friends, yet she didn't answer. 'Oh crap... I spilled soda on you.'

Instead she pushed herself back to her feet without his assistance and frowned in suspicion. Just who was he? She briefly looked at her white singlet to recognise the splash on her chest. She flushed in embarrassment and covered her chest with her arms – clumsy fool.

'Let me help you He began but Laria didn't want to hear it. Her first instinct was to snap at him for crashing into her; however, there was a voice in the back of her head telling her that it would be wrong to do so. 'Do you need my jacket or-?'

'I'm fine,' Laria cut him off curtly and walked around. He was still on the ground; Laria noticed the unbuttoned leather jacket that he was willing to offer her.

Finally, her eyes went to Brodie who seemed to frown at the fallen boy. Laria couldn't help but step away. To them, it looked like she was running in embarrassment, but in reality, she felt like she was running from something much more frightening.

Laria knew the exit at the back of the Silver Roots would give her some space. It surprised her that she wasn't bombarded with concerned friends; Laria preferred it that way.

Her thoughts were cut off by an ominous feeling. It was like something was watching her yet Laria couldn't make sense of it. Despite her instincts demanding her to flee, Laria wanted to investigate.

With a cautious step, Laria made her way towards the sound behind the dumpster. It was just weak echoes of moans and as she got closer the panic built in her chest.

I have to see what it is, she told herself firmly, clenching her fists to force away the nervous feeling in her gut. Something was telling her that misery was all over this alley, but there was something even deeper that seemed... intriguing.

As Laria finally got a view of the scene, she almost wished that she hadn't. She immediately ran towards the bleeding man as she called out for help. 'Hang on!' Laria demanded fiercely and her hands went over the man's chest to stop the bleeding. He was covered in bite marks, scratches and countless bruises. 'You'll be fine!' But she knew that she was lying to herself and the man; there were too many wounds for her to save him.

'You.' The man's voice made Laria take her gaze off the wounds to meet his eyes. She flinched when she saw that they were gold, but it was clearly her imagination. They were brown the next moment. 'The fire is strong in you... Alfero...' He coughed out blood, spraying it on Laria's soda-soaked shirt.

How did this person know that she was an Alfero?

'Hey! Stay with me!' Laria shook the man's body and gritted her teeth to stop herself from screaming. She didn't know this man, but she felt she had to be responsible for him.

'You can't die, please!' But it was already too late.

His laboured breathing settled, and he seemed to be at peace as he died in her arms. His eyes shut as his final breath left him. Laria began trembling.

Thunder cracked the sky and Laria heard a growl. She jolted at the sound peering over her shoulder to see something move in the shadows. Her eyes could barely catch the shape of it, let alone discover what the creature was. It was the only sign of life besides her. But just like that, the creature was gone, disappearing from her sight until it would strike the next time.

This world was filled with a lot more darkness than Laria was led to believe.

CHAPTER 2

The trail was dead.

Zanobi Adkins sighed to himself and pushed the black shades over his eyes. He hadn't been far away when he got the report that there was an animal attack. As soon as he got there, Zanobi knew it would become complex. Humans heard the commotion and hoped that they could take photos of the body.

'Did you find anything, Deputy?'

Recognising the cold voice of his superior, Zanobi turned towards the woman. She was short, even for a woman in her forties, with strawberry blonde hair tied in a complicated braid and grey eyes as hard as stone. With her badge attached to her belt, everyone knew who the stern woman was.

'Nothing Sheriff Cyler.' Zanobi's answer only angered the petite woman. But then again, it was hard to please Nadia Cyler. Slowly, he pulled away his shades to reveal his olive-green eyes and spared a glance towards the girl that was being comforted by her friends. 'Laria Alfero found the man barely alive.'

Nadia still didn't seem pleased. 'They always have to be involved in this mess.'

Running a hand through his curly, auburn hair, Zanobi scoffed, 'As Lucien's daughter – I'm surprised that she hadn't become involved sooner.'

'Did you notice anything odd about today?' the sheriff

questioned, and Zanobi looked back at the Laria Alfero. She was with Brodie, who had the same look as his serious father as he wrapped his arms around Laria. The Laurence boy was alone, scowling momentarily before turning away from the scene. In the background, the hooded woman was watching with awareness in her midnight coloured eyes.

Four of the true descendants were together.

'Do you think there's a Uniter in our midst?' Zanobi wondered, turning towards the sheriff with a raised eyebrow. 'One has not appeared in over a hundred years – why would one show up now?'

'Remember that their arrival is based on mental connection,' Nadia replied, swiping through her phone. 'If there is one, it could be any one of them that were in that bar. What we need is to find the Beast.' The Beast was a code name for the killer that had been attacking the town for months now.

'What would you have me do?'

'Give the body to Leon.' Nadia turned away swiftly. 'I will call the Mandati Dux. Another life and it was so close to human civilisation. I do not believe that the Beast cares.'

'Why would they?' Zanobi asked in return, looking to the spot where the hooded woman once was. She disappeared from his sight. 'But if what you say is true... then we might need to find the Uniter – we are unsure of his intentions after all.'

Nadia was about to reply, yet a voice cut her off.

'Laria!'

Laria's head snapped up with a startled yelp. 'Mum?!'

Lesley Alfero looked much like her daughter when it came down to the long brown hair but in her late-thirties, Lesley developed fine lines of age over her face. Her vibrant green eyes never left Laria.

'I told you I would come here as fast as possible,' Lesley said and embraced her daughter. Laria awkwardly patted back, but immediately the woman exchanged a glance towards Zanobi. 'Just wait a moment Laria.'

A frown formed on the girl's face, but she said nothing as Lesley grabbed Zanobi's arm and dragged him to move out of sight from the crowds. She clenched her hands tightly when they were alone.

'Zanobi.' Lesley's voice seemed soft as she spoke, but her green eyes were filled with a harsh determination. 'What happened?'

Zanobi's gaze didn't falter. 'Another shifter has been killed by the Beast. Surely the blood on your daughter's clothes gave you that much of an indication.' Lesley didn't flinch from his blunt tone. 'You realise what this means, right? Our friend is after the true descendants – meaning your daughter.'

'But I can't let Laria know about the bloodlust,' Lesley replied fiercely. 'She wouldn't believe me.'

'You're a witch; a witch from Salem to be exact. Can't you conjure up a simple spell?'

The woman scowled. 'My powers have been severely weakened since I left that life behind. I remember what happened with Chris and the fire.' Her eyes coated with an everlasting guilt. 'I couldn't let anyone come to attack her – not again.'

'You might have to tell her something,' Zanobi said firmly. 'Because the *sheriff* suspects there to be a Uniter in town.' Lesley's eyes briefly widened as she took in the sudden news. 'If there is one, then it's only a matter of time until your precious daughter will find out and it won't be the easy way.'

'May I have an opinion in this matter?' interrupted a new voice and Zanobi scowled when he recognised the smooth voice. Lesley's hard features softened upon of the arrival of their new guest.

'Haroni Ladas,' Zanobi responded with a heavy voice. His sarcasm added the tension in the air. 'What do we owe the pleasure?'

Their guest was a tall and lean man in a suit. His brown hair was short that had too much gel in it and brilliant, cerulean coloured eyes filled with centuries of wisdom. A twitch of a smile formed on his cleanly shaved face.

'Deputy, you do not sound pleased,' the man responded with a mere chuckle and Zanobi's eyes narrowed harshly. Everyone knew this man's face. Haroni Ladas; school students knew him as the older brother of their school principal Tracy Ladas. Humans knew him as the mysterious, rich man with women following his trail. Yet Zanobi's acknowledgment of the man was deeper than that and Zanobi loathed him.

'Don't stall, *Fallen*,' Zanobi snapped and Lesley merely frowned in concern. Of course, Lesley and Haroni were friends ever since she arrived into town, yet even she was a fool to not see the true face of the man. It was the way he drew people in, charming them with words and empty promises. He was not to be trusted.

'Now we're bringing out the harsh words,' Haroni answered casually, the smirk never leaving his face. 'I may have an idea to help dear Laria in her case of losing control.'

'What is it?' Lesley asked her attention no longer on Zanobi.

Haroni's eyes sparked with amusement. 'That my dear is a very simple answer.' He stepped towards the woman with a confident stride. 'Send her to Cheyenne to stay with her brother, Christopher. She will be away from your Beast.'

'No.' The woman shook her head. 'I couldn't put Chris in danger like that... not after the last time it...' A shred of sympathy went in Zanobi's chest as he saw guilt fill her expression.

'Besides it doesn't keep the Beast away from the other descendants,' Zanobi responded when he thought back to the three others. A sigh escaped him and Zanobi reached for his forehead to manage his incoming headache. 'The best we can do right now is find the so-called Uniter and make sure that no one besides the selected few of us finds out.'

Haroni merely raised his eyebrow, but he didn't respond. Knowing him, the man was most likely constructing a plan to go against them. However, Zanobi knew he had to act fast to find the Uniter – or else the next attack could be even closer.

***

'Brodie?' Laria noticed that he had his undivided attention on where her mother and the deputy were. At the moment, he appeared identical to his father, and Laria wanted to know more. How did Lesley and the deputy know each other?

Jenna, Maya and Heather had left, saying that they needed to head back before nightfall. Laria simply let them go. They were better off not knowing how she felt about the scenario.

But her mood dampened once she recalled the dying man in her arms. It was his blood that stained her hands and even though she didn't end his life, Laria felt like she should've done more. He could've lived if she had only been louder or faster. His dying words haunted the back of her mind.

The fire is strong in you... Alfero...'

Even when she was questioned by the police, Laria never gave them the final words that he said to her. For some reason, they were meant to be only for her ears. She didn't even have the courage to tell Brodie what she heard, and he was the closest one to her.

Speaking of her best friend, Brodie wrapped a comforting arm around her shoulder with concern in his gaze. 'Are you alright?'

Slowly Laria met his eyes and she couldn't help but think of the boy that spilled soda on her. If it hadn't been for him, then perhaps Laria would've never had to worry about the man dying in her arms.

Then again, she would've never heard the words that stirred something in the back of her mind.

'I'm fine.' Laria brushed Brodie's concern away, seeing her mother returning from where she'd dragged the deputy away. However, there was another face in the crowd that Laria knew that made her frown with suspicion.

Haroni passed the pair, winking. 'I will see you soon my dear.'

A scowl reappeared on Laria's face. Creep.

'Let's go,' Lesley said towards Laria and she offered a smile towards Brodie. 'Do you need a lift back to your house Brodie?'

'No,' he replied politely. 'Dad's on his way here. I'll be fine.' Lesley seemed convinced and Laria followed her mother towards the car, but not before she spotted the boy that crashed into her earlier. His brow furrowed as he looked between the scene and her, yet he remained beside a woman, one that Laria assumed was his mother.

There was something odd about the boy. Laria frowned again and kept a cold gaze on him, even when Lesley pulled out of the car park.

***

The sky cleared up for the night, but Laria's thoughts weren't as lucky. Her body fell on the bed from exhaustion and she was asleep in an instant. Yet even in her unconscious state, her mind was flashing with images. Once Laria found herself in the plains, she knew that she was dreaming. This place was something she could only recall while sleeping.

It was always beautiful. The plains were vast and the

forests surrounding the plains seemed endless. There were lakes, rivers and smooth hills, and the sun above her settled nicely in the sky, allowing the warmth to soak her skin.

This world was a world that Laria felt like she belonged in.

It was in the next second that Laria saw the boy that bumped into her at the bar. He wasn't facing her, yet Laria recognised his leather jacket flapping in the wind. Something nudged her hand and she looked down to see a flash of red tangled in her fingers.

Red string?

The string dangled through her fingers and floated with the wind, but the strangest part was the green glow. Laria's eyes narrowed and lifted the string for a better view. What could that mean? Laria looked back at the boy and noticed that the red string was being held by him.

And just like that the boy was gone, replaced by a field of fire. Despite it not being real, Laria could feel the heat against her skin and she froze with fear. It destroyed everything in its path, consuming the once pure grass around her.

'Misery,' whispered a familiar voice and Laria turned around only to step back with shock. It was like staring in a mirror. The doppelganger of Laria merely raised a brow, looking towards the flames with a sneer. Amber eyes replaced the chestnut. 'Fire causes misery. That is who we are.'

And just like that, Laria wrenched herself from sleep. The cold sweat clung onto her body like a second skin, yet she didn't focus on the sweat. Her body trembled, trying to shake off the feeling that she just stared at death in the eye.

Whatever her dream was, it certainly felt like it was reminding her of the dying man's message.

CHAPTER 3

'Wake up or you're going to be late.'

Hearing the familiar voice, the dark-haired boy let out an exhausted moan and pulled the blanket over his head. Standing by the door was a woman with the look of age on her pale face. She crossed her arms over her chest, narrowing her bright blue eyes as her black wavy hair bounced around her shoulders.

'Jason.' This time the woman spoke in a warning tone. She strolled silently to the end of his bed and tore the blanket off his body.

'Damn, it's too early...' Jason voiced his thoughts out loud, rubbing his eyes, the same blue as the woman's. 'This whole fresh-start thing is not going to work if you wake me up like that Mum.'

The single mother, Mae Amarel, gave a threatening glare. 'Jason, you and I both know that moving was the best option. Come on, you're nearly eighteen – you should start acting like it.'

As Jason pulled himself up from the messy bed, his eyes met with his mother's stern glare. 'If I started acting my own age, I would be drinking and partying like every other teenage moron.'

'You do party and drink Jason,' Mae corrected as she turned and walked away before Jason could retort to her statement. As Jason huffed to himself, he heard her voice. 'Hurry up and get dressed before I send you to school half naked!'

Jason looked down to see that his torso was bare, his shirt

taken off in his sleep due to the heat of the night. He ran his hand through his curly hair, brushing it back as he took in a deep breath.

New start. At the moment it didn't felt like much – after his first night in this strange town there was already a death. A death that probably would've been discovered later if he hadn't bumped into the girl.

'*Jason!*' Hearing Mae's voice cry out made Jason shake his head out of the clouds and let out a heavy sigh of exhaustion.

Getting dressed was easy. He threw on a pair of black jeans and a grey shirt for the day. Jason went out of the room and greeted his mother again.

'Ready for breakfast Mum,' he announced with a goofy grin.

After an intense stare, Mae gave up. 'You look a lot like your father,' she said, chuckling softly and she gestured the cabinet. 'Go make cereal, I'm too lazy to make you breakfast.'

An action that Mae missed was the fact that Jason had stiffened automatically. He had never met his father, but Mae had always spoken about him as if he was a good person – this instantly angered Jason.

But he brushed it away, like always. Instead, Jason sourly grabbed some cereal to feast on. He didn't want to think about his old life. The people back in the city were convinced that he belonged with them, like a cult. As usual, Jason wolfed down the cereal that he poured for himself and finished preparing for the day.

When he was ready for school, Mae took one critical gaze towards him before she frowned at an observation. She reached up to play with his curly hair. 'You really need a haircut Jason.'

'Nah,' Jason replied as he brushed past Mae. 'I like my hair like this – it's better than the short hair in my opinion.'

Mae rolled her eyes before she allowed him to exit the building. 'Whatever you say kiddo – don't blame me if kids start beating you up because your hair looks girly.'

'It doesn't look girly,' Jason retorted.

Mae rolled her eyes again and smiled jokingly. 'Whatever you say, girly hair.'

Jason didn't remove his scowl. 'You're my mother, you're not meant to tease me.'

She chuckled and said, 'Well, you know better than anyone that I like to break traditions.' Finally, Jason removed his scowl, huffing quietly as he headed to the car and allowed Mae to drive him to school. The drive to the school campus was quiet, but Jason stared out of the window to see the numerous trees off the side of the road.

Jason felt nervous as the car parked and he sighed when Mae cut the engine. 'Thanks Mum, I can handle it from here.'

'I know you can,' Mae replied with a faint smile. 'I'll pick you up from here.' She showed a smile, before she patted Jason's shoulder with confidence. 'Try to not get any boys flirting with you because of your girly hair.'

'Oh, ha ha,' Jason retorted sarcastically as he opened the back passenger door and grabbed his bag. 'You're funny.' He closed the door and waved goodbye as she drove away.

His nerves returned, but he confidentially looked towards the school building. He couldn't let Mae down today; she had to pull a lot of strings to get him into this school. She had to leave her life behind in order to move.

There were some things that haunted him. Back then he didn't have many friends. It wasn't that he didn't try, but rather he couldn't. He stayed away from prying eyes, focusing on his study. Through studying, Jason managed to raise his grades and tolerate the strange looks he received from others.

Pushing the past into the back of his mind, Jason stepped

into the front office, and the first thing he noticed was the receptionist. She had her attention on the computer, but she managed to eye him with a polite smile as he approached her.

Before Jason could introduce himself, the receptionist spoke, 'Jason Amarel?'

'Do I stick out that much?' Jason wondered with a sheepish grin.

'It's a small town and most of us recognise a new student when we see one,' the woman replied, pulling out a few papers to hand to Jason. 'I'm Kylie Andrews.' Jason raised an eyebrow suspiciously as he accepted the paperwork. 'That's your timetable, a map of the campus, your locker code and pretty much everything you need.'

'Thank you,' Jason replied awkwardly and looked at the paperwork. 'I hope you have a nice day.'

Kylie smiled again. 'Thanks Jason. I hope you do too.' Just as he turned around, Kylie called out his name to get Jason's attention. 'Welcome to Golden Cliff High.'

'Thanks,' he replied, leaving the front office and heading to the school building. It wasn't a large building and there weren't many people pouring through – well not compared to his previous school. Looking around the doors to find his room number, Jason felt stares on him.

They probably recognised him as a newbie. Either that or Mae was right, he did have girly hair for a guy. Checking his timetable once again, Jason saw that his first class was his Math class. It didn't take him long to find the room that he was searching for, and he walked in without another word.

The teacher, that was sitting by her desk, looked up with her bright green eyes before she quickly noticed who she was talking to. 'I'm glad that you came to this class Jason,' she announced, pushing herself to her feet to shake the boy's hand. Jason awkwardly smiled back but steeled his confidence and showed the woman his timetable.

'Thanks, I guess.' Jason felt foolish that he was the new kid and didn't know what to say in front of this teacher.

'I'm Teah Kenta.' She allowed Jason to take a seat. 'Anyway – the rest of the class should be here soon.' He nodded simply and took a seat at the front corner, glad that the teacher wasn't going to tell him where to sit. As soon as he sat, he pulled out a single book and pen so that he could jot down notes.

Soon enough, the students poured themselves into the classroom and saw Jason with shock in their eyes. He wanted to hide from them, uncomfortable at the attention from the other people.

But not everyone cared apparently.

The last student to enter the room was the only one that didn't take an interest in Jason. His chocolate brown eyes held no muse as he took his seat in the back. Jason turned back to the final student with a curious frown. He appeared withdrawn, with short brown hair and an unreadable expression.

It didn't take a genius to figure out that he probably noticed Jason but didn't really care. But still, there was something about him that felt... odd.

'That's Seth Laurence,' said the classmate beside him. 'Doesn't talk much – he sits at the back of the class and doesn't have any friends.'

'That's not true,' another muttered. 'Remember that Maya Rosa chick? She's started hanging out with him before the break.'

'Maybe they're dating,' the first replied casually before he went back to listening to the teacher.

Jason still kept his eyes on the silent boy, questioning if this Seth really was a good or bad person. Normally people who kept their distance away from other students ended up being psychotic.

Jason was startled when the brunette shot a glance at him. There was something about his dark eyes, unreadable yet filled with knowledge. He couldn't tell what it was, but the boy just gave off a mysterious aura.

A smirk had flashed on the boy's face, before he returned his attention to the board. Jason felt uneasy at Seth's smirk, but he looked back towards the board when it disappeared and was replaced with a serious frown.

Miss Kenta had greeted the class and gave a brief reminder on Jason being the new kid. He was glad that he didn't have to do an introduction. The teenager barely listened to what the teacher had to say, watching her write equations on the board.

Jason saw Seth in the corner of his eye. Seth had been quiet – just like his neighbour had mentioned to him earlier, but he wasn't writing anything down.

Before Jason could turn to confirm the information himself, the bell rang, and the students immediately packed their equipment. Jason flinched at the sudden noise, but he regained his composure and he followed the other students.

'Now remember class,' Miss Kenta continued with a smile, 'do your homework.' She waved her hands and allowed the class to leave for their lunchbreak. It seemed that the school allowed one first small class, a big break and three final classes before leaving for home early. It wasn't too bad, Jason realised. At least he would be back home sooner.

Jason spent his first lunch on his own, getting familiar with the landmarks and occasionally checking his phone. He didn't know why, but the feeling of Mae calling kept his motivation for looking at the device. Every time he pulled out his phone, he felt a flip of disappointment upon realising that Mae had yet to call him. He looked up and a shudder escaped him as he recognised the football players with cheerleaders by their sides.

The lunchbreak went quicker than he hoped, and Jason was on his feet again fumbling for his timetable. He was roughly pushed out of the way at times and Jason took the chance to find a decent spot to read.

These students are so impatient, he thought, looking around when he found a spot to look through his timetable to read what he had next. Since it had been Math first, he would have–

'The English room as at the other end of the hall.'

Hearing the deep voice, Jason wildly turned to see Seth Laurence standing behind him with a mask of empty emotion. For a moment, Jason's eyes went down to read the timetable to prove that he did indeed have English next. The boy's dark eyes met with Jason's, recognising the uncomfortable feeling in his chest.

Slowly, Seth showed the familiar smirk. 'I'm Seth Laurence – welcome to Golden Cliff High.'

Jason was too stunned. Didn't the classmates say that he didn't talk to anyone?

Seth's smirk dropped and Jason wondered if he said his thoughts out loud. 'You should really ignore what people say when it comes to gossip.' He didn't appear to be angry – his expression was empty. 'It's a noisy place here and I dislike it.'

Before Jason could reply, Seth had already turned around and left him standing alone. That was strange. Seth was just complicated to figure out. Jason recovered from his shock, moving out of the way from some people only to bump into another.

However, Jason managed to knock this person off their feet. He reacted immediately and grabbed their arm as they looked at him. 'Sorry.'

His eyes instantly registered the face; long brown hair, chestnut eyes and pensive features. Jason couldn't believe his luck. The same girl that he crashed into the day before was in front of him and recognition sparked in her gaze.

'You.' Her voice was low, but not angry.

'Sorry,' Jason replied, and he realised what he had said. 'I mean... again – sorry for bumping into you... two days in a row.'

It took the girl a moment to compose herself and Jason wondered what she was thinking. After all, she was the one that was humiliated the day before and found the dead body. Jason couldn't help but feel sorry for her.

'It's fine – this place is crowded and yesterday I wasn't paying attention,' the girl finally answered before her features settled. A sigh of relief escaped Jason's lips. Good. One thing his mother taught him was to never anger a woman since the consequences were dire. 'So, you're the newbie?'

'Does everyone know about me?' Jason asked with a chuckle, scratching the back of his neck nervously.

The girl chuckled. 'Just a few of us care.' Her laugh made him briefly smile and she added, 'Laria Alfero.' She raised her hand for Jason to shake and he was completely stunned by the introduction. Here he thought that she would've hated him for crashing into him.

'Well, I'm Jason...' he introduced himself, slowly accepting Laria's handshake. Her hand was tiny compared to his and it felt comforting. 'Jason Amarel.'

'So what class do you have next?'

If anyone knew this school, it would be this girl. 'Got English next with some Paul Hunt fellow.'

'What are the chances? Me too,' Laria replied with a smile. 'He's a decent guy – smart when it comes down to poetry which is good because I'm hopeless at that stuff.' She led Jason towards the room. He felt comforted that she was okay with him knocking her off her feet. 'Have you met anyone that you would hang out with?'

'Well, I met a few people,' Jason answered calmly. 'Including this guy, Seth Laurent or something...'

Laria halted her movements to look towards Jason. 'Seth Laurence?'

'Yeah.' Jason scratched his ear nervously. 'Do you know him?'

'Not really – just in one of my classes,' Laria answered as she calmed herself and began leading again. 'One of my friend's talk to him as well. He's... hard to read.'

So, it wasn't just him that felt that way about Seth? In a way, Jason was glad. 'Okay,' Jason replied with half a smile. 'I will be suspicious of him if he's offering me candy and a free ride in his van.'

The female turned back to face Jason with a smile. The signs of distress from the day before were gone, much to Jason's relief. 'You better.' They entered the room together, and Laria gestured towards the old man filing through the work. 'Anyways – go talk to the teacher and come sit by me if you want.'

As she went to her desk, Jason looked towards the elderly man that was apparently his new teacher. With a frown, Jason went to show the timetable and allowed the man to check it. In the corner of his eye, he saw that Laria was sitting in the front row and unpacking her bag

'Welcome to Golden Cliff High my name is Paul Hunt – take a seat wherever you want.' Jason walked next to Laria and took a seat beside her. He didn't know why, but he felt like she was different from the people of Cheyenne.

As the teacher went on with his class, Jason tried to listen to what he was saying. It ended up being a giant blur, and Jason tilted his head back to stare at Laria. She focused her attention to the teacher, listening to every word that spilled out his mouth. At least someone was enjoying it.

The class finished sooner than he thought. Jason packed

his books and recorded the information that Mister Hunt wanted him to remember. He prepared himself to leave, but a hand tapped his shoulder and Jason turned around to see Laria with a smile.

'Thanks for showing me class today. And again, sorry for crashing into you.'

Laria rolled her eyes. 'I said it was fine already. What class do you have next?'

After checking his timetable, Jason frowned. 'Gym.'

'Sorry,' Laria said sheepishly and scratched the back of her head. 'I have Chemistry, but the stadium is at the far end of the campus.' She pointed ahead of her as she hung her bag over her shoulder. 'I would take you there, but my teacher is an ass.'

Wow. It was the first time he heard her curse. 'I understand,' Jason replied after blinking away his surprise. 'I'll see you around?' It seemed like a promise, and Jason somehow knew that she was thinking the same thing.

She agreed and went in the opposite path. Jason watched her disappear behind a crowd of students and followed Laria's directions. She wasn't wrong when she said that he wouldn't miss the stadium. It was a large basketball court with a volleyball net set up in the centre.

Jason huffed. Of all the sports it had to be one where he had to focus on aim. But he went to the woman in charge and the second she turned to face him he flinched when he noticed the old scar going over her right eye. It was large enough to be seen for the distance.

'May I help you?' The single hazel eye narrowed in his direction and Jason felt his composure falter. Her dirty blonde hair was short, tied behind her head in a low ponytail and she wore loose clothing. She looked like someone that just came out of the army in order to teach class.

'My name is Jason Amarel.' He noticed the single eye widened briefly at the sound of his name. 'This is my class.' After scanning him from head to toe, Jason wondered what her deal was. Was she expecting someone taller? Offering the timetable, the woman raised her hand to dismiss him.

'I'm Tara Forte – go and wait until the other fresh meat arrives.' And arrive they did. There were twenty students; more boys than girls yet Tara didn't seem fazed. 'Alright you guys know the drill – two teams and show me what you have.'

Two captains were chosen for each team; both of them were jocks that Jason recognised earlier yet only one of them had his eyes set on him. Like he suspected when they started picking for teams, Jason was alone in the class and most likely destined to be picked last.

'Newbie!' said the jock that wasn't leering in his way. 'You're on my team.' Jason seemed to take that as a good sign, making his way towards the redhead. The other captain had blonde hair, so pinpointing him was easy.

Then the volleyball game began. Their court was serving and it was clear that the opponent was underestimating him. When the blonde-haired captain shot the ball in Jason's way, he acted with his instincts. His clenched fist smacked the ball into a spike and it hit the ground with a loud thud.

Jason's team cheered while the blonde-haired captain remained glaring. Blue eyes met blue and he wondered if there was something mentally wrong with the jock.

Their game ended when the bell rang, and it was tie. Jason took the chance to sneak out of the gym and make his way towards the final class that was in his timetable. He didn't remember putting in Law Study, yet he didn't complain. It could be fun.

'Hey, Newbie!' shouted a voice and Jason cursed when he found himself responding to it. It was the blonde-haired guy;

the one that had enjoyed staring at him. Judging by the irritated scowl, it wasn't going to be a decent conversation.

Jason swore to Mae that nothing bad would happen, so he kept casual. 'What's up?'

'You bastard,' the jock said harshly. 'Don't look at me like you're the king of the world.'

'I'm not,' Jason responded, sensing the audience growing. With a sigh, Jason settled and tried to get out of the guy's way. 'Look. I'm busy and quite frankly, not in the mood to start drama.'

A sneer formed on the jock's face. 'You don't know the rules around here, *Newbie.*' With the tone of his voice, Jason had to refrain from rolling his eyes. He couldn't believe that the stereotypical jock was picking a fight with him. 'I saw you looking at my girlfriend.'

This ass had a girlfriend?

'He was!' cried a girl *Just who did this girl think she was?* 'He was looking at me!' Great, more clichés.

'So we have a liar among us,' the blonde hissed and clenched his fist, preparing for a punch. 'I don't take too kindly to idiots who stare at my girl and lie about it.' But before he could make a move, a paper aeroplane flew in front of him to cease the argument.

Jason's eyes were wide as he stared at the object in their way. He wasn't expecting something like that.

'The hell?!' The jock seemed just as alarmed, but his harsh tone was covering it.

Jason looked back to see that Laria had been the one to throw it; her expression was flat.

'Stop screaming, Vegetable.' Laria's voice seemed casual. It was then when Jason realised that Laria wasn't alone. She stood with a taller girl, her black curly hair tied back, her blue eyes irritated. 'We can hear you from the other side of the school.' A few chuckles came from the audience, Jason's lips twitched at the comment.

'Alfero,' "Vegetable" hissed, his attention with the girl going towards the other pair. 'What the hell do you want?'

'For you to get a better name would be a start,' Laria answered with a smirk, earning a snort from the raven-haired girl beside her. 'But leave Newbie alone.' Great, now she had taken up the nickname. 'He wouldn't stare at Sara even if he were a sex crazed idiot.'

'You jealous or something Alfero?' The girl – Sara – sneered. The question made Jason exchange a glance towards Laria. Would she have been jealous?

'Please,' Laria responded with a scoff. 'I pity you. But you tell me something for once Sara Maraca. If I hit you hard enough, would you start rattling?'

Sara's hand suddenly clutched Laria's collar and pushed her into the lockers. 'What did you say?!' She kept Laria pinned by the lockers with a snarl of fury. Just as Jason prepared to intervene, he felt the raven-haired female grab his arm.

'She's defending you Newbie,' she explained with a rough voice. 'The name's Maya. Just let her deal with this.' And Jason did. Laria was still under the girl's grip, unmoving despite everyone was chanting in the background to fight.

'I heard that a man was found dead in your arms yesterday,' Sara announced dully and Laria's eyes narrowed. It must've struck a nerve. 'So why are you still roaming the school when you're an obvious killer? Maybe your mother got a deal with the deputy – it would be the only logical reason why she pulled him away.'

Now that was low.

'Screw you Sara!' The raven-haired female snapped, stepping up to the pair.

'You don't know the half of what happened,' Laria hissed

warningly. 'So I suggest you shut up.' The signs of anger were clear enough for Jason. As seconds passed, the audience began to grow nervous at her hoarse voice.

'Face it Laria, you and your family are pathetic – no wonder your dad's dead.'

He didn't even know Laria, but at that moment he could tell that she snapped.

Laria reacted, latching Sara's wrist with a constricting hold and twisting it. Sara let out a yelp. She released Laria, but Laria didn't loosen the vicious hold.

'Laria...' the other girl whimpered weakly. 'Let go of my wrist... it hurts...'

'Oh it hurts, does it?' Laria's voice was soft. 'I haven't even begun to make you suffer.'

'What... is-' Before Sara could finish, Laria used the opportunity to suddenly pin the girl on the opposite side of the lockers. "Vegetable" was shocked while Jason stumbled only to be caught by Maya.

'Stay back,' was the only thing that she said, before going towards Laria.

But as soon as the fight started, it was over.

A woman stepped forward, clamping her hand on top of Laria's shoulder. 'Stop fighting.' Her voice was collected and cold. It was the same voice that introduced him to Golden Cliff High; the school principal, Tracy Ladas.

With blonde hair swept into a bun, she looked superior and stern. Her cold blue eyes were on Laria like she was a criminal. Every student recognised the woman; most of them even backed away and went to class in order to avoid a scolding.

'You two are heading to my office,' Tracy decided and gestured for the fighting pair to follow her. They did, but they were keeping to themselves.

The trio left together and most of the students had run off. This gave Maya a chance to offer a coy smirk towards Jason. It was a look that worried him.

CHAPTER 4

This wasn't the first time Laria and Sara had been sent to the office, however usually it had been about fierce arguments or a slap mark. This time, Laria was in trouble. Tracy could be a prison guard in a remote island full of the most dangerous of criminals. Her cold exterior was what made her so intimidating.

It didn't make it better that Sara's father, Max, was glaring down at Laria. The only thing that made her feel safe from the weatherman's wrath was Lesley and the school counsellor Takon Falls.

Takon was a tall man with stubble and wavy brown hair that reached to his earlobes. His eyes were his main distinctive feature, appearing brilliant amber that hid behind his rectangular framed glasses. When Laria began to feel nervous, the man pulled out his pen to write down observation notes.

'Sara,' he said and spared a glance towards Sara's frightened face. She flinched. 'I need you to tell me what your story...'

'It was pretty obvious,' Sara hissed in response as she shot a glare towards Laria. 'That girl is a complete psycho that would attack me just for opening my mouth!'

Anger surged through Laria's actions as she shot to her feet. Her audience tried calling out her name but she didn't acknowledge their existence. 'Have you ever heard of provocation you idiot?!'

'Sit down.' Tracy's cold voice held authority, silencing the pair.

'Principal Ladas – can't you see what this school is full of?' Max snorted at the sight of Laria before he turned towards the principal. 'That child is a menace!'

Lesley's vibrant green eyes hardened as she stepped in front of Laria. 'Max, I know that you love your daughter but never insult my child in front of me.' Max only glared.

Takon, the only neutral party looked between the girls before he huffed. 'Look... I know that I shouldn't judge, but Laria did mention that Sara insulted her.' When Sara was about to protest in denial, Takon lifted his hand to silence her. 'Why don't we ask her ourselves?' His amber eyes met Laria's and she felt spooked at the intelligent gaze.

'She insulted my dad,' Laria muttered after a short silence. She noticed Takon stiffen but she paid it no mind. He knew how she felt about him.

Sara glared back at Laria. 'It still doesn't change the fact you almost snapped my wrist!' She lifted her arm to see the light bruises all over the forearm. 'You looked like you could've killed me!'

I did that?

'Come on Sara,' Takon gently interrupted. 'You really don't mean that, right?'

For a moment it looked like Sara hesitated in her answer. The next second, she snorted in disgust and turned to look at Takon.

'Of course I mean it,' she snapped at the man. 'Why would I say it?' Laria almost felt that she was betrayed, but for what reason? Even if Sara was the one at fault, Laria did want to kill her.

'Enough.' Tracy motioned the girl to be quiet before she glared at Laria. She flinched at the cold glare. 'Laria and Sara, I am going to prepare your punishments right now.' She straightened her posture and glared at the duo to prepare for their punishments.

Whatever Tracy was going to state, Laria knew that she just had to suck it up. She couldn't explain that she was ready to murder someone in a heartbeat. Laria didn't want to go through the feeling again.

***

Jason leaned on the wall of the office with a concerned stare.

'Why are you worried?' Maya asked leaning by the opposite wall. Her intense blue eyes met his and Jason couldn't help but look away from them. It had been Maya's idea to ditch their classes in the first place to see the outcome of Laria and Sara. 'My name's Maya Rosa...'

The familiar name clicked in the back of his mind. 'You're Seth's other friend, right?' Jason wondered as the girl nodded with a smirk forming on her face.

'Yep, we don't talk that much but we're still friends,' she explained. 'I heard he's the one that approached you first?'

'I would've thought that Seth told you to never listen to rumours,' Jason replied cockily. 'So how did you guys become friends in the first place if Seth isn't a talker?'

'We were partners for a lab assignment.' Maya shrugged her shoulders dully. 'He was pretty smart and he tutored me with my maths to get my grades up – in return I showed him how to play basketball.' She grinned before it was replaced with a scowl. 'Though he really didn't use that knowledge to knock out Taro.'

Taro. That must've been the guy that Laria called Vegetable. However Jason noticed something, from their interactions. 'This isn't the first time that Laria has got into a fight with Sara.'

A snort escaped the girl. 'Hell no. We've been archenemies

since the first grade. There's no way that our feud is going to vaporise anytime soon.' She let out a quiet chuckle and approached Jason with a sly smirk. 'It began when Laria was playing by the swing set and Sara thought that she could do whatever she pleased so she knocked her off.'

He winced. 'It looks like you have you have your own history with Sara.'

'Yep,' Maya continued with the scowl deepening as she nodded. 'Our parents knew each other so we were forced to get along. But my mum died shortly after my dad left, so Sara called me poison and excluded me. Around that time, Laria had been struggling to cope with Sara's teasing and we became friends shortly afterwards.'

'I'm sorry.' Jason suddenly blurted out. Surprise flashed over her features as Jason continued. 'Sorry about your parents and sorry about Sara treating you so harshly.'

'It's fine.' Maya shook his apology off like it was nothing. 'And I know that if I keep thinking about that sort of stuff, I would be dragging everyone down with me – I'm not that kind of girl.'

'I see.' Jason nodded his head and looked towards her. 'So you and Laria go way back, right?'

Again, Maya nodded. 'But not as far as Brodie – man... those two are inseparable. He's the only one that knows everything about Laria. I bet you my college earnings that if he had been there, he would've stopped Laria before she even got a chance to say Alfero.'

'Brodie?'

'Brodie Forte,' Maya answered. 'You know... Miss Forte's nephew?'

'This is my first day here.'

'Point taken,' Maya chuckled dryly. 'You'll be fine after a week here or so. We don't have much to do.'

Just as Jason was about to reply, the door opened revealing a familiar adult. It was the school councillor that Jason had heard about. The man flashed both students a smile before he vanished into the hallways. After that, Jason saw Laria walking towards Maya with an expression of alarm.

'Maya.' Laria's eyes locked to Jason and she felt a smile forming on her face. 'Jason... What are you two doing here?'

'I was worried.' Jason's answer seemed to surprise himself. 'Also... I wanted to thank you for... defending me back there – you didn't need to.'

'Taro's an ass,' Laria responded after giving a pointed look towards Sara. 'It was worth it.' Sara merely huffed in response.

It was Maya who asked in inevitable question, 'So... what's going on?'

Both Laria and Sara exchanged glances before Laria spoke up, 'For me... I'm gonna be suspended for three days for bruising Sara.'

'What? That's not fair! Sara clearly started it,' Maya snapped, before shooting a glare towards Sara. 'What about you princess!?'

Sara rolled her eyes. 'Stop whining Maya. I'm getting in school suspension because I *started* it.'

'Well I'm glad you two are alright,' Jason spoke up, ignoring the glares from the girls. This made him uncomfortable. 'I'm heading back home – school's only got half an hour anyways.'

'Me too – I'll give you a lift Newbie,' Maya piped with a smirk. 'Anyways, Laria I'll come visit you during your suspension.' Without warning, Maya dragged Jason away with her, but he heard something that gained his attention.

'*I know you're hiding something Alfero, I saw your eyes change colour.*'

'*That's stupid – stop pissing me off more than you already have.*'

Just as Jason turned around to clarify the conversation himself, he saw that Laria was walking away from Sara. Just what was this place hiding?

***

After making his way through the town without the attention spreading, he finally made it to the Alfero residence. Standing with him were two other men. With a chuckle, he pulled off his hood to reveal his short black hair and crimson eyes. He waved a hand to his followers. They exchanged glance before they climbed over the fence.

His phone buzzed in his pocket and he immediately checked the caller before pulling the device to his ear. 'Charmi – I told you that I could pull this off.'

'Shut up Edward.' The familiar English accent rang in his ears and he smiled.

'Are you always this bitchy to people, or is it just me?' Edward teased. His eyes widened at the sound of a car pulling up on the street and he immediately went to hide in the nearest bushes. He saw the car pull up in the driveway. 'Charmi, I believe that we will be striking at dusk.'

CHAPTER 5

Again, with the strange dream.

Jason in the mental paradise. The red string in her hand. All of it disappearing in the fire and the doppelganger.

However unlike last time, the doppelganger seemed more lenient with conversation this time. The amber eyes followed Laria with a sinister smile.

'Did you enjoy causing harm to that wretched girl?' the clone questioned, her grin turning slightly sadistic. 'I know I did.'

'You're delusional,' Laria spat back and ignored the pain in her hands when she clenched her fists. 'Now tell me what the hell does this all mean?' The fire was still raging in the background and her desperation was getting in the way of her fear.

'Isn't it obvious Laria?' the doppelganger wondered snidely. 'I am you – your true self. I've been trapped in the deepest part of your subconscious that hungers for the misery of others.'

'It's not true!' Laria snapped, her eyes narrowed sharply and she felt her stomach tighten. After hearing more laughter, Laria's irritation grew. 'Leave me alone!'

'Very well then,' the copy decided with a simple shrug. Laria was surprised that the strange being managed to cooperate for once. 'Just so you know, the more you deny me and your desires, the harder it is going to be for you to control me.'

'Stop it,' Laria demanded with a hint of anger. Just about everything the clone said was true but dark. She had the thoughts of hurting people, to make everyone suffer at her feet while she laughed at their misery.

'You really think that cheap words are going to get you to deny me?' Laria gritted her teeth angrily. 'Your fears only make me stronger, speaking of which... I hear that your greatest fears open the gate that the witches locked me with.'

Instantly, Laria felt her confusion cloud her mind. Gate? Witches? Her dreams were always filled with strange mysteries. Was this normal for dreams to end up like this? However, just as Laria went to reply, the world swirled around her and her eyes fluttered open with alarm.

Laria sat up from her bed and checked her surroundings, realising that it was her plain, old room that she had passed out in after coming back from school.

Again with the same clueless dream. Two times in a row, ever since finding the dying man on the street. It was probably time to talk to someone about this issue. Laria sighed heavily to dismiss the thoughts and brushed her hair out of her face. Either she needed to seriously think on how she was going with life or she was going to get it.

Suddenly, Laria overheard the sound of smashing glass and a familiar scream. A frown crossed her face as she got to her feet and rushed into the kitchen. Just as Laria entered the room, she froze.

'Laria!' Lesley was held back against her will by a cloaked man with crimson eyes. Her mother attempted to break out of the hold but the mysterious man held her back with ease. 'Laria get out of here!' Laria didn't have time to question because two men suddenly jumped at her.

They were too quick for her natural reflexes; both guys grabbed each of her arms and pulled them back painfully.

'What the heck is your problem?' Laria snapped, fighting against the hold of their grips. Her gaze went to the crimson eyed male. 'Leave us alone you creep!'

'Shut up,' one of the men ordered, tightening his hold on her arm.

'My, my.' Laria's anger shot up when the crimson eyed male pulled off his hood. He revealed himself to be a male in his mid-twenties with dark messy hair and a shaved face. 'Such anger is unbecoming of a girl such as yourself Laria Alfero.'

'What would you like? A cookie?' Laria asked sarcastically, before she spared another glance at the men.

The thought hit her; the images of their dead bodies hanging by the wall. She smirked to herself at the thoughts of their blood staining the carpet; the thoughts gave Laria a sense of relief. It was an interesting thought to have their misery all over their faces before she ended them.

'Laria no...' Lesley whimpered, her eyes filling up with guilt as Edward told her to quieten down.

'I'll give you a final warning,' Laria ordered. Her voice didn't sound like her anymore. 'Get lost.'

The angered tone from Laria surprised all three men and it gave Laria her an opening. She used her adrenaline to lift the first man off her and she threw him. Before the second man could react, Laria threw him on top of the first.

After hearing a yelp of pain, Laria was no longer in control of herself. This wasn't her, but as long it got Lesley safe, she didn't care. As Laria looked down to her palms, Laria noticed that her nails appeared somewhat sharper then they should've, resembling claws. Her vision changed, but not in a bad way; Laria could see finer details.

'What the hell is happening with me?' Laria whispered to herself, before she realised she liked this feeling. In her mouth the canines became sharp and pointed, like an animal.

Her strange new vision looked towards the man who sneered in response, before she raised a clawed finger towards him. 'Who are you? I want to thank you for bringing me out.' Laria didn't sound like that; she never had a tone filled with cruelty.

However before Laria could get answered by the man, she heard a shout of disapproval from Lesley. It was a split second later when Laria snapped out of the episode and she was in control of her movement again. Lesley smacked her head against the mysterious man's and she rushed towards Laria to grasp her. As Lesley held her, Laria started blinking furiously.

'Laria,' Lesley spoke in a firm voice as she cut off Laria's puzzled thoughts. 'Leave us... now...'

Laria's eyes widened as she turned back into the frightened teenager. 'But I can't go!' She didn't want to leave – it wasn't right.

'I can handle Edward,' Lesley retorted with a sudden protectiveness.

An invisible force sent Laria through the air and she yelped as she hit the opposite end of the house. Pain shot through Laria's body as she recovered from the attack, but she widened her eyes when she saw something in Edward's hands.

It was fire. Was her mind playing tricks on her? No – it was true.

Laria was completely dumbfounded at the small flame that danced in between his fingers. What the heck was going on? Laria's head was filled with words – words that weren't her own. The fight between the duo began, the man shot fire from his fists like it was a part of him. Laria was sure that she was seeing things when she moved the flames out of her way to hit the wall.

The flames licked at the walls and burnt anything that stood in its way, which made Laria's heart pound rapidly.

These flames – they terrified her.

Just as Laria took a step towards the duo, fighting with each other with skilful blows, Lesley waved a hand and the invisible force pushed Laria again. It wasn't as rough, but Laria's head smacked hard into the wall and she felt Lesley's presence from the random attack.

'Come with me!' Laria whispered desperately as she reached out her mother. But the fire was too close. She needed to leave otherwise she would be no help at all.

Tears stung Laria's eyes, but she had to obey the silent command. Her guilt ate at her heart as she left the door wide open and ran.

She felt her feet trip and Laria smacked into the ground with a painful thud. 'Help!' Her voice was unrecognisable as she screamed. 'Someone help!'

'No one will save her.'

If things couldn't get worse, Laria suddenly paused at the sight of Haroni. When did he arrive? However, upon sensing the strange feeling in her gut, Laria immediately backed away.

She felt her fear overcome her body. 'Get away from me!' The instinct in her gut now told her to run away and that's what she did. Laria's body trembled in protest as she found the remaining strength to flee; she ran a list of friends that lived close by.

Brodie; he would help.

Sparing a glance over her shoulder, Haroni wasn't moving. Suddenly the newfound strength sapped away and Laria slipped on the road.

Before her body could smack into the ground, two strong arms clasped around her frame and secured her. In fright, Laria looked up to see the one that caught her and proceeded to hit him as hard as she could. How did he-?

'Easy there dear – we wouldn't want anything to happen

to your pretty face,' he spoke with the familiar smile that she loathed. Her exhaustion got the best of her, relying on him as her legs buckled.

'Haroni,' she breathed before tightening her hold on him. 'Don't kill...' Blackness filled her eyes and she lost consciousness.

***

I'm on my way! Brodie thought as he rushed through the familiar streets. His sharp nose caught the scent of smoke and he looked into the sky with alarm. The cloudy sky was polluted with black – the kind of black that made him feel sick to his stomach.

The roads were filled with fire brigade vehicles and the wailing sound echoed into his ears. At the sight of the familiar building burning, Brodie rushed forward.

'Laria!' he cried with panic, gaining the attention from the rest of the firemen. Brodie ignored their gaze. They looked towards Brodie's direction with alarm and one of them let out a call. Laria wasn't with them.

'Hey! Hey! Someone, get that kid! It's too dangerous!'

'Wait for me Laria!' A bulky figure tackled Brodie into the ground and he pushed himself to reach the house. 'Let go of me,' he snapped viciously as he tried to move. 'Laria!' More of the bulky firemen took a hold on Brodie and halted his struggles, but it didn't mean that he didn't try.

'We need you to stay here!'

'I don't care!' He roared fiercely as he attempted to struggle more. 'I need to go in there and save my friend! I can't just let her die, damn it!'

'Don't be foolish, that's why we're here. There's no need of you to play the hero!' the fireman snapped at Brodie. 'We will save your friend, but until then...!' An explosion erupted from inside the building, throwing everyone off their feet.

'There's no way any of us can get in there,' one of them explained. Brodie was meant to be protecting Laria... she was his friend... there was no way that Brodie could forgive himself if anything had happened to her.

'Alright, let's hose this place down – there's no chance of survival, but we pray for a miracle.'

Most of the firemen did their job and attempted to hose the single house down. Even though he had stopped moving, Brodie didn't feel the men letting go of him. They probably thought that he could still bolt unexpectedly. He didn't care – his eyes remained on the burning building as distress clogged his throat.

'Laria,' Brodie whispered hoarsely. 'I'm sorry.'

CHAPTER 6

News travelled fast.

Seventeen hours since the incident, and Jason only found out in the morning by listening in on a few whispers. He recognised the names that were mentioned, and he had to stop himself from questioning out loud.

It was only a day ago when Laria was standing in the hall ways, pinning Sara on the lockers with an almost sadistic glint in her eye. Last night, there was a fire in the Alfero residence.

Only Laria survived the fire.

From what Jason had gathered, her friends had been with her throughout the whole night, refusing to leave her side. He had to visit her at one point, but Jason wasn't sure if she would like to have strangers by her side and not her loved ones.

'It looks like you know with the rest of the school.' The sudden voice made Jason jump. He turned to see an expressionless Seth. 'Don't worry – Laria's a tough girl, you'll see.'

It wasn't long until Jason finally accepted Seth and looked away from him. 'Did you guys ever talk?'

'No, we did not,' Seth replied bluntly as he went through his locker. 'But I can tell she'll pull through this.'

A light smirk crossed over Jason's face as he turned to look at the quiet student. 'I thought you weren't meant to judge a book by its cover, you may get the wrong impression on them.' It was Seth's turn to smirk but it quickly flashed to its neutral expression.

'I don't judge people, Jason,' Seth explained as he leant on the lockers 'I observe their body language. It's the only way I can have a proper conversation with someone. The eyes rapidly blinking, the nose occasionally twitching with a lie – it's how I know.'

As Jason absorbed the information, he joined the stare with Seth and frowned. 'What about me then? Tell me what I am thinking about.'

Seth's dark eyes met Jason's, and again, he had felt vulnerable in front of this boy. Just by watching him, Jason could feel the piercing stare following his every movement. However before Jason could speak up, Seth had already looked away.

'You're too worried about Alfero – stop worrying about her,' Seth admitted. Jason dismissed his companion before he finally turned to see the three faces he never thought he would see at this time.

Out of the trio that appeared, the male was the first to notice that Jason was looking in his direction. It instantly occurred to Jason that it was Brodie Forte and he looked exhausted.

It wasn't long until Brodie stopped with the two females, looking towards them with a tired gaze. He whispered something and they responded with pats of sympathy before he slowly stumbled towards his locker, which meant that he was approaching Jason. He felt something jolt his heart as he felt a hand on his shoulder.

'Watch your back Jason,' Brodie warned huskily and made Jason shiver. 'This mess just got complicated.' Just as Jason was going to retort, Brodie walked away to prevent him calling out to him.

'Yo, Jason,' Maya called waving lazily. Jason turned back

to see that Jenna was yawning as Maya crossed her arms over her chest. 'Does Seth know anything about last night?'

'Yeah,' Jason replied numbly, looking away from his key chain to glance back at Maya. 'He went to class if you're looking for him.'

'Nah... Jenna and I have our class first anyways,' Maya referred to the blonde who lightly smiled at Jason's gaze.

'We haven't met officially,' Jenna spoke kindly opposed to Maya but Jason saw that both had friendly intentions. She held out a hand with the pained smile. 'My name is Jenna Sommers, it's nice to meet you.'

She seemed nice. 'Jason Amarel.'

'Sorry,' the blonde whispered as she pulled away. 'I'm not normally like this, I'm meant to be happy twenty-four seven.' She shook her head to dismiss the thoughts before flashing a forced smile. But it wasn't long until her smile slumped back into a frown.

'It's understandable,' Jason replied with a boyish grin.

'Well, my dear friend Maya and I are heading to class.' Jenna reminded, dragging Maya along. The raven-haired tomboy followed along willingly to Jenna's leading, not before waving back with a yell.

'I'll see you later Newbie!'

Jason let out a huff of irritation. Newbie. That nickname was going to haunt him for a while, wasn't it?

***

It was a bright room, and her body felt like jelly. At first, her mind was full of countless questions. Laria's scrunched expression deepened at the sound of a heart monitor. Hearing her own heart beat from the monitor, Laria finally remembered everything that had happened.

Throughout the hours, her memory had been foggy due to

the medication that the nurses presented her with. Her friends had been with her at the time, watching over her. As Laria turned her head with a wince, she saw someone that gave her a reason to let a tear escape her eyes.

Chris was leaning on a chair, his face concealed by his hands and his dark hair was a mess. Just by seeing his distress, Laria could tell that he'd found out everything that happened the night before.

I can't believe it...

It had only been a few hours ago, when Laria was screaming out for someone to help her. She ran into Haroni, who only frightened her and caught her as she passed out. However, it looked like the untrustworthy male had done himself a good deed for once; he must've taken Laria to the hospital while she was unconscious, leading up to the current events.

Speaking of Haroni, where did he go?

'Laria.' Instantly Laria looked over to see Chris. His green eyes that were once filled with life were bloodshot. 'I'm glad you're alright.'

'I'm not,' Laria replied with tears filling her eyes again. 'She's gone Chris, and I couldn't do anything about it.'

Chris slowly grabbed Laria's hand. 'I share your pain little Ria...' She refused to look at him in the eyes. 'Dad's gone and mum's gone... we only have each other now.' She was afraid – afraid of the men that had attacked them, the man with the crimson eyes and the hands filled with flames. 'Look Laria... there's something that you have to know.' He paused for a moment to turn around. For a moment, Laria looked up with Chris to see Haroni leaning by the door frame.

'It looks like she still doesn't know,' he mentioned gruffly as he pushed himself away and approached Laria. Laria avoided his stare, hoping Chris would send him out. 'I'll take it from here Christopher.'

'What's going on?' Laria questioned, at the duo with a hint of seriousness. 'I want to know the truth.'

Haroni was almost silent, but he let out a cool sigh and took a seat on Laria's bed, much to her displeasure. His eyes were flashing with distress. 'Very well.' He kept his azure eyes following her every detail but he began the story. 'Do you know the story of the Navajo tribe?'

'How is that explaining anything?' Laria demanded with a scowl, wincing at the feeling of her sore body.

'The Navajo tribe is famous for the origin of skin walkers,' Haroni answered as if the question was about the weather. 'It started centuries ago. The tribe had fallen ill and the magic came with a price for four healthy humans within the tribe. Your ancestors are a part of this same tribe my dear, do the math.'

'You're insane,' Laria hissed when her heart rate picked up. 'I may have a hint of Native American but not one from Utah. I'm not a skin walker!'

'Deny it as much as you like,' Haroni replied with the smirk she was beginning to hate more each time. 'Tell me, how much do you really know about your parents' origin?'

His question stunned her into silence. She wasn't sure about her father – but she knew that her mother's ancestors came from England.

'The town founders came from Utah my dear. In this town, the rectocs were once referred to as gods – however in reality, they are the demons always getting their way with a deal... they used different forms to appear as something more, in other words... they had the ability to shape shift.'

That wasn't something Laria never heard from the stories of the tribe. 'What on earth are the rectocs?'

Haroni didn't appear surprised by Laria's question. 'Truth

be told, they are still much of a mystery. They were banished to from an unknown realm, responsible for giving power to those who asked. They were the ones that gave the skin walkers the ability to use magic, eventually leading to transformation of the animal.'

It still didn't make sense. 'Even if what you say is true,' Laria said harshly. She looked at her brother who hadn't spoken to deny it. 'The Navajo stories indicated that you had to break laws in order to turn into a beast.'

'Not in this story my dear. The founders in this town happen to all have the gene to be a skin walker. The Laurence family, the Rosa family and even the Forte family.'

'I don't buy it,' Laria denied and shook her head. Despite saying it out loud, she knew that there was a chance for it to be true. The dying man in her arms, the shadow of the beast and even the mysterious dreams. They were trying to lead her to something.

'Our mother was never a descendant of the Alfero family, but she originated from a town similar to this one. She was a witch. She could perform elemental spells. Like her, I've started my practice of magic. I'm a warlock.'

'But I...' Laria whispered as she looked over to Chris. 'I thought I was going crazy... it didn't make sense that I wanted to kill Sara...' She looked towards Haroni who had barely moved. 'Brodie and Maya go through this every day?'

'Not exactly,' Haroni replied with a considering frown. 'My dear sister and I can sense presences on the school campus. We don't know much about Maya but it looks like she has kept herself under the radar – whether it had to do with her human side remains a mystery and Brodie had a human mother.'

'Right.' Laria looked away with despair. 'Who was that shifter that went after us? Surely he didn't come over for a tea party.'

'Rectocs don't roam in this world anymore – they are sealed up, unable to escape their prisons.' Before Laria could say anything, the man lifted his hand to stop her questions and continued. 'But it doesn't mean that the world is at peace. Several skin walkers go along with their bloodlust and they don't hesitate to kill humans for mere amusement. The man that was after you – he wanted you to lose control of yourself completely.'

'I wanted to kill them, so doesn't that make me evil as well?' Laria asked, looking away as she forced the memories of Sara out of her mind.

'Many shifters will forever have that feeling,' Chris answered. 'Heck, even though I'm more like our mother, I still have that feeling from time to time. Since Dad was a shape shifter, he was meant to have the feelings all the time, yet he had no intention of killing humans.'

It was rare when she heard something about her mysterious father. When she did hear about him, Chris always regarded him with a lot of despair. Since Laria was only an infant when he passed away, Chris was the one who had the strongest bond with him.

'But let's get down to business,' Haroni spoke up to interrupt the duo from their talking. Laria scowled in his direction. She hadn't forgotten how much she loathed this man, 'You need to get out of Golden Cliff – since you're a late bloomer, and exposed.'

'What are you talking about?' she questioned hastily. 'I'm not going anywhere, no matter what you say – that man killed my mother.'

'But Laria!' Chris interrupted. 'You won't be able to stand up to them; I won't let you lose your life like our parents did!'

'Chris.' Laria looked over to her brother with distress in her eyes. 'I can't forgive myself, so there's no way I could allow that man to get away with murder... What do you mean by late bloomer?' She turned to Haroni with annoyance in her expression.

'Obviously you have yet to transform... like a skin walker does. Common transformation is only a single predatory animal such a bear, coyote or a large cat. Late bloomers are when they have yet to transform into their animal counterpart.' Haroni simply answered with a shrug. 'I know that it may not seem like much but you are better off living with your brother.'

'Cheyenne...' Laria slowly turned to Chris, and she understood. 'You said you had an internship over there...'

'Yes,' Chris confirmed. 'I did say that — but when I managed to gain access to control my magic, I was told by our mother to move to Cheyenne so that no one could harm you guys trying to get me.'

'But our mother is dead,' Laria argued fiercely. 'You're really just going to leave her behind like she's nothing to you?'

'Don't say it like that,' Chris retorted. He leaned close to Laria who had flinched under his desperate stare. 'I want to avenge mother as much as you do, but I'm too weak. You also have little power.'

'I'm not leaving,' Laria decided firmly as she glowered at her brother. 'I'm staying, and I will train here no matter what you say, Chris.'

Before Chris could argue, Haroni raised his hand to silence her brother. He looked frustrated at first, but he slowly cooled down enough to stop himself from speaking. As Laria watched the exchange, she couldn't help but wonder their relationship. Who on earth was Haroni Ladas to control her brother like that? And why did he have so much confidence in the way he acted?

'Very well,' Haroni said. It made Chris look over to him

with a look of distress. 'Christopher, I understand why you want Laria to come with you, but I see why she wants to stay.' He met her gaze and softly added, 'She cannot just leave her home behind.'

'Thank you,' Laria said sincerely.

Haroni lightly smiled as he stood up from her bed. 'Alright, if you don't want to stay with your brother then it's fine. I've come up with the simple solution.' He looked towards Chris with a reassuring glance. 'Until she is eighteen – she will live with Tracy and myself.' And her opinion of him completely shattered in mere seconds.

'What?' Laria hissed. 'I would rather stay with Brodie and Leon – I've known them longer and I trust them.' She expected Chris to defend her, but he was silent.

'Laria, dear.' Haroni looked towards Laria with an amused smirk. 'You may not have gathered during this whole time, but I am your legal guardian. Since you don't want to leave with Chris, the next best thing is me.'

'No deal,' Laria growled with a glower. 'I don't trust you.'

'You do not have to,' Haroni replied, completely unfazed by Laria's warning. 'But your mother did when she made me your godfather. So I can promise you that I will protect you while you harness your powers.'

Laria fell silent as she stared back at Haroni, unable to speak for the first time. She couldn't be so sure why her mother trusted him, but if she did, it should mean that Haroni wasn't the man Laria thought he was. After all, she trusted Tracy but sort of feared her.

She stared at his unusually bright eyes. There was something about him. He wasn't a shifter like he had just introduced, but Haroni Ladas was something that wasn't natural. 'What are you?'

Slowly the man smirked and his eyes flashed back to their

mysterious blue gaze. 'Well, you have to wait and find out, dear. I'll speak with the nurse to discharge you.' As soon as he left the room, Laria looked towards Chris with guilt.

'Chris...' her voice quivered, 'I'm sorry that I have to do this.'

Chris grabbed her hand with a smile. 'I understand... I don't like leaving you here, but with Haroni and Tracy you will be safe.' He brushed her hair behind her ear. 'I wish to ask you a favour.'

'Anything, Chris,' Laria replied desperately as she met his gaze.

'Kill the one who did this to mum. Make sure that he's miserable.'

She was determined to make him pay. 'I will Chris,' Laria swore with the flash of her suddenly amber eyes.

***

I have to stay calm, Brodie told himself as he entered his home. Out of all the families that lived in the town, the Fortes had the greatest riches. They had the house that held the parties and the large property that everyone could get drunk in.

Brodie went through the house in silence, his eyes wandering down the walls, recognising the old paintings of his ancestors. His estate was huge, but it always appeared to be empty. The thoughts were only for a moment, because he had dismissed the portraits and moved up the stairs to meet a door. He immediately gave a knock and patiently waited for a response.

'Come in Brodie.'

Hearing the elder's voice, the cinnamon-haired teenager pushed the door open. It creaked as he made his way into the room. His hazel eyes flashed in recognition of the figure in front of him. The familiar man that sat behind a polished desk, the mirroring hazel eyes glancing back at Brodie as he nodded in greeting.

'Hello, Father,,' Brodie said in a calm voice.

Leon Forte was a man in his late thirties, with curly brown hair and light hazel eyes. He looked like an older version of Brodie but Leon had a stern face. He stood tall like his son, but his figure was thinner due to the years of keeping away from society.

In Brodie's opinion, they weren't the closest duo, but they had the mutual care that the father and son were meant to have. His mother had died during Brodie's birth, so he didn't know if Leon had been a different person before. It didn't bother Brodie as much as it used to, because he could tell that Leon cared for him.

'Do you have any news about her recovery?' Leon asked. Of course, Leon had cared about Laria as well – since she was a friend of Brodie's.

'She's a bit shaken up, but she will be okay,' Brodie replied coolly as he stepped closer to his father. She had survived, but Lesley didn't manage to escape. It didn't make Brodie feel better that Laria was going to live with Haroni of all people. There was something about Haroni that Brodie didn't trust. 'Do you think she will accept this part of her life?'

Leon looked out of the window. 'Let us hope so Brodie.' the man continued softly before he poured himself a scotch. 'It would be a shame to lose someone like her. She's strong – like her father was. We should just leave it at that.'

Laria was special to him; Brodie wouldn't forgive himself if something had happened to her. He kept his eyes locked with his father's and he slowly agreed. 'You're right... I shouldn't worry about her.'

Leon took a sip of his drink before he went back to focus on his work. 'Finish your work – tomorrow we're going to have to visit the Mandati Dux.' Brodie nodded in agreement and turned away from his father to leave the room. 'Shut the door behind you,' Leon said and Brodie followed his orders, closing the door as he exited.

So much had happened during the day. Brodie let out a sigh of frustration before he went up to his room. He had hoped to all the gods that existed that Laria was alright, and hopefully not too upset with him when she found out the truth.

Everything he had done was to protect his best friend.

CHAPTER 7

The music from the radio distracted Laria from her angry thoughts. She stared out the window of Haroni's black Chevrolet Camaro, passing through the forest.

After she was discharged, Chris took his car and told Laria that he would return. She didn't know how long Chris was staying, but at least he was with her.

With a sigh, Laria spared a glance towards Haroni before she glared out the window to listen to the unfamiliar music. Maybe Haroni was into listening to eighties music; he seemed to be quite cheerful about the songs.

She rolled her eyes with a grunt, but she didn't want to be caught by him so she kept her eyes away. It was strange; Laria had never considered that she was going to be living in the same house as her high school principal and her untrustworthy brother.

'You know,' Haroni said after a minute of silence. Laria scowled at the interruption. Even though he was doing more than enough, Laria still didn't understand why she couldn't trust him. He was her godfather after all, another shocking story that she had not known. 'You have yet to ask me questions about your own heritage.'

'I gathered that,' Laria responded quietly as her chestnut eyes focused out of the window, 'as Chris said that my mother was a witch it meant that she hadn't gotten the "bloodlust" like me. I already realised that my father was the shape shifter because he was an Alfero, and there was no other way to give me the bloodlust.'

'You're pretty smart,' Haroni complimented with a light smile as Laria shot a glare at him. He clicked the indicator and took a turn to a deserted area. 'No curiosity about the shifters?'

'Of course I have questions,' Laria snorted, folding her arms over her chest. 'Are the shifters able to do that mind reading stuff? And you said something about them not being able to transform until a certain time. How does that work?'

'Dear me,' Haroni said. 'You are a curious little dear.' He looked over to Laria and she had on her infamous scowl. 'You make me feel like an encyclopaedia, and that "mind reading" as you put it isn't true. The way the skin walkers communicate is by telepathic communication by projecting their thoughts into another's mind. And yes, but your animal transformation must come as a need, not a want.'

Laria snorted in spite and kept a suspicious glare in her eye. 'What the hell is with these annoying "sensing" feelings that I'm getting?' Suddenly frustrated by the sharp smell, Laria scratched her nose and hoped it would go away – unfortunately it didn't.

'Ah, that is your enhanced senses kicking in,' Haroni answered with a smug smile. 'You have all of these emotions, abilities, and senses going through your system and it's all going to pile on you at once.'

'Great,' Laria muttered as she scratched her nose again. It had only been a few hours and she already hated her situation. 'Why did I have to be the one with this curse?'

'Relax dear – you have half a year to spend with us... I bet you that the day you leave, you will miss me.' His blue eyes flashed with recognition as he let out a chuckle. 'Here it is...'

If Laria had the chance to have a drink, she would spat it

all over the window in front of her face. It was a mansion, roughly the same size as Brodie's house but Haroni's was white. Brodie's estate always had some sort of darker theme to it.

At the thought of her best friend, Laria felt a little sad. Brodie was probably worried sick about her, and Laria was stuck in the same car as a potential sociopath. She promised herself that when she got into the building, she would call Brodie to let him know how she was doing. Hopefully Brodie hadn't murdered the entire hospital when he found out that she wasn't there anymore.

'Home sweet home,' Haroni spoke up to interrupt Laria's thoughts. He smiled and allowed her to open the door to take a better view of the mansion. 'Don't worry about any enemies finding you here,' he reminded as Laria took a look towards the long road that they just came from. 'If I am not here, then my dear sister is. No one would dare attack.'

The garden surrounded the drive. It was neatly trimmed with a blue Porsche parked out the front. Laria instantly recognised the Porsche as Tracy's since she was the only one that drove it to school and warned students not to touch it.

As they walked up to the front, Haroni opened the doors revealing a large room. The first emotion Laria experienced was astonishment. her eyes lit up as she saw the spiral staircase.

The walls looked like they were made of marble and a giant chandelier was in the centre of the room.

'Combat room is in the left,' Haroni pointed to one large room that had paintings and swords hanging over the walls. 'Dining room on the right; we cook the food ourselves, but sometimes enjoy take away.'

Haroni took Laria upstairs and gave her a tour. 'Bathroom is the first door on the left, Tracy's room is down at the end, and mine is just next to the bathroom. Your room-' Haroni opened the closest door to him and showed the large room. 'Will be the temporary guest room, until we can buy back everything you had lost.'

Laria was definitely shocked. Her previous room was probably less than half the size of this room and now she going to be sleeping in it. Her bed was a queen size with white, clean sheets – it wasn't meant to have much since it was only a guest room. There was a large window that faced the backyard, which wasn't as big as the front but there was a forest behind.

'Look.' Haroni grabbed Laria's shoulders with a hint of comfort. 'I know this may be too much – you've been through a lot with Lesley's death and learning the truth behind your heritage, but I promise you... Laria Alfero, I will not let you be alone anymore.'

No sooner than Haroni said those words, Laria felt her energy sap and her legs lost the strength to stand. Why on earth wasn't she able to walk? As her body fell, Haroni swooped her up and lifted her body like it was weightless, to place her on the bed. She felt her fingers instinctively clasp his shirt so that she wouldn't fall, afraid that he would drop her if given the chance.

'What are you?' Laria whispered as he smiled and brushed her hair back. She loathed this man, yet he only got her curious more than anything.

'Laria, I thought I told you,' he said with amusement as her vision went dark. She squirmed unnaturally as she felt his hand stroking her face. *You are going to have to wait to figure that one on your own.*

***

Haroni smiled as he saw Laria's chest rise and fall. His

prediction was correct about everything piling on top of her; she probably couldn't handle to physical stress so her body gave way to absorb the new transformation. He remained watching his goddaughter until he heard her mumble a curse.

Maybe it's her instincts fear of what I am – after all, an instinct from a skin walker often comes from their ancestors.

As he went down the stairs, he saw Tracy staring up at him with a serious gaze in her eyes.

'How is she?' she questioned softly, sparing one of her serious glances towards the rooms.

'She's coping – for now at least,' Haroni answered. It was something that Laria had to deal with on her own and he felt hopeless. He couldn't offer her a shoulder to cry on because she didn't trust him; the most that he could offer her is a home. She probably wouldn't like to stay any longer than she had to.

'Is it time to contact the others?' Tracy wondered, before Haroni shrugged lazily.

'Do whatever you want dear sister,' he retorted as he brushed passed Tracy and went out the door. Before he could escape however, Tracy grabbed his arm and halted his movements instantly. The siblings' eyes met, but Tracy was the one to speak up first.

'Do not leave her behind,' Tracy growled softly. 'You brought her here. She's *your* responsibility, not something that you can dump when you're done with her.' She tightened the hold on him and her eyes brightened in warning, 'We protect the innocent lives here and don't let them suffer any more than they already have to. We are angels for a reason.'

'Fallen angels,' Haroni corrected as he shrugged his sister's hand off him. 'We are fallen angels for a reason dear sister. Maybe you should remind me why.' He left the mansion and pulled out his phone. Laria wasn't the only one that was affected by Lesley's death.

With a hum of approval from the inside of his car, Haroni felt his mind wander. A lot had happened in the past few days. While the man's death was a reminder that Laria was not safe, Haroni knew that the Beast would not go for her directly.

Not until she was ready.

'Ah, Lesley,' he hummed and tapped his fingers on the steering wheel. 'I don't know anything about raising a daughter... you should've given the godfather position to Leon. At least Laria would've been with her childhood friend.' As Haroni parked the car at the Silver Roots, he locked it and saw the familiar face, drinking his sorrows.

'Christopher,' Haroni said as Chris turned around, with eyes wide before smiling with recognition. Haroni caught up with him. 'Laria is safe – she's just sleeping it off back at home.'

'That's good,' Christopher replied and followed Haroni into Silver Roots. The duo took a seat by the bar. Chris curled his fingers. 'I wish that I didn't have to be here,' he said in distress.

'It's too late to be worrying about that, Christopher,' Haroni explained before he turned to the bartender and ordered a scotch. The glass was put in front of him and filled up with the familiar beverage. 'I'm taking care of Laria until she's old enough to move out. I can tell that she isn't happy about moving but she's dealing.'

'I know Laria,' Christopher admitted with a light shrug. 'I just think that she's feeling guiltier than I am.'

'She will be fine – a leader is always burdened by the death around them. No matter what – it is a trait that you share with your ancestors,' Haroni assured as he took a sip. Christopher didn't respond.

***

'Are you ready Brodie?'

As he glanced from his reflection to his father, Brodie noticed the black suit he wore for the funeral. Even Brodie had a suit of his own; identical except for the grey tie that Brodie wore instead of Leon's black one.

'Yeah,' Brodie replied softly as he approached his father. Leon's expression was empty. 'I'm ready.' The duo left the estate; Brodie silently looked out the windows and considered what it was like for her.

When he was born, Brodie lost his mother but they really didn't have a bond. Laria however, lost both of her parents and she loved them unconditionally. Brodie couldn't help but wonder that if she knew the truth about her own mother.

No sooner than he thought of it, he dismissed it. If she didn't know the shifter heritage, then she was most likely clueless about the witch side.

Brodie was a shifter since birth, naturally he surpassed shifters; especially when it came down to strength. His transformation was like breathing to him and Brodie was beginning to master his family's gift. When he became friends with Laria, Brodie swore to his father that he would never share the truth about her until Laria became one herself.

It took her nearly eighteen years.

Even as a descendant of the Forte bloodline, Brodie never had the bloodlust's urge to kill. He had the tolerance of people and loved to exercise.

'We're here Brodie,' Leon spoke up as he parked the car. Many recognisable people and shifters headed inside the church, but then Brodie saw the one he was thinking about.

'Laria...'

His voice was a quiet whisper, losing composure as Laria walked in with her elder brother, her expression hidden. He knew exactly what she was thinking – Laria didn't want to be near anybody, but she needed someone beside her. She wore a black dress that he had never seen before. Leon cleared his throat, making Brodie snap out of his daydream.

'We should head inside,' he declared, and Brodie followed along obediently. In the corner of his eyes, he smiled gently in Tara's direction who politely replied with a nod.

'Father, I wish to go see Laria,' Brodie declared as they entered the church to see that Laria was speaking with someone. He couldn't tell who it was, but he could see that the other figure had black hair.

At first, Leon's gaze went to Laria and for a moment, Brodie would've sworn that his look softened. Was he feeling sympathy towards Laria? However it was gone in the next second. 'Very well,' Leon said, departing to take a seat.

Just as Brodie came close enough, he finally recognised the voice of the one person that was beginning to irritate him. To control his anger, Brodie curled his fingers into a tight ball to distract himself.

Then he heard them.

'Sorry about your loss Laria, it must be hard.'

'Yeah it is,' Laria's voice responded. 'I just want to move on from this and there's only one way to do it.'

From his position, Jason raised a curious eyebrow towards her. 'Which is...?' he thought. Brodie decided to step in. It was his job as the loyal best friend to step in after all. He wrapped an arm around Laria's arms protectively and showed off a devious smirk.

'Hey,' Brodie spoke up confidentially and saw that Jason's eyes widened in shock. 'Look, we're all here because we're helping Laria move on.' He turned to Laria, who suddenly appeared speechless at the sight of Brodie. 'Let's take a seat, we wouldn't want to be rude to the dead.' It didn't take long for them to find a seat at the front.

'Brodie...' Laria was still staring at him with alarm. 'It's true, isn't it?' She observed Brodie with a curious gaze. 'You're a shape shifter as well.'

'Sorry I didn't tell you,' Brodie quickly replied as he faced the front. 'It was something that I wasn't allowed to share with you.' He spared her a boyish grin but kept his attention on his father. 'But this isn't about me. This is about your mother, the mother that you loved.'

Laria looked back at him with pain filling her eyes, but she gently grabbed his hand. 'Thanks for being here with me Brodie. And thanks about Jason, I felt uncomfortable that he wanted to know if I would move on by killing my mother's murderer.'

Instantly Brodie looked over to Laria. That wasn't something that Laria would normally agree with. 'Wait... What are you planning-?' Unfortunately, he was cut off by the Father, who began the service.

'Lord hear our prayer.'

Brodie was never one to be religious; in fact he believed there was more to Heaven and Hell that the bible let on. So he kept quiet as the majority of the church repeated that phrase throughout the service. He spared a glance to Laria, who was desperately trying not to sob but occasionally wiped her tears away from her face.

'*Laria,*' he spoke telepathically towards her, making her look up with alarm. It looked like she still didn't know much about being a shifter. '*It's okay... I'm here with you.*' To assure that he was telling the truth, he tightened the hold he had on her hand.

She smiled faintly and she leaned into his frame. '*Thank you, Brodie.*'

She was a natural. He didn't say anymore, making sure that she didn't leave his grasp until she was called up to talk about her mother. She pulled away from Brodie's hand and headed towards the platform in front of countless figures of the town. Brodie knew Laria, he knew that she was naturally good at public speaking but watching her up there with tears in her eyes – it was the first time in his life that Brodie knew that Laria was nervous.

'To you,' she began shakily, 'Lesley Alfero was a friend, a colleague but to myself and Chris – she was our mother. She taught me to stand up for myself, to be kind to others that need it. Her heart was pure, like an angel sent from heaven.' In the crowd, Brodie noticed that Haroni lightly cleared his throat. However Laria ignored the minor interruption and continued, 'I'm sorry that I wasn't strong enough...' She left the stage and took a seat next to Brodie.

As she sobbed, Brodie kept a calm expression when he wrapped his arms around her to embrace her. For the first time in his life, Brodie never thought that she would look so frail until that moment when she sobbed in his arms.

***

Many people left, but one of the few that stayed was Zanobi. After the long and boring funeral service, some of the men took the coffin and put it in the car so that they could bury it in the graveyard.

He pulled at his tie uncomfortably with a mutter of annoyance. His friend really knew how to strangle him with this ridiculous thing. He sighed, keeping his hands to his sides as he approached Laria. She barely knew him, but Zanobi was well aware of her father.

Tracy, who remained by Laria's side, was the first to notice his presence, followed by Haroni. A surge of annoyance spurred in his chest, yet Zanobi merely nodded in greeting towards the stoic faced Leon.

It was Laria Alfero. She looked like she was a mess, but Brodie Forte was standing beside her in a comforting position and Leon approached them just as Zanobi arrived.

Haroni smirked, knowing that his smile only irritated Zanobi more. He brought the quiet Laria to his side. 'This man is Zanobi Adkins. You may recognise him.'

'I do,' Laria said and for a moment Zanobi wondered if she knew him from her past. 'You were the guy that mum dragged away when I found that man.' Of course. There could be that as well.

'Hello there.' Zanobi offered his hand which Laria shook. 'I'm sorry for your loss Laria.' He met a gaze with Leon Forte and saw the serious expression. It was normal for Leon to give him a heated glare, the duo never really got along.

'Thank you,' Laria replied softly and she pulled her hand away from him. 'Are you going to teach me about the shifters?'

'Yes,' Zanobi promised as he pulled out a card from his pocket to let her take it. 'There's my contact details. Just call me when you feel ready to discuss.' He left the small group behind to head out.

The phone rang as Zanobi prepared to leave and he checked the number. It was a new ID. He didn't expect Laria to call him so fast. Before he could confirm it himself, Zanobi quickly turned around to see if Laria was calling but she wasn't.

The only thing that he could assume was a random caller. So he hung up the phone, letting it fall silent and Zanobi felt the sunlight overcome his face with a harsh glare. He pulled out his sunglasses and covered his eyes when he got a message.

Zanobi paused for a moment and went to check the message.

Zanobi, don't say anything.

Looking back at the church with a frown, Zanobi only

came down to one conclusion.

It was Leon Forte.

Leon managed to read the number off the card and give him a warning about telling Laria the truth. But Zanobi knew that Laria was going to find out everything eventually. It would be better sooner than later, just in case the bloodlust did take over.

CHAPTER 8

Laria twirled the card that Zanobi Adkins gave to her in her fingers with uncertainty. He was a kind man and she felt comfortable around him. While she wanted to go back to school, Laria was still technically suspended.

With a sigh, Laria looked up at the television again to see that the Beast struck again and to a random couple. She didn't know who the killer was, but she could tell that they were no longer animal attacks – they were done by shifters alone.

Laria needed the training. Without another word, Laria dialled the number off the card and waited patiently until a deep voice picked up on the line. It was so sudden that Laria almost dropped the phone in shock, but she managed to hold herself.

'Hello, this is Zanobi Adkins speaking.'

A smile automatically formed on her face. 'Hi, Zanobi... It's me, Laria, I just want to know if you're busy this afternoon.' She would have at least a few hours since it was quite early in the morning, but Laria honestly couldn't be stuffed getting out of the mansion at the moment. Haroni left her alone for a change, and Laria was taking advantage of his mysterious actions. But this stranger felt supportive. Laria couldn't explain it.

'I'm free at two today, I will meet you at the Silver Roots then.'

'Thank you,' the brunette replied before she hung up her

phone. As soon as the phone bounced on the couch, Laria immediately grabbed the remote to turn off the television. She heard the click and leaned back.

She felt like she was going on a date with a stranger. Sighing again, Laria pushed herself up from the couch and headed to the bathroom to get ready for her first outing in days.

Today was the day that she was going to learn more about her heritage.

After having her shower, Laria tied her hair back, ignoring the rebellious strands that refused to pin back. Her summer clothes were the closest thing to decent she had here.

Laria nodded to herself in approval as she looked at her own reflection. She didn't look like a girl that was mourning for her mother's death – but rather she looked like she was on a mission. To be fair, Laria wanted to know how to fight as soon as possible.

The sooner she learnt to control her powers, the sooner she would be able to stand against her enemy. Edward was lowlife scum; he went after her mother when Lesley was only trying to get Laria out of it.

Remembering her promise to Chris, Laria clenched her fist. He will die, no matter what stood in her way. Laria wondered how Edward's head would look if she had torn it off and hung it on top of a Christmas tree.

'Laria!' Haroni's voice interrupted her dark thoughts and she shuddered in disgust. One thing for her to have those kinds of thoughts in her head, it was worse that hearing Haroni's voice actually made her grateful. She scowled but opened the bathroom door to glower at the male that was downstairs with a large plastic bag. During her time here, Laria knew that Haroni had secret hobbies. 'Laria, good... Are you alright?'

She rolled her eyes; she was seventeen not seven. 'Yeah I'm fine.' He seemed to nod in approval and he went towards another room but it made Laria only curious. At first, she leaned down to see but her eyes lost sight of him and she instinctively followed him down stairs. 'What are you doing anyways?' she questioned, following the sound of his footsteps as they entered a new room that Laria hadn't seen before.

It was a basement that was under the stairs and Laria couldn't believe that it was her first time seeing the room. True, she had only been in this house for a bit over a week, but she had still had plenty of time to explore the building.

'Be careful,' Haroni called out as Laria saw another set of stairs in the basement. His voice echoed eerily from below and Laria took her time going down the unrecognisable stairs. 'There's a step higher than the rest at the bottom.' Since he warned her, Laria was able to take extra caution.

For a basement, it was surprisingly clean and organised with Haroni covering up a canvas with a thick curtain. He smiled in greeting and Laria gazed around the rather large room. It looked like he had more things covered up by giant blankets or curtains, yet Laria couldn't see what was under them.

'What is this?' She was tempted to pull up the curtain of the closest canvas to her. With a quick peek and Laria held in a gasp when she saw the painting from behind. It wasn't finished, but it was a painting of a blonde, nude woman.

'That is called Broken Wings,' Haroni said and gestured towards the lady's shoulder blades. It took Laria a moment to realise that blood trailed down to where the wings were supposed to be.

'You're an angel.'

Haroni merely smiled. 'The correct term for me would be

fallen, meaning banished.' Just as Laria prepared to ask more, she noticed that he went to cover it back up without remorse. While it was an excellent painting, Laria noticed that he appeared conflicted upon staring at the art.

'These aren't finished?' There were a lot of unfinished works.

'Some call it artist's block,' Haroni replied as he took out his art equipment placing it on a large table to the side. 'I call it – I do not want to do this painting right now, I will finish it later.' He explained his goal and focused his attention on her. 'Do you have something to do today Laria?'

'I'm meeting with Zanobi,' she announced which made Haroni smile. 'I was wondering if you could drop me off to Silver Roots.'

Haroni petted Laria's head and chuckled lightly. 'Sure – it's no problem, I have to go to work anyways and I'll drop you off on the way there.' No sooner than he mentioned he had work, Laria looked towards the stranger with a hint of shock.

Throughout the time Laria was aware of him, she didn't know anything about Haroni's life, including an occupation. 'Where on earth do you even work?'

'It's just a simple job to occupy myself,' Haroni implied as he finished packing away. 'I know how you feel about me let alone about me having a mysterious job, but I promise you that I won't be murdering you.'

Like that made feel Laria any better. 'Still doesn't explain why you have a dark room.'

A chuckle escaped his lips. 'I come here to paint the pictures of my assassinations.' Surprise flashed in his eyes as Laria snorted lightly at his comment trying to stop herself from laughing but it was already too late. He smiled and wrapped his arm around her shoulders as he led her up the stairs.

***

Sitting in Silver Roots alone wasn't an uncommon thing for Zanobi, but when he was alone, more people found it pleasing to talk to him. His phone vibrated and for a moment, Zanobi thought it had to be Laria, but he saw who the sender was from and smiled lightly. It was his friend asking where to meet.

Meeting place – you know where that is don't you?

Not even a minute later and Zanobi's phone vibrated again. He checked the messaged and chuckled at the response.

Of course I do, jerk!

Instead of writing one big long message, he simply gave a short reply. She hated to be teased, but sometimes he couldn't help it.

As the text got sent, the door opened with a ring of the bell. Zanobi turned to see Laria strolling in to Silver Roots with a nervous look on her face. Zanobi lifted a hand to get her attention, which it did, and she immediately passed by the tables to meet him.

'Good afternoon Laria,' Zanobi greeted as Laria took the seat and twiddled her thumbs nervously. 'It's been good living with the Fallen I suppose?'

Laria looked nervous and scratched the back of her head. 'He's been decent enough.'

'That's good.' A waitress came with a drink. Zanobi took his bourbon and offered Laria one. She smiled at his offer but she quietly refused, and the waitress left their sight. 'I also understand that your brother, Chris, has disappeared back to Cheyenne?'

'Yeah,' Laria responded with a serious expression. 'He said that he wasn't strong enough to stay – Well neither am I, but I'm not leaving my home for Edward.'

His eyes flashed with curiosity of the girl as he finished his drink and stood up. 'Very well, we should get going – we have a lot to cover today.' He grabbed a few notes from his wallet and placed them on the table. Laria obediently followed. 'So tell me Laria – do you feel different since you have begun your shifter quest?'

'I have,' she said as she explained her situation. 'I can see more, smell more and even hear more.' She leaned in and kept her voice quiet. 'Is everything heightened?'

'That's exactly right,' Zanobi answered as the duo escaped Silver Roots and roamed through the streets. 'Now, I should really explain how shifters are.'

'What do you mean by that?' Laria's frown only indicated her confusion, yet Zanobi found himself easily answering.

'All of the shifters in Golden Cliff are commanded by the six duxes, or leaders in the human language. They organise the supernatural deaths and causes to make it look natural to prevent exposure. Many of us are descendants of the tribe hundreds of years ago, but there are some that are like our ancestors – with their power willing to consume them and we call them the true descendants.'

'That's because of the bloodlust, right?' A nod indicated that she was correct.

'The other kind of shifters have easier control. Their transformation is harder but they have the built-in instinct to protect a true descendant. We don't have a name for them, but they are as much as a descendant as you.'

'So... I'm one of the descendants that are like my ancestors?'

'Your father was the same,' Zanobi claimed and he flashed a grin. 'And since your revelation, the duxes have been calling you the Last Alfero.'

'The Last Alfero?' That sounded like more of a taunt if anything. Her brother was technically an Alfero as well.

'Well your brother isn't a shape shifter. Despite the knowledge of a few Alfero shifters, you are the youngest. Your father was once known as the Last Alfero before he had you and Chris.'

Suddenly, Laria felt uncomfortable at the topic of her dad. She didn't know the guy – but he seemed to be respected enough to be spoken of. 'What about you?' Laria asked. 'Do you know about your ancestors?'

It was nothing that she needed to worry about. 'I was orphaned at my birth – my mother was a witch, and we didn't know much about my father except for the fact he enjoyed one-night stands.' They stopped at a single house at the end of the street with the lawn neatly cut.

'So you don't know which family you're from?' Laria's eyes softened in sympathy. 'That must've been hard.'

Zanobi put his shades. 'It was a long time ago. Descendants all over the world have similar situations as I do.' He nodded his head towards the house. 'Do you know this building?'

'Yeah,' Laria replied as she nervously looked away from the house. 'It's meant to be a haunted house. We were told as children not to go there. When I got older, I just ignored the fact that there was a spooky house.'

'Well this house isn't haunted if it makes you feel better,' Zanobi assured and entered through the gate. 'We have a busy schedule ahead.' Laria widened her eyes in shock but she followed along just in case she got caught loitering in front of the house.

'Zanobi!'

He ignored that she was struggling to keep up with him. The house's indoors remained as it always had; there was nothing but an old bookcase and a smashed chair to give the impression that this house really was haunted.

'Zanobi, we're not allowed to be in here.'

'Relax – we're in the right place,' Zanobi promised and he

easily pushed the bookcase to reveal a stairway. Her eyes seemed to focus on the clichéd hiding spot. He gestured for Laria to walk in front of him, but she only gave him a glare. 'Very well.' Zanobi entered the stairway and allowed his companion to follow him.

'Where are we going?' Laria asked as they made their way down to the basement.

'I have to introduce you to the duxes – like I said before,' Zanobi replied simply as he finally reached at the bottom of the stairs. He flicked a light switch and it revealed Laria's squinting eyes as she adjusted to the sudden glare. 'I will speak with them first; you will have to wait here.' She didn't look happy as Zanobi turned away from her and headed to a new room.

Zanobi closed the door behind him, his green eyes flashing with familiarity as he stared back at the six familiar figures. They were sitting behind a long table, watching Zanobi with looks of annoyance or blank expressions.

The first to speak was a young, pale skinned woman with messy, raven hair. Her blue eyes were unique, dark as the night sky on a cloudless night. She smirked at Zanobi. 'Bout time ya came here Zanobi – what took ya so long? Did the brat give ya a hard time?'

'Tahani,' Zanobi replied, 'I believe that you would've been no better.'

'Spare me the chat Zanobi,' she said and ran a hand through her short hair. 'Kids ain't my thing.'

'Alright then.' Zanobi immediately turned to the man that was at the back of the room. 'I brought her, Mandati Dux.'

Takon Falls raised his amber eyes and smiled with acceptance. 'Well done Zanobi, you should bring her in now.'

'Wait a minute Adkins!' Nadia interrupted with a scowl. It was strange to not hear him being referred to as a deputy within this building, but it was the only time Nadia permitted it. 'Adkins – you invited all of us in this meeting, only to meet the trash!?'

'She can probably hear us, Venatione Dux,' Zanobi spoke up as he exchanged a look at the sheriff of the town. This woman barely trusted anyone, but she cared about the peace of Golden Cliff.

'I will speak my mind whether she wants to hear it or not,' the woman responded. 'She was the same girl that found that dying man. How do we know that she isn't the monster we've been searching for?'

'Nadia – take a chill pill,' Tahani spoke up to interrupt the mistrusting woman. 'We all came here to meet Laria Alfero. Don't start blowing up. She's the last Alfero ain't she?'

'Watch your tongue Rosa,' Nadia shot back, glowering at the woman. 'You are no better. All you want to do is fight her to tame your ridiculous bloodlust – it is a miracle that you are the Ungue Dux.'

'It's because I'm good at my job,' she explained and ignored the second growl. The two females never got along because of their opposite ways. 'If I fought the kid, she probably wouldn't put up a fight. Let's get over ourselves and meet this kid.'

'I happen to agree with Ungue Dux,' a tall male with wavy, black hair spoke up. He wore a white lab coat and round glasses. 'I want to meet this Alfero – she will be an excellent specimen to see why she didn't follow her witch side,' he cackled madly.

Zanobi inwardly groaned at the arguing duxes. Laria was probably getting tired of waiting for these morons to get a hold of themselves. He knew it was impossible sometimes.

'Huh,' Tahani said with realisation as she looked over to the man with the glasses. 'Yer the last person to agree with me

Jyle. Tell me that yer not planning to cut my head open when I turn my back.'

'Of course not,' the scientist snorted. Not many people agreed with Tahani. 'I wouldn't waste my time on mindless brutes; I'm interested in finding out more information about the recent Alfero – who happens to be a late bloomer for your information.'

Before Tahani could retort, Takon slammed his fist on the table. Silence went through everyone in the room as they turned their attention towards him.

'That's enough!' he snapped, glowering over everyone as his eyes flashed yellow. 'Zanobi requested us to come here. Let us not waste any more time.' His eyes darkened back to the original amber. 'Bring her in.'

Each of the shifters spared curious glances with each other but they all nodded in silence. Zanobi didn't refuse, turning away from them to open the door for Laria to enter.

She walked right in like a nervous animal, her eyes wary of each figure until her eyes met with Takon's. Recognising him instantly, Laria froze in her spot.

'Takon...' Laria whispered with shock, just as she looked towards the third figure and Zanobi understood. It was Brodie's aunt Tara, the Potentia Dux.

'Hello Laria – I am sorry for your mother,' Tara spoke softly.

'Yes Laria,' Takon spoke up as his eyes flashed with determination. 'As the duxes of Golden Cliff, we hide everything supernatural from humans.' His eyes narrowed sharply and he stood up. 'We want peace.' He looked over towards the remainder of the duxes with a serious gaze in his eyes. 'I am the Mandati Dux, Takon Falls.'

Nadia was the next one to introduce herself. 'Sheriff Cyler, the Venatione Dux.' She showed her badge in proof. 'This means that I have authority to lock you up if you break any law – human or shape shifter.'

The middle-aged man with short brown hair beside Nadia offered Laria a smile. Unlike Jyle, this man didn't have a threatening look across his face but rather a gentle expression in his chestnut eyes. 'Hello there,' he said with a faint Spanish accent. 'I'm Hugh Salve the Medicinae Dux; pleased to make your acquaintance.'

'Uh...' Laria's cheeks were red and Zanobi could tell that she was nervous. He rolled his eyes as Laria tried finding something to distract herself. 'Thank you... '

'Don't worry, ya get sick of the accent eventually,' Tahani said with a snort. Laria raised an eyebrow in surprise at Tahani's blunt attitude. Zanobi silently chuckled at Laria's surprise. It was only the beginning of Tahani Rosa. 'The name's Tahani – Ungue Dux.'

Her lack of explanation made Zanobi surprised. Usually she would've offered a fight. He knew that Tahani was thrilled by fighting. She sometimes used the bloodlust as something that should be accepted, but it worried him.

After all, she had it with her for at least eighty years now.

A sinister chuckle from Jyle interrupted Zanobi's thoughts. 'My name is Jyle Grenth, the Scientia Dux and I have one rule for you – no refusal in my experiments.'

Laria's eyes almost popped out of her head due to the honesty of the crazy man. She hid behind Zanobi and his eyes only darked with annoyance.

'Very well.' Takon clapped his hands together to gain everyone's attention. 'Zanobi, I wish for you to take Laria back to Haroni's mansion while I discuss our next plans for strategy.' The male obeyed immediately, taking Laria's arm to drag her out of the room.

'Why do you guys speak in Latin?' Laria wondered. 'You

say most words in English then you say dux.'

'The rectoc's native tongue was Latin,' Zanobi replied instantly. 'As we gained the gift from the rectocs, we learn the way they speak. But I have noticed the younger generation doesn't speak as much Latin. It is possible that we are slowly becoming more human – besides, many of the translations of the names do not sound good in English.'

***

'Father?' Brodie spoke up and entered the room. Leon scowled and gestured for his son.

'Brodie, I have some disturbing news.' Leon looked up to see Brodie's puzzled expression. 'The Beast has attacked again. One of us.'

'Another death?' Brodie repeated. 'Did we know this shifter?'

'I did,' Leon curtly replied and filled out his paperwork. 'The Mandati Dux ordered me to figure out the killer by examining the body.' Again, surprise flashed over Brodie's face and Leon kept his gaze serious, 'Brodie – the S.H.O. have not informed us of sightings from the shifters since Lesley's death.'

'What do you mean?' Brodie wondered, ignoring Lesley's name. 'Do you think that they've starting to figure out the sensors?'

'It would be impossible,' Leon responded warily before he took a drink. 'I have gone through the reports – only three unregistered shifters came when they went after Laria and only one left. The two that were with Edward were disposed of. These deaths are not caused by enemies outside Golden Cliff.' Leon's eyes met Brodie's whose heart was thudding in his chest.

'Father...'

'The Beast... has being among us, all this time.'

CHAPTER 9

It had been nearly two weeks since Laria had gone to school, but she had to return. She would be lying to herself if she didn't want to go back to school. Spending her free time at Haroni's was driving her crazy and she needed to see her friends again. With a nervous grip on her bag, Laria strolled towards the campus.

'Is that her?'

Apparently, the supernatural hearing was against her will – no matter how much she didn't want anything to do with it. They were talking about her.

'That's her... The one who lost her mum in that fire.'

Anger poured in her system and Laria was tempted to tear the idiot's face off for talking about her mother. But as soon as she thought of it, her mind dissolved the negative thoughts. There was no way she was going to get anyone's trust if she kept thinking about killing someone every second.

Laria took a deep breath and with great concentration, she managed to block out the voices around her as she entered the building. Her eyes found Maya immediately, but she was talking with Seth. It appeared that they were having a decent conversation, but Seth's dark eyes rose up and met with Laria's.

He spoke softly to Maya – it was impossible for Laria to catch it but it had to do with her because Maya's head turned to see Laria. At first surprise flashed through Maya's face, but then she suddenly smiled in gratitude and returned the grin.

But something stopped her – the realisation that Maya was a human. Laria assumed that she hadn't been – strange.

By the time Laria regained herself, Seth spared Laria a warning glare before he disappeared into the crowds of the students. She wanted to ponder on his strange behaviour but paid it no mind – if Seth wanted nothing to do with her then Laria shouldn't force it on him.

As Laria reached Maya she flashed a smile. 'Hey Maya.'

'I can't believe you're back.' She gave her half a hug. Considering Maya never hugged anyone, it was a rare treat. Laria took it to heart and hugged her friend back. 'How's everything? I thought you were going to move in with Chris and leave us!'

'No way,' Laria retorted with a smile as they pulled away. 'I've got some interesting news to tell you though.' She looked around warily as if the devil himself was around but she focused back on Maya. 'Do you know Haroni Ladas?'

'Our principal's brother, of course,' Maya replied as she frowned in confusion.

'Yeah well he happens to be my godfather.'

It didn't take long for Maya to process the information, but when she did her eyes went wide and they looked like they were about to pop out of their sockets. 'Shut. Up.' Laria nodded in agreement and Maya let out a gasp of shock. 'No way... Haroni Ladas is your godfather?'

'Since I was in the hospital when I found out, it didn't come much to a shock to me because they drugged me up.'

'That's something... and you hate the guy.'

'Not exactly hate,' Laria began but she was interrupted by the school bell. As soon as the bell went off, she flinched at the high pitch sound and covered her ears. 'What class do we have now?'

'Geography,' Maya replied with a groan of annoyance. 'I hate Geography.'

On the way, there was a blockage of students that stood in their way which made the duo stop momentarily. As they waited, Laria saw Maya from the corner of her eye and tried to not show any expression. Maya probably had questions about the incident, but thankfully she remained silent.

But none of it mattered to Laria. Her old life was gone. Lesley wasn't coming back. Chris wasn't returning either.

'Hey...' Maya's voice brought Laria out of her thoughts. 'What's going on in the office?'

Laria felt her senses kick in upon seeing someone's hooded figure. She couldn't see the face, only recognise the hood. Was it the stranger that she always saw in Silver Roots? If so, then Laria had no idea on why the person was there.

'That's strange,' Laria agreed with a frown of puzzlement. 'Why wear a jacket in summer?'

'I have a strange feeling,' Maya muttered uneasily. 'I never get these feelings around other people... do you think that this is some transfer student?'

'Two new students?' Laria wondered with a raised eyebrow. 'I didn't realise that our school was slowly getting popular.'

'Maybe.' Maya shrugged before she began to pull Laria away. Laria didn't refuse the pull, staring blankly at the office before she turned towards the path in front of her. 'Let's get going – the blockage is gone.'

As Laria spared one final glance at the person's back, she was tempted to eavesdrop the conversation but she immediately stopped herself. The curiosity was gone when Maya brought her to the classroom and they took their seats out the front.

The teacher raised an eyebrow towards them and Maya

apologised about their lateness with a fake enthusiastic voice. One thing that Maya excelled in was the art of deception – she was great with lying and faking enthusiasm. It was a rare treat for everyone who knew that she was lying.

'It's fine,' the teacher dismissed them before he locked eyes with Laria. Of course, Laria hadn't been to school in two weeks because she had been recovering. 'Glad to see that you're back Laria.' The teacher had already turned away. 'You will need to catch up; exams are coming up soon.'

They began their lesson instantly. Both Maya and Laria struggled with the beginning of the class as the teacher went on with the lesson. Laria was slightly frustrated that the teacher was going too fast, but she kept it to herself. It wasn't anyone in this class's fault that she was behind.

A knock on the door interrupted the teacher, and he suddenly paused to look at the entry. Kylie Andrews stepped into the room with a warm smile and she whispered something to the teacher's ear. Feeling the curiosity, Laria closed her eyes and forced herself to use her enhanced hearing to eavesdrop on the situation.

'We have another new student,' Kylie mentioned. She left the room, spoke to a mysterious figure and Laria heard the sounds of heels clicking to announce that the office lady was leaving.

'Everyone,' the teacher said calmly motioning for someone to enter the room, 'we have a new student. Please make her feel welcome.' Whispers echoed around in the room as Laria and Maya exchanged a curious glance.

As the figure stepped into the room, a wave of alarm Laria her like a truck. Why did it have to be her? It could've been anyone on this earth. she recalled every detail about the woman.

'Laria?' Maya said softly. 'It looks like you've seen a ghost.'

Seeing a ghost would've been better, Laria almost said, but she quickly checked the details to confirm the appearance herself. The ivory skin that made her look pale, her short, raven hair that almost resembled a bird's nest and her most noticeable feature – the midnight blue eyes that gleamed with a sense of thrill.

'Damn it...' Laria muttered with annoyance, seeing the jacket hood was off her head and now resting on her back. A black singlet was concealed under the jacket with knee length tights and dirty joggers on her feet. The woman waved lazily in their direction.

No doubt about it, Laria knew that this was the woman from the office.

'What's up?' the woman muttered with a bored expression forming on her face. Her midnight gaze met with Laria's and a teasing smirk extended on her face 'The name's Rosa.' Colour drained from Laria's face and the woman's smirk only widened. 'Tahani Rosa.'

***

Zanobi impatiently knocked on the door of the office. It took a lot for him to get mad; but once it involved *her*, Zanobi could no longer hold back. Just as he was about to knock again, Takon revealed his face behind the door and frowned.

'You're not meant to be here.'

Zanobi ignored Takon's voice and entered. 'What the hell is this, Mandati Dux?'

Takon's amber eyes remained neutral. 'I do not understand-'

Rage flashed in Zanobi's eyes. 'You know I don't buy that crap!' His fist clenched in denial. 'The Beast; we only just found out about his treachery because of Laria.' He glared outside the window. 'You're sending Tahani to do it. She'll be a target for that bastard!'

'I understand your situation Zanobi,' the dux announced when he took a sip from his coffee cup. 'What was the promise that you made to her all those years ago?'

When Zanobi met Takon's eyes, he stiffened. Zanobi remembered the day as if it was yesterday.

They were all orphans, the two raven haired girls that tightly held each other with fright as the rest of the town tried to slaughter them. Back then humans knew of their existence and the humans loathed the shifters. A man had found them and cornered them in a dark alley. Before he could lay a finger on either of the siblings, Zanobi interrupted by slamming a rock on the back of the human's skull, saving the two girls.

'I will not hurt you,' Zanobi swore that night.

The older one of the girls had a fierce look in her midnight eyes that faintly flashed with an icy blue. 'Back off!' she snapped protectively. He didn't move. 'I don't care if yer human or shifter, I told my parents that Kaeylin wouldn't get hurt!'

At first, Zanobi had been shocked at the girl's declaration. Even though she nearly faced death, she didn't show any sign of fear – a Rosa trait. 'I promise that no harm will come to you or your sister,' Zanobi announced offering a hand to help the girls. 'But I cannot promise this if you don't come – please.'

He remembered seeing the elder one glower with distrust, afraid that he would rat them out just to save his own skin.

'Tahani...' the one named Kaeylin said. Her eyes were a lighter shade of blue, a more natural blue than the other girl.

'Fine,' she spat, accepting Zanobi's hand. He knew from that day onwards he would protect them.

'I had promised them,' Zanobi muttered with a shaky voice as he tried shutting out the memories, 'that no harm would come to them but I broke that promise... when Kaeylin died. Tahani became the Ungue Dux to avenge her sister.' It made things worse when they had a spat that separated them.

He had promised to protect them, that no harm would come to them, but he failed.

'That's why,' Takon replied softly to see Zanobi glower back in his direction. 'The Ungue Dux needs to have the responsibility. It will help her grow and confront the past in order for the both of you to move on.' His eyes remained gentle with sympathy. 'Out of all the shape shifters, she can easily control the bloodlust and will be able to teach Laria.'

He'd found her, he taught her everything that he knew. She loved learning and her fighting improved vastly as opposed to Kaeylin, but it gave Tahani more reason to train.

'I understand,' Zanobi muttered with submission.

'Great.' Takon stood up and showed Zanobi out. 'Now don't come back in here, just because I lead the shifters it doesn't mean that I am the boss of this school.'

Zanobi scoffed as Tracy Ladas appeared in his mind. *Of course.* 'Very well.' Zanobi's eyes flashed warningly to Takon. 'But if anything happens to her...'

'She's tough Zanobi,' Takon assured. 'If anything, I feel slightly concerned for Laria.'

***

What on earth is she doing here? She asked herself as Tahani was staring at the front with a look of boredom. The teacher instructed her to take a seat, but it didn't stop the curious gazes of the other students.

'Just what exactly is with that woman?' Maya asked from her seat, looking towards Tahani with a hint of wariness. As if she heard, Tahani spared a glance towards Maya and scowled.

Everyone looked in Tahani's direction with a frown and

silently debated her name and her slightly older look.

'*Oi.*' Laria could recognise Tahani's rough voice – it was similar to Maya's. '*Tell her to stop looking at me. I'm not a bloody museum piece.*' Suddenly snapping out of the thoughts, Laria reached up and tapped Maya's arm to get the girl's attention.

'I don't like her,' Maya admitted with a glower. 'There's something off 'bout her.' Her eyes went soft and she clenched her fists in anger.

'Looking at her won't make it go away,' Laria suggested with a small smile and Maya smirked back. The tomboy immediately proceeded with the suggestion, focusing back on the work.

At least that issue was over.

'Now remember everyone, finish it off by tomorrow,' the teacher announced as the bell screamed out to declare that class was over. Maya packed her things quietly as Laria watched the other woman grumble under her breath. Laria had to know, she had to know why Tahani here in the first place.

'Laria?' Maya said.

Laria looked towards she, raising an eyebrow in curiosity. She noticed the wary look in Maya's eyes before Laria answered her silent question.

'I've got to talk to her,' Laria admitted; she couldn't think of an excuse. Maya's eyes hardened but Laria flashed a fake grin. 'What's the worst that could happen?' A thousand things could.

'Fine but be careful,' Maya seethed in Tahani's direction. 'I'll see you at Chemistry with Seth and Brodie.' She turned away and left the room with the remainder of the students. Even the teacher disappeared after class, and it was only the two of them in the same room.

They stood alone, the silence thickening with tension.

Tahani quietly packed her bag when Laria stood next to her. It wasn't long until Tahani pretended to notice, looking up and mocked a gasp. 'Wow. Scary. Coming to threaten the new kid already?'

'Don't play innocent Ungue Dux,' Laria said coldly, recalling the woman's title. 'You don't strike me as the one who goes to school for fun.'

Silently Tahani scoffed. 'Now Laria – please tell me that isn't the way yer talk to ya magister.'

'Magister?' Laria's eyes widened when she realised the translation of the word. 'As in teacher? Does that mean that you're the one that's training me?'

'Yup,' Tahani retorted as she popped the 'p'. 'Ya look like ya 'bout to unleash hell on earth.' She finished packing her bag and flashed a snarky grin. 'Orders from Takon – I have to train ya by crashing at the angeli house.'

And this woman was staying at Haroni's place. Laria couldn't have found anything worse. 'But... you're...'

As Laria trailed off, Tahani raised a hand. 'Relax.' She relaxed her grin. 'I'm not gonna be like the other uptight morons – for one, ya gonna call me Tahani and nothing else!' Surprised by the woman's declaration Laria leaned away from her close face. 'I'm one of the few that has bloodlust willingly. Training ya might give me something to do.'

Laria felt all hopes sink like the Titanic. She really was going to die.

'Final thing.' Tahani kept her eyes stern and she glowered at the exit. 'I don't want backchat, if I hear that sort of talk from ya or ya little pal, I'll definitely beat ya into next week. Yer clear?'

'Crystal,' Laria responded with a confused gaze.

'Now run along.' Tahani looked away and waved her hand towards the exit. Just as she prepared to leave, Tahani called out her name again. Laria turned, she recognised the smirk. 'I'll see ya in Chemistry with the rest of ya pals.'

Laria's eyes were wide as she witnessed the woman jump out of the window. Tahani was definitely going to be the death of her.

***

'Hi Jason, listen – I have some business that I have to take care of. For today you have to walk home, I'll see you at dinner.'

As the response, Jason deleted the voicemail. The books that he had remained in his locker and Jason closed the door. With a soft sigh, Jason put his phone back in his pocket and headed out.

This day was quite the shocking day for him. First, he had found out from Seth that Laria returned to school. He wasn't sure how to respond to it if he was being honest with himself. Yet that wasn't all, it happened to be the day that another student started at Golden Cliff High.

Apparently, her name was Tahani Rosa. Just like Maya's last name, so it was clear that the new student was probably related to Maya. However he noticed that Maya was distant, so it was most likely a coincidence.

His thoughts were interrupted by smacking against someone's shoulder and Jason halted in his tracks immediately to see that Brodie. He stiffened at the sight of the other male.

'Amarel,' Brodie said, meeting his hazel eyes with a spiteful glare.

Jason kept a stance. 'Forte.'

It felt like the school around them lapsed into silence, freezing in motion to watch the duo's intense gazes. Unfortunately, Jason pulled away uneasily. He didn't know what Brodie's problem was, yet he couldn't do anything to stop it.

Without another word, Brodie's eyes moved away from Jason and he stepped around him as if he was infected.

At that moment, Jason just wanted to go home and sleep. He sighed and headed out of the school grounds. The sun was still bright against the town, and Jason walked himself home.

He was passing the forest when he heard something growl. Jason stopped in his tracks. Staring in the direction of the sound, he saw something move in the trees and his eyes widened with alarm.

Whatever the creature was, Jason was in no mood to play with something that was possibly dangerous. He moved quickly, trying to stay on the main roads with houses. Jason kept moving, but he still heard the sound of soft growls behind him, but he refused to panic.

His was grateful when he arrived at the house, stepping on the porch with a smile. Nothing stalked him home, but it still felt like there was something watching him. Jason's smile dropped when he noticed that the door was opened.

Mae said that she was going to be late. He stepped closer to the door, and his eyes spotted the dents on the door that he didn't see the last time he looked at the door.

Someone had broken into his house.

'Damn it!' Jason narrowed his eyes and pushed his way side, picking up a phone to start dialling the police. At the horrible smell of blood, Jason raised his arm to his face and continued to inspect the house in case the guy was still in it.

That was when Jason tripped over something. It dawned on him instantly... it wasn't a something he tripped over but a someone.

'Jason...' Mae's voice brought him out of his trance, but he couldn't think. Stab wounds littered her body and Jason realised it was a miracle that his mother was still breathing.

'Mum, who did this to you?' Jason begged the woman,

attempting to pick her up himself. His hands were stained with her blood as he held her.

'Jason.' Mae got his attention again with a hard stare. 'You have to get out of here, he's not gone and he intends on killing me and taking you!'

For once, Jason felt anger towards his mother. 'What are you talking about? There is no way I'll leave you behind,' he snapped as he tried to grab her. 'Look, we need to get you to the hospital, who was the psychopath that did this to you?'

'Jason just listen to me for once!' Mae demanded in and with a wince she managed to push an envelope in Jason's hands. 'Read this letter first and find Leon Forte. He will help.'

'But Mum!' At the sound of a growl, Jason suddenly halted his actions and saw a hooded man walk towards them. Fear flashed Jason's eyes as the man's crimson eyes met his. He stumbled back.

'Kid Amarel – I have no idea why you are a part of them.' The crimson-eyed man sneered in delight as one of his hands was suddenly filled with a raging fire. Jason felt his hand tighten on the letter but he refused to leave Mae behind.

'Who the hell are you?'

'Call me Edward,' the man replied with a sadistic sneer. 'I was sent here to kill that woman behind you and then take you.' In a flash the man who had introduced himself as Edward was in front of Jason and had pinned him to the wall. 'Does this make you angry? That you're unable to save her?'

'Let her go!' Jason coughed, trying to pull his iron grip away.

'It's the thrill I enjoy; the screams of agony, the panic, the desperation.' Edward raised his other hand, the hand that was filled with flames and it suddenly shot out to Mae. Jason's eyes widened with horror as her screams deafened him. Jason had lost his strength. Her shrieks were ear-splitting, and Edward didn't move his hands until she fell quiet. 'The thrill of taking a life away with my bare hands.'

And just like that, Jason's mood switched. Rage flared in his system. 'I'll kill you!'

'That's it... get in line!' The man suddenly pulled back as a gunshot rang through the air, dropping Jason in the process. Jason looked up to see that Edward was sneering at a familiar face.

'Seth Laurence – your family is still alive, is it not?' Edward wondered with a sneer of excitement. Seth pointed the pistol towards Edward; no emotion on his face. 'It will be fun when I burn your parents' corpses.'

'Leave now,' he said with a flash of his yellow eyes. *Wait yellow?* Jason thought. *They were brown…* When Edward took a threatening step towards the unmoving Seth, there was no fear in Seth's eyes. 'I missed on purpose – it will not happen a second time.'

Finally, Edward stepped down with a sneer. 'Very well, but I will be back.' With that threat, he flashed out of sight and Jason returned his attention to his mother. The flames died down to reveal her charred body.

'I apologise,' Seth noted, lowering the weapon to examine the body. 'I was too late to save her.'

'What was he?' Jason demanded furiously turning to Seth. 'That man had flames in his hand and he killed her!' His shoulders shook in protest. 'How did you find me? I never told you where I lived.'

'You want to know?' Seth questioned sternly. Jason gritted his teeth. Of course he did. 'I will make it blunt.' Jason raised his head, his face full of sorrow. 'I read your mind and happened to be close.'

'What?' Jason choked out.

'I can read minds,' Seth clarified as if he was talking about the weather. *This whole time Seth knew his thoughts?* 'And I still do now,' Seth explained with a flat expression. 'Now you would probably understand why I keep myself from the rest of the humans.'

'H-Humans?' Jason stammered, trying to understand what was going on. People didn't call people, humans. It sounded unnatural – and it sounded like Seth himself wasn't "human".

'I will explain the things you need to know,' Seth said looking down at Jason. 'But I will ask you this in return... What do you have in your hand, Jason?'

Now realising that he still had the note in his hand, Jason looked at the letter and felt his heart sink in depression. Whatever this was, there was a feeling that Jason wasn't going to like it. He slipped the note away and shook his head.

'It doesn't matter,' Jason muttered. Not anymore. 'I can't even begin to think what Mae had written in here...' His eyes met with Seth's and he spoke up. 'Just explain to me what happened.'

CHAPTER 10

Brodie sat on the roof of his house, watching the sun peek over the trees. His hazel eyes squinted at the light but they adjusted. The view was a rare sight and he took advantage of it.

Another day. He thought as the light managed to reach him. The bottle of scotch in his hand was nearly empty as he watched the sunrise. With a sigh, Brodie took a final swig from his drink and stood up from his spot.

Finally, Brodie jumped from the roof of the mansion and landed smoothly on his feet.

Shifters that had training could handle long falls, but Brodie wouldn't deny the shooting pain through his legs from the impact. He stripped off his clothes piece by piece, feeling the sun's warmth cover his olive skin. It felt like he had just stepped in a bath filled with warm water.

As soon as he stood naked, he closed his eyes and concentrated on the pain, the thing that suddenly made his bones snap. Brodie's eyes flashed opened, revealing his light brown eyes instead of their normal hazel. He didn't cry out as pain shot through his jaw. His canines extended to sharp needle like teeth and his bones snapped into place. Brodie felt his body drop to the ground, groaning at the agony of his bones reforming.

His hands halted his fall and Brodie clawed the dirt underneath his fingertips. The senses were first; magnifying to his awareness. As a chill shot through his spine, Brodie recognised the feeling of his fur starting to spout from his back. It felt like goose bumps that shot through his body, and Brodie's hands forced themselves into paws.

His throat let out an inhuman growl, and his eyes noticed the sandy fur shooting through his thinning figure. Black spots sprouted with his sandy fur, and Brodie regained his footing after his balance shifted. He felt his breath escape his lungs when he looked at his new form. Instead of standing as a human, Brodie stood as the fastest land animal on earth.

Brodie adapted to his father's animal form and turned into a cheetah.

A scent caught Brodie's attention, making him growl softly to track down the alluring scent. The scent trail led him through the forest, keeping concealed behind the trees.

Before Brodie could find the source, it had disappeared into thin air. He paused in consideration, looking around him as if there had been something to block his senses. If he was blocking Brodie's senses, it meant that this shifter was using an animal pelt from their tribe to cover their tracks.

Instead of heading back to the estate, Brodie felt his limbs move swiftly into a run through the forest around them. His eyes took note of every single detail, relaxing at the feeling of the dirt being kicked up from behind his paws. He felt satisfied that he could run without worries, sensing the blood rush through his veins and felt the repetitive thump from his chest.

'Brodie!'

His thoughts returned to himself, recognising his father's voice, calling him over to get to school. With a low growl, Brodie went back to his father without hassle.

Leon was holding Brodie's clothes, glowering in his direction. 'You tracked it again, didn't you?'

Brodie let out a small growl of agreement, before he focused on morphing back into his human form. He silently flinched at the pain from his bones cracking. The stern look in Leon's eyes didn't faze as Brodie lost the fur and stood back up in his human form.

'I tried,' Brodie explained as he accepted the clothes, 'but the scent disappeared again – he must be using a pelt.'

'I will discuss this with the Mandati Dux. We might need to have more people on this.' Leon narrowed his eyes and picked up the empty scotch bottle. 'I would have to get more of this I assume?'

'Yeah,' Brodie said as he finished dressing and pulled the twigs out of his hair. Leon's eyes remained stern as he held out Brodie's school bag for him, which he took. 'I'll see you later, Father.' As Brodie retreated from his father, he felt his fists clench by his side. He had to do everything in his power to help Laria and his father.

***

Three days passed.

Jason blocked out Kenta's voice as she tried to explain the lesson. His eyes flickered in the direction of Seth sitting beside him, who was watching the teacher. But that wasn't the thing on Jason's mind as he watched Seth listening. It had been three days since his mother died. Three days since the discovery of the shifters. Three days since Seth revealed himself to be one of them.

This world was filled with supernatural creatures, but Golden Cliff was the home to shape shifters. They weren't like television shifters. In fact, they had the desire to kill.

And more importantly, they were real.

At first, Jason couldn't believe it – who would when they were told that the town's legends suddenly revealed themselves? But he thought about the strange things that had occurred in this town ever since he came here. How could Jason ever deny that?

He wanted to know why a shifter killed his mother. He wasn't anything special. Ever since he spoke with the Sheriff, Jason found out that they were going to keep Mae's death quiet and it angered him. Mae had every right to a funeral, but they told him there will be a small service. The police force wanted to catch this killer off guard.

He didn't say anything until the sheriff dragged him away and demanded answers. She introduced herself as Nadia, and that she was a shifter. So he proceeded with her wishes, telling the woman every detail he recalled. Nadia took notes, but then asked him to stay with Seth since he would be able to track the killer down.

In a surge of anger, Jason clenched his fist until his knuckles turned white. He hated it – there was a feeling deep down that begged for him to ditch class to find out more about Edward. Jason really wanted to kill this guy for laying a finger on his mother.

'Stop thinking about it,' Seth interrupted with a whisper, glancing in Jason's direction. 'I know that you demand justice, but you're not the only one who has lost a parent to that man.' When Jason met Seth's eyes, he felt like he was suddenly hopeless and he slumped from his position.

'Why?' Jason asked softly, keeping a hard gaze on his blurred lines. Why him?

'We will find out,' Seth swore with a serious gaze. 'But until then – we can't do anything. You are just a human but the fact you were wanted concerns me.'

Jason raised an eyebrow in suspicion, but he decided to let it drop for now. His eyes kept finding themselves wandering to the door; his desperation to get out was getting to him. He tried to focus on something else, so he didn't try to escape. The clock, the scratching of pens on paper, the responses that each student made in Latin that happened to translate to vengeance.

Please... Jason thought with horror, trying to get his head out of the thoughts. In the corner of his eyes, he saw that Seth had kept a stern stare but Jason didn't care. Again, Jason tightened his clenched fists and felt his fingernails dig into his skin.

He had to get out. Everyone was mocking him for letting Mae die. They didn't stop laughing. No one was there to help him. The room was beginning to shrink and trap his body in the small space. Edward was laughing with excitement as everything burned.

'Jason, you have to calm down,' Seth warned, but Jason wouldn't hear it. He couldn't be here anymore; the air was starting to get hot as if the classroom were alight with flames.

Jason pushed himself up from the desk. At that moment the bell rang and made the remainder of the students pack their bags. he stormed out of the room, ignoring the voice of Kenta. The panic was still in him, his heart racing with adrenaline as students around him crowded him.

They taunted him, saying that he wasn't able to protect his mother. That he didn't deserve to live after he let his mother die.

'Excuse me?'

A single voice caught Jason's attention and everything around him settled. The hallways no longer felt like they were on fire, his panic vanished. He looked around warily, noticing that the students weren't laughing at him. Jason gazed at the one who spoke to him, calming down at the sight of her and felt his held breath leave him.

Her hazel eyes were the first thing that he had noticed

about her; the fact that they were full of life and devotion. She had her light brown hair tied up in a ponytail with a few loose strands that were too short to be pinned back with the rest of her hair. The girl in front of him frowned in.

'Hey.' She spoke softly as her frown deepened. 'Are you alright?'

Jason cleared his throat nervously and straightened his posture. 'Yes... I'm fine.' He immediately pushed away his other thoughts and scratched his head. 'What makes you think that I wasn't okay?'

The girl leaned in. 'You looked utterly terrified,' she explained before adding, 'and you're lacking a bag.'

'Right,' Jason realised and his cheeks turned warm. He should've known that he left his bag in the room with Seth. 'My friend has it at the moment.'

Staring at the petite girl in front of him, Jason could help but smile. For once in the past three days he felt better. There was something in the air around her that settled him.

'Jason!'

He flinched at Seth's voice, sheepishly turning to see him with an annoyed scowl. 'Hey, Seth... sorry about that – something just...'

'Forget it,' he replied stonily and passed Jason his bag. 'I understand.'

Before Jason could ask, the girl quietly muttered, 'I need to be heading back to class.' She moved around the duo and walked towards class until Jason realised that he forgot something.

'Hey wait!' Jason gained the girl's attention as Seth stood next to him in silence.

She paused and tilted her head. 'Is something wrong?'

Jason flashed a grin towards the student. 'I don't know your name!'

Slowly she answered back. 'Heather Verdas... It's nice to meet you Jason.' She waved shyly and headed into the crowd, leaving the duo standing in the middle of the hallway.

Jason immediately turned back to Seth. 'How long as she been here?'

***

Edward ignored the dirty looks from his colleagues. The streets were filled with countless people, but only half of them had recognised his crimson eyes. He entered a large white building, sneered at the glares. It amused him that his own allies hated him.

At the sight of a familiar face, Edward smiled wickedly and approached the receptionist. He noticed that the woman's icy blue eyes met with his and she hissed. Seeing her familiar red lips curse under her breath, Edward leaned on the counter.

'Charmi,' Edward greeted slyly. 'Red is a lovely colour on you. It suits you,' he said referring to the red dress that hugged her curves.

With a snort, Charmi went back to work. 'As if you're going anywhere with that lame attempt of flattery Edward.'

Edward showed a childish pout. 'Charmi, I can handle the fools that think they're so tough but do you have to treat me like dirt?

Charmi dismissed him with her accent clear in her tone. 'I can treat you any way I want. I wish for you to be dead, but it looks like you survive another day.' She moved her eyes away from him and focused on the computer. 'He's angry by the way.'

'I'm aware,' Edward retorted with a scowl. He hated the fact the he had failed to bring any of them, especially since two of them were protected. The third child that he orphaned was still living happily despite having no parents to depend on. 'All of them are stubborn.'

'I think it's amusing to see you mad,' Charmi said as she went through a few files and handled him a piece of paper. 'Unfortunately, you don't have to do anymore orphaning; apparently the duxes aren't backing down.'

'Very well,' Edward agreed and clenched his jaw. 'Besides it's within all of them – they are true descendants after all.'

'I don't see it,' Charmi explained as she looked back at him with a sneer. Edward remained silent as she let out a chuckle. 'You give those children something to fear... but it obviously wasn't enough to unleash the bloodlust.'

'You're wrong there,' Edward said and it suddenly stopped the woman. 'Laria Alfero, her bloodlust was activated before I came along – she only needed one reason to snap.'

Charmi's face turned serious for a moment, her eyes met with Edward's and he heard it. The screams of agony went through his brain. He growled in frustration to hold his head, seeing the images of the men that had done him wrong.

'You're a bitch,' Edward growled as he tried to shut his eyes. Even when he closed them, he could remember the pain of countless needles being injected into him. All for the purpose of science, they said – to advance the human research.

'Trust me Edward – we won't fail.' Charmi leaned forward and the smile formed on her lips. Just as the woman smiled, the images of Edward's past vanished and he scowled at her. He hated feeling so weak around Charmi Forte, of all people. Her powers to bring up the subconscious memories were flawless.

Edward shook his head to get rid of the thoughts. 'You're a bigger idiot than I remembered if you think that's going to bring the four true descendants to our side.'

'I never said I was going alone.' Charmi stood to her feet.

A smile was brought to her lips and she snorted with amusement. 'I think that the look of horror is a great expression as well.' She left the main room and headed out, leaving Edward to growl to himself in annoyance.

'You'll regret it Charmi,' Edward muttered. 'You'll wish that you listened to me.'

CHAPTER 11

'Let's go, one more round then we head to school!'

With a look of determination in her eyes, Laria watched the Ungue Dux with an observant gaze and processed the situation. One thing that Laria had learnt by fighting Tahani was that she didn't hold back. 'Sure.'

A cocky smirk crossed over Tahani's face. She chuckled lightly as Laria brought up her fists in a defensive position. 'Sweet.' Tahani's hand darted towards Laria; wrapping her cold fingers around the offending limb and pulled it above her head. Laria smirked at her accomplishment as it exposed Tahani's ribs and aimed a kick.

However before Laria could meet her foot with Tahani's side, the dux used her strength to flip Laria over her and smacked her into the ground. Hitting the ground made Laria release the grip that she had on Tahani. But then, Tahani wrapped her legs around the single arm and pinned Laria in a painful position.

There was no breaking out of the arm bar. Laria tapped on the ground. 'You win again.' The pain vanished in the next second as Tahani let go and pushed herself to her feet. 'I can't believe that after a month training with you, I still haven't gotten the best of you.'

Tahani snorted. 'Are yer stupid? This ain't a movie, there's no way ya gonna pass someone who fights back in the pits.'

When Laria first heard about the pits, she had been rather

confused. But over time, she learnt that the pit was a hidden place in the town where people went to fight. Shifters went there all the time to vent out their frustration but a lot of humans attended to fight or place bets. Currently, Tahani who had been the shape shifter in training for years had been the woman's champion for three years in a row.

Then there was the issue of time. Since shape shifters aged slower the more they killed, Tahani would have to hide in the abandoned house with the other duxes. Sometimes they moved away, but it was different for Tahani.

'If ya do beat me, it would be because I'm dead,' Tahani reminded, raising a hand over Laria to offer her a boost. With grudging respect, Laria accepted the offer and Tahani pulled Laria to her feet. 'Stop pouting – I'm not training ya to be the strongest, I'm training ya so ya can learn how to control that bloodlust. Fighting soothes the beast within – yer don't wanna snap.'

'By teaching me Muay Thai? I thought there would've been some Latin styled fighting that I would've automatically learned.' She noticed that Tahani went to the bench of the combat room to wipe the sweat over her face with a towel.

It had been nearly two months since Laria had learnt about the existence of shifters. She was physically stronger thanks to Tahani's training and Laria adapted to her new nature. It wasn't much of a curse to her anymore. However Laria still had no signs of transformation, or any hints of her abilities.

The only thing that Laria had was bloodlust and it was tough to control. She wasn't exactly impatient about these abilities, but Laria would rather have a chance to defend herself from the real monsters out there.

Monsters like Edward.

'As much as that sounds awesome, it doesn't work that way,' Tahani said and passed Laria a clean towel. 'Our strength mostly comes from instinct, so we naturally learn to communicate like the rectocs. Fighting is all on us.'

'Speaking of the rectocs... how were they sealed?' Laria asked and Tahani's curious expression coloured her features.

'The rectocs,' Tahani muttered under her breath as she turned to face Laria with a serious expression. It was a new thing to see. 'They were sealed up by a stone called the Corvena – the origin of our gift. It has a lot of power and that includes sealing. As soon as the rectocs were sealed the stone was separated into four so that no one could easily revive them again. We call 'em Azu, Verm, Rel and Viri.'

'Who sealed them?' Laria asked, and she noticed Tahani's expression turned nostalgic.

'It's kind of complicated-' Tahani began but her eyes looked up and she flashed a grin. 'Good morning to ya, Angeli.'

Angeli was the nickname that Tahani gave to Haroni. Judging the deep thoughtful look in his eyes, Laria wondered if he took it personally.

Haroni shook his head to dismiss any lingering thoughts and he waved towards the duo. 'I see training is coming along rather nicely.' He noticed as Laria nodded in agreement. 'Perhaps soon I will start teaching you how to fight with a sword.'

'What about a gun?' Laria suggested with a raised eyebrow. 'We don't live in the dark ages after all – what happens if an enemy has a gun and tries to shoot me?'

'We'll do whatever you feel more comfortable with,' Haroni promised before he checked his watch and chuckled quietly. 'Anyways, I came here because Tracy demanded for you two to come along and get ready. You know how she is.'

'Man, Tracy Ladas does not like me.' Tahani chuckled at the thoughts of the blonde. Even though Tracy was often cold, she seemed to act colder in front of Tahani.

'Alright,' Laria agreed and put the towel over her shoulder. She pulled her sweaty locks back and cringed with revulsion. 'I need a shower too - I'm sweating like a pig.'

'Ya gotta beat me first,' Tahani announced, smirking as she pushed Laria, making her crash into ground. As Laria fell Tahani took off up the stairs and disappeared from Laria's sight.

'Wow,' Haroni chuckled lightly and offered a hand. 'She's full of energy.'

'Do you ever wonder why you let her live here?' Laria asked Haroni as she grabbed his hand and helped herself up. 'I mean she drives Tracy through the roof, especially when you two drink together – then she proceeds to take forever just to go for a damn shower.'

'Seeing my dear sister angry is highly amusing,' Haroni noted as he wrapped a comforting arm around Laria's shoulders. 'But she's training you. You enjoy her company because you feel like you're not alone and if you're happy, then I'm ecstatic.'

Shaking her head lightly, Laria let out a soft chuckle. 'As much as I hate to admit it, I know that you're right.'

***

'So tell me, how did the movie end?' Heather wondered with a smile as Jason smirked cockily and shook his head. The duo walked the same path to school, since Jason had only lived a few houses away from her.

Since Mae had passed away, they'd had a small service in Mae's honour and Jason got everything in Mae's will which included her house, her car and the money in her bank account. It was a fair bit, and Jason silently promised himself that he would keep it, but it didn't help that he had to stay with Seth.

'No way,' Jason replied. 'I don't give spoilers; I'm not one of those people who will ruin a movie.'

'But it's different when I want you to tell me how it ends,' Heather explained with a smile which only made Jason shake his head with a chuckle. 'Come on, please tell me.'

'I already said I'm not going to tell you,' Jason retorted and dodged a soft looking swat from his female companion. 'Just watch it, and then we can talk about it.'

Heather stopped pestering him with questions and she settled down. 'If I don't like it... then don't blame me.'

'You'll love it,' Jason promised with a smile. His gaze went to the school campus. As always, the school building looked overpopulated with students.

Jason rolled his eyes but they ended up squeezing through the giant crowd. He checked the time on his phone before he remembered what he had. 'I have English first up, I'll see you later, okay?'

Before Heather could reply, Jason left her with a smile. She was a great person to be around, but sometimes Jason felt that he was too nervous to be near her for too long. For a moment, he wondered what was going on until he recognised Laria with Tahani Rosa.

'Laria,' Jason called out, getting the duo's attention. The brunette waved cheerfully and beckoned him over while the other woman scoffed. During the month that Tahani had been around, she often disappeared but whenever they were in class, Laria was seen with her.

'Hey Jason,' Laria said with a smile. He smiled in return and he realised that she looked different. Not in a bad way of course.

After realising that he was staring at her, he shook his head in dismissal. 'Sorry,' he muttered and looked away with a light frown. 'So did you end up doing your essay?'

Both of the females widened their eyes in realisation, but Laria was the one who voiced out her thoughts. 'Not yet.' Laria scratched the back of her head nervously. 'How about you?'

'Me?' Truth be told, Jason hadn't given it much thought. It was an essay about the characters of *Macbeth*. 'Not much, but I'll get there soon. Mister Hunt is collecting them by the end of next week.'

'Great then Tahani said with a smirk. "Cause I haven't done anything on that dumb Spearshake essay.'

'Tahani,' Laria spoke as if she was trying to explain it to her simply. 'It's "Shakespeare" – don't you know your history?'

'I don't care about history that has nothing to do with me,' Tahani snapped coldly.

'Tahani,' Laria scolded before she faced Jason sheepishly. 'Sorry Jason, Tahani's a bit blunt.'

'Don't apologise for my behaviour,' Tahani growled and Jason flinched. There was something about this woman that seemed strange. 'If he doesn't like the way I act, then he can leave the both of us alone...'

He wanted to scowl, but he chose not to so he didn't spark any flames. If Laria was friends with this woman then who was Jason to judge? She was already friends with someone who hated his guts; there was no problem with him dealing with another.

'Don't worry about it.' Jason shook it off and it surprised Tahani. 'After all, she's not like your other friend. I mean, I like Maya and Jenna but your other one.'

Laria's frown formed on her face. Her thoughtful expression deepened with concern. 'Brodie's causing you trouble? It doesn't sound like him.'

'He makes it clear that he hates me.'

Instead of pressing on the matter he recognised the teacher calling them in. 'Come on.' He decided as he walked ahead.

Jason took his seat at the front as always and he met Laria's gaze with a faint smile. She looked like she was confused by his confession as she sat next to him. Her face formed a scowl as Tahani smirked cockily and took a seat away from them, but her features softened when she passed a gaze to Jason.

Jason found a pencil and doodled on one of the books, keeping his mind away from Laria. It worked for the first half of the lesson, but as soon as he felt something brush his arm, Jason knew that their silence was over. A small, folded piece of paper slid into his view.

Curiosity got the best of him, taking the small note to read. His eyes recognised the small writing that belonged to Laria.

Jason, tell me... how is Brodie bothering you?

At first, Jason did want to her to know how Brodie had been behaving. However he didn't want to separate two friends just because one of them was making his life miserable. Jason refused to tell her, but his muscles frozen in place when Laria rested a hand on his.

'Please Jason,' Laria whispered with pleading eyes, making Jason flinch in concern. There was no way he could refuse a second time.

'Brodie is... different with me,' he began gently as Laria kept a focused gaze. Jason took it as a sign as her listening intently and he continued, 'I don't know how to explain it...'

Laria's eyes narrowed seriously. 'I promise you that I had no idea that Brodie was treating you that way. If he keeps causing you trouble, just tell me alright?'

Jason flashed a smile at her offer. 'Alright.' He agreed and just as he did so, the bell rang to announce that class was over. Everyone packed up their books and Jason stood from his spot. His eyes met hers as he offered a warm smile. 'I'll see you later then, right?'

Laria stared back with uncertainty on her face, but it wasn't long until the worry disappeared. He relaxed at her accepting look.

'Alright then,' she answered and flashed him a smile. Jason seemed stiff under her stare, but she merely offered a wave. 'I'll see you later.'

He nodded. 'Yeah.'

***

'I can't believe that ya not letting me stay with yer friends,' Tahani reminded as Laria led her to their final class for the day. They had just had their lunch and as always, Tahani went to go off on her own for a bit. The only conclusion that Laria could come up with was the idea of being with Takon to discuss their plans.

'My friends don't like you,' Laria responded. 'In fact, Maya once assumed that you were going to kill someone and make them look like they ran away to never come back.'

'That little brat,' Tahani muttered as she crossed her arms over her chest. 'That girl ain't a true Rosa if she's fearin' me.'

'Look, I know that I have no chance in changing you,' Laria started with a frown and made Tahani look in her direction. 'But please, can you stop with that?'

The dux appeared innocent. 'Stop doing what?'

Laria's scowl deepened. 'Stop threatening people – I know that you're strong, but those are my friends you're threatening and when I'm protecting the ones that I care about, I won't hold back.' Suddenly Tahani stopped and Laria copied her movements, the latter harshly glaring at her.

'Ya think that it's that easy? If ya ask me nicely that it might go ya way?'

Laria felt herself gasp within a heartbeat and suddenly found herself trapped. She tried to break out of the pinned position between Tahani and the lockers but Laria knew that it was pointless.

Tahani's eyes flashed warningly. 'Listen Laria,' Tahani said coldly as Laria resisted a shudder from the temperature drop. The grip that Tahani had on her didn't loosen. 'I came here to train ya.' As soon as Tahani released Laria, she felt her senses recover from the attack. 'I didn't come here to give a damn 'bout the humans – let alone yer sorry band of friends. Ya don't tell me what to do... at all.'

As Tahani turned away and entered the closest room, Laria felt her chest and noticed the cooler temperature of her skin compared to the rest of her body.

'*Laria!*'

Jenna rushed in and suddenly hugged Laria from behind. Laria felt relief when she sensed Jenna, glad that they shared a class. Being in a class alone with Tahani would've made her feel awkward. Especially after that confrontation.

'Hey Jenna,' Laria replied as she pulled herself away from the blonde. She noticed that Jenna had a wide grin as always but it suddenly dropped when Jenna observed Laria with an elevated gaze. Laria frowned, knowing that look of Jenna's too well.

'Is something wrong Laria?'

The conversation with Tahani ran through her head. There was no telling on how the dux would've acted over such a request. From the first time they met, Laria knew that Tahani was blunt and rude, but she didn't expect her to be cruel. It meant that her friends weren't safe near Tahani and Laria had to make sure she protected them.

'Nothing important.' Laria dismissed the words and the duo headed to class together.

'Hey, I noticed Mister Embers has been acting up,' Jenna realised as she went through her daily conversations. 'It's like he...' Laria managed to dismiss the small talk and pretend to listen, keeping focused on her sight. As Laria stood in the classroom, she noticed that Tahani was leaning at the back seat with a bored look in her eyes.

Why was Tahani so complicated?

'–There's something wrong with Tahani.' Suddenly gaining interest, Laria perked an eyebrow as Tahani closed her eyes. Laria knew that Tahani could easily overhear the conversation, but the dux didn't do anything to interrupt them.

'How so?' Laria wondered as the duo took their usual seats together. 'I'm not very good at reading people, you know that Jenna.'

'Well – for one, she's angry at something, most likely herself.' Jenna explained. Immediately, Laria looked over to Tahani and felt curiosity crawl in her chest. 'Her eyes have this desire; she wants redemption – the closure that you both need to move on.'

As Jenna continued, her voice slowly faded out of Laria's mind and she began to feel it. She kept her gaze on Tahani until the dux opened one eye to glower at Laria.

'*Stop staring,*' the dux ordered with a silent growl and Laria glanced at Jenna. For the moment, Laria had forgotten that Tahani was able to sense everything that went on around her. '*Tell ya friend to shut up too – she's dead wrong 'bout everything.*'

'*But something did happen, didn't it?*' Laria silently returned and spared a look towards Tahani, who snorted in annoyance. Jenna was about to continue but she fell quiet as David entered the class with a heavy look in his eyes.

'Sorry I'm late students,' he began. 'I got held up in something – I have a busy schedule for today so I'm just dismissing the class.' Students cheered in excitement. 'But.' The students who celebrated suddenly stopped their cheering when David met a gaze with Laria. 'I wish to speak with Tahani and Laria.'

Why them two?

Jenna looked sympathetic but she packed her bags with a guilty look in her eyes. 'Sorry Laria but I need to finish my math assignment.' She spared a glance towards Tahani who went to the teacher's desk. 'I'll see you tomorrow?' As soon as Laria nodded, Jenna headed out of the room with the rest of the class.

'Alright David,' Tahani spoke up with a scowl as she turned to the history teacher. 'Ya sending students home and bringing us ol' shifters here. What the hell is going on?'

Suddenly shocked at Tahani's comment, Laria looked over to the dux with disbelief. Did she just announce that she was a shifter? David was a fan of history, and the myths of skin walkers would be the greatest thing that he would ever hear.

'Sorry,' David muttered sheepishly which made Laria's jaw drop. He chuckled. 'It seems that you failed to inform Laria about me, Ungue Dux – especially after a month.'

Laria's eyes grew wide. 'What?'

'Ah.' Tahani clicked her fingers with a smirk covering her features. 'That's what I forgot,' she said and waved a hand. 'Laria – this is David Embers; he hunts shifters.'

'He's a hunter?' Laria asked, mildly surprised at the new information.

'Yes,' David confirmed, lifting the collar of his shirt to reveal a tattoo with three markings that appeared like claw marks. 'Humans were aware of shifters and rectocs. But shortly after the treaty over sixty years ago, humans turned you guys into stories such as the disappearance of the tribe. Only a selected few were chosen to know the truth no. We're a council that is dedicated to protecting lives known as the Shifter Hunting Organisation or the S.H.O. This is our confirmation as hunters.'

Laria took a seat. 'So you knew about me this whole time?

Do you know anything else that I have to know?'

'Not really.' The teacher shrugged it off. 'I just cancelled class today because I got a hit.' He raised his hand to flash a phone. 'All over Golden Cliff, there are sensors that can track shifters, including outsiders.'

'You track our enemies with a phone?'

David raised an eyebrow. 'It's an app – come on Laria, we're in the twenty-first century. You can do everything with a phone nowadays...' He hid his phone in his pocket and his expression went back to serious. 'Now, back on topic – there's an outsider that has been around town but it hasn't attacked. I fear the worst.'

Tahani shrugged quietly which left Laria confused. There was a shifter around and they were doing nothing? Before Laria could do anything, the dux grabbed Laria's shoulders and held her back. Laria struggled against the hold, but Tahani's hold was iron.

'Stand down Laria,' Tahani warned. As Laria shot a glare, Tahani's gaze was darker. 'That's an order Laria.'

'Fine,' Laria spat coldly and looked away. 'Just get me out of this grip.' With a cocky smirk, Tahani dropped her hands and returned her attention to David.

'Now, as for the shifter, I'm not sure what the intentions are,' David continued to explain. 'This guy is bouncing around as if he's looking for something.'

'Or, in this case, someone,' Tahani announced with a blank stare which made Laria turn towards her with wide eyes.

'It's not Edward,' David informed as Laria began to feel panicked. 'But we can track someone through their bloodlust desires; it is someone that is obviously a lot more skilled than Edward.'

Laria kept her eyes wide as the duo conversed. There were people just as dark as Edward was? Sure, they were an army full of bloodlust warriors, but Laria had been under the assumption that Edward had always been the most ruthless one.

'Why?' she finally asked to interrupt the conversation. 'Why do they want me? There are plenty more shifters that are capable of bloodlust, and I can't even transform.' Both David and Tahani spared a glanced towards each other, before they focused on Laria.

'It's not just you,' David said as Laria shot him a look. She remained quiet as her teacher began to explain. 'The true descendants are always targeted.'

'Beside the point.' Tahani stepped in with a distant stare out of the window. 'Yer wanted because yer an Alfero.' She passed Laria a serious look. 'The last Alfero to be exact, they want yer to be on their side for reasons that I don't even know.'

Laria felt her throat go dry. It explained everything, why her dreams kept reminding her that something had been sealed by a bunch of witches. She knew this, but she didn't know why every time she heard it – it still sounded like the worst news in the world. 'But... I'm just...'

'Like David said – it's not just the Alfero family,' Tahani reminded and crossed her arms over her chest with a scowl. 'They've been after the true descendants for years – even I have to be careful around them. Now there's a story that ya should know, something that's grave and has a lot to do with ya history.' Laria stared back at Tahani with alarm. 'When the humans did know 'bout us they killed.'

'Killed?' Laria whispered, ignoring the bad feeling. Then it dawned on her. 'The massacre that you were talking about.'

'Killed the true descendants that they knew 'bout,' Tahani clarified which made Laria suddenly stop in her tracks. 'Many shifters were dead, including your ancestors – the survivors lost control of themselves from their loss. They killed anything for the sake of vengeance, rage, misery and even for the thrill. That's when the enemies discovered unlocking a shifter's bloodlust by killing a family. Their connection.'

Laria found the will to speak again. 'What about you?'

Laria could had sworn that Tahani had become a different person for a moment. The look in her eyes turned serious and her face was filled with a desire Laria couldn't make out.

However it was quick, Tahani's face went blank again. 'Not really.' She shook it off with a shrug. 'Everyone knows that I only use my bloodlust for fun and there's no losing control of that anytime soon.'

***

'Brodie – I will return, stay here and don't track anyone down.'

Those were the last words that he heard from Leon before he'd left Brodie alone that night. He laid back on his bed, staring at the ceiling with an uninterested gaze. At first he had thought it had to do with the heat in his room, then he realised that it had to do with more. Sleep wouldn't come to him, even when he took off his shirt.

Years of training as a shape shifter gave him a fairly strong build. Ever since Leon left with rage forming on his face, Brodie wondered what his father had been doing this whole month. They hadn't encountered each other during the time since Leon had been busy with examining the dead body and Brodie had gone to school. For a moment, he had been tempted to go down the basement, where his father had been working but dismissed it.

The door was coded, and Brodie didn't know his father that well.

Since Brodie's estate was rather large, he had a decent sized room. It had his queen-sized bed on one side and a large mirror showing his reflection on the other. He kept a pile of old stories on his table and he had no paint on his walls.

'What's wrong father?' Brodie asked to the space above him. Like he expected, there were no sounds that would indicate that he was getting an answer anytime soon. With a sigh, he pushed himself off the bed and rubbed his sweaty forehead.

When he last saw Leon, he could literally feel the anger emanating from the him. He shoved something in one of his drawers before he rushed out and ordered Brodie to stay put. It wasn't bloodlust or anything; Leon had the look of hatred in his eyes and was determined to kill something.

But once again, Brodie didn't know his father well enough.

However, he respected his father's wishes and never disobeyed him. Everything that Leon owned and kept away from Brodie was concealed with the drawers – even though he was curious, he honestly would rather have his father open up.

He sighed again with worry but decided to find out his father's whereabouts. Relying on the sense of smell, Brodie was an excellent tracker, his eyes remained hard as he left the house and walked alone until he heard unnatural growls.

Immediately Brodie rushed, ignoring the heart pounding moment when he turned into a dark alley and halted in his tracks.

A large, white wolf stood on top of his father's body.

CHAPTER 12

Brodie had felt fear before, but it was never so intense. His father should've been strong enough however this time was different. There was something that turned Brodie's nose off. It was like he was facing death face to face.

'What the hell are you doing to my father?!'

The white wolf shot its head up, revealing the amber eyes that Brodie recognised too easily. It snarled in his direction.

The Forte's are finished,' the wolf began with a deep voice. Brodie heard his voice in his mind, and then the beast looked at Leon who was choking in his own blood. *'Goodbye Leon Forte – as you rot in hell, you will realise how you failed not only your children but Laria Alfero.'*

Brodie's anger failed to diminish. 'Hey!' he snapped, getting the wolf's attention once again. Anger licked at his spine when the wolf's eyes glinted dangerously. 'As if I'm going to let you get away with this!' His eyes flashed brown to activate his power but to his surprise, nothing happened.

'Brodie, no!' Leon shouted, 'He's too strong for your hypnosis! It won't work.'

Brodie wanted to refuse his father, but he really saw the situation.

'Damn it – I can't do anything like this!' Brodie hissed, just as he clenched his fist. Without thinking, Brodie let out an angry yell to attack the wolf. The wolf growled deeply, jumping away from Brodie's form, and leaping at him from a different angle.

It hit Brodie with surprise, knocking him into the ground in a life-threatening position. All the wolf had to do was crush his windpipe and Brodie was gone. He stared at the wolf's amber eyes and saw a man behind them. However, Brodie was surprised when the wolf backed away.

'*You are trash Leon Forte,*' the wolf announced. '*That's why you can't even tell your son the truth.*' Brodie pushed himself up when the beast backed away. But before he could do anything, the shifter was gone.

Hearing a groan from his father snapped Brodie out of it. He rushed towards Leon with panic and cradled his body.

Leon cursed in agony. 'You have to go after-!'

'No, Dad,' Brodie snapped which shocked his father. 'If you die then our efforts will be for nothing – please don't give up yet.'

Leon cringed in pain, but he managed to speak up again, 'I found him... the Beast...' Just before Brodie could tell him to save his energy, Leon stopped him. 'But that isn't important... I feel like I should tell you the truth.'

'The truth?' Brodie shook his head. 'Not the time father – right now I need you to stay alive more than anything, I'll pull you up-'

'You're not my only child Brodie.'

Suddenly, Brodie stopped his actions and felt the air finally go cold. What did Leon just say?

'You have a twin... I separated you when Deborah died.' Brodie felt his throat dry up, unable to believe the sudden turn of events. 'Brodie, I do not have long... we both know that...'

With an angry determination, Brodie shook his head in annoyance. 'I don't want to hear it! Keep your energy and the Medicinae Dux will heal you when he gets here!'

Leon chuckled dryly and stared up at the sky. 'For someone who had great respect for me, you sure have a hard time listening.' Then Brodie felt his father's mirror ability of hypnosis in the back of his mind. Leon was always the stronger one.

'No!' Brodie knew what it was. He felt his body sway, then he suddenly collapsed on the cold floor of the night with the thoughts of the giant wolf with amber eyes and his dying father.

***

The buzzing from her phone woke Laria up the next morning, stopping her long-forgotten nightmare from continuing. Her hair was in a mess, but she pushed herself up to grab the phone and she saw the contact information.

'Brodie,' Laria spoke up.

'*Laria...*' Once she heard his voice, she couldn't recognise it. Brodie's voice was hoarse to her ears. *We need to talk... Bring the Ungue Dux with you as well.*' The phone went dead and Laria pulled away.

Before Laria could get out of bed she heard a familiar rough voice. 'I guess ya got the announcement from the Forte kid.' Laria jumped with a startled yelp when Tahani appeared by her window with a serious stare.

'Tahani, how the heck did you get up here?' Laria snapped, standing on her bed to glower at the dux. Tahani chuckled lightly, slipping into the building and pulling a twig out of her messy hair.

'I just came back from my run if ya so damn worried,' the dux replied with a smirk as if she had read Laria's thoughts. 'So we're needed at the Forte Estate to discuss some news – Takon's orders.' Her eyes suddenly turned serious, glancing back at Laria with a hint of sympathy. 'Yer aware of Tara's brother?'

She recognised the name. 'What about Leon?' Her eyes

went wide in realisation and she grabbed the collar of Tahani's shirt. 'What happened?!' Laria loved Leon. There was no denial – he was simply the father that Laria never had.

'I don't know myself. Takon didn't tell me the details,' Tahani explained curtly as she stared down at Laria. When Laria dropped Tahani's collar, Tahani brushed the shirt and headed out of the room. 'So it's obvious that it's serious enough to bring a dux or two. Be ready in ten – I'm driving there.' As soon as she left the room, Laria sighed heavily.

She went to the bathroom to get dressed and fix up her messed-up hair. As soon as she stepped out again, Tahani had been waiting behind the door with Haroni's keys flashing in her hands.

'Is Haroni letting you drive?' she asked sceptically.

'There's a bunch of things that ya don't know 'bout me,' Tahani declared with a smirk. She led Laria out of the mansion to get in Haroni's car.

Laria's eyes were suspicious as the dux took the wheel; Tahani said nothing as she started the engine and began to drive. At first, Laria thought that she was going to die – however Tahani calmly drove out of the driveway and went on the road without a hassle.

It seemed that Tahani noticed the surprise in Laria's expression. 'Yer really don't know anything 'bout me Laria.' The dux was right; Laria didn't really know anything about Tahani. 'Actually... do ya know where that Forte kid lives?'

Tahani listened to Laria's directions without protest, but when she pulled up in the large driveway, the duo noticed that there were several pulled up cars.

'It looks like it's more than just a little picnic,' Tahani noted when she turned off the car. Laria stepped out of the vehicle with Tahani and frowned.

'We need to see what happened.' Laria ignored Tahani's

warning call as she pushed herself through the small crowd and found the familiar flash a cinnamon brown hair. Recognising Brodie, Laria struggled to catch up. She found him sitting on an armchair with Tara and a group of unfamiliar faces.

The unfamiliar figures gave wary looks towards Laria and some even whispered. But it didn't matter to Laria, she had learnt to block out everyone's voices that were about her.

Brodie noticed that she arrived and Laria flinched at his bloodshot eyes. 'Laria...'

'Brodie,' Laria responded with a worried tone. 'What happened?' At first, Brodie remained silent; it felt lethal. Her eyes stung and she lost composure. 'Tell me Brodie!'

'Leon's gone, Laria,' Tara announced from Brodie's side. 'Leon had contact with a shifter that had been sighted around town and went to take it on.' She couldn't breathe – not Leon, he didn't deserve it. 'He's dead Laria...'

'Brodie,' Laria began as Brodie turned away. She ignored the rejected feeling in her chest. 'I...'

'I need to be alone Laria,' Brodie admitted and once again, Laria heard the deep croaked voice that didn't belong to her best friend.

'But you called me,' Laria protested in irritation. 'Brodie, you were there when I needed you... so please tell me, what happened?'

He went back to look at her, and the pain was clear in his face. 'Just leave me alone for a bit.'

Laria felt anger coursing through her. She'd known Brodie for years and she understood the secret part of his life. Yet Brodie wanted to abandon her just because he wanted to deal with the pain. It wasn't a thing that she could accept.

'I can't!' she argued. 'I won't just leave you just because you don't want to talk to me. Aren't we friends? Don't we support each other no matter-!'

'Enough!'

Laria suddenly stopped speaking as a hand shot out to grab her shoulder stunning her into silence. Zanobi's tall frame towered over her but he gave an air of authority.

With a scowl, Laria backed down. 'Zanobi.'

'He had just lost his father,' Zanobi reminded Laria which only made her angry. 'If he wants to be alone with his family, you just have to understand.'

She wanted to disagree, but Zanobi was right. With a weak sigh, Laria followed Zanobi out of the estate. In the corner of her eyes, Laria noticed that Tahani had looked onwards but didn't bother to say anything.

***

Zanobi strolled through the property with Laria. It was a nice forest to go through; the only thing he had to complain about was there was no path. Laria followed in silence.

'You're worried,' he noted as Laria looked his way. He was good at reading people, especially adolescents. 'It looks like it has to do with more than the loss of your father figure.'

'Leon was the father I never had...' Laria whispered and looked away.

'You know the story of the massacre?' Zanobi questioned, looking back at Laria as she nodded in agreement. 'Because of your current loss, every shifter has been on edge with the sudden deaths. You and Brodie have yet to lose yourself.'

She didn't argue back.

With a sigh, Zanobi decided to tell her something for a distraction. 'Fifteen years ago was when your brother began to realise his origins.'

'I was about two years old then...' Laria explained as Zanobi silently nodded in agreement. 'I thought that Chris had his powers later on.'

'Like shifters, witches from different families have different abilities – especially your mother. Your brother developed early. However you were a different case; you had nothing. Your family was attacked by shifters, they were obviously intending on getting Chris to turn on their side.'

'But he was a warlock...' Laria realised and it dawned on her.

'When he showed no signs, you did Laria.' Zanobi pointed out seriously. 'Your eyes looked like an animal's and the shifters retreated without any signs of traits.'

'So my bloodlust was sealed by the witches until they returned,' she finished Zanobi's story and naturally, Laria let out a shaky breath of agony. The enemy knew that she was a true descendant from the day that they tried killing off her parents. 'How do you know so much?'

'I was there of course,' Zanobi answered. Laria felt the surprise flash in her eyes but she remained silent. 'You were the daddy's girl, always hiding behind Lucien as if he was going to scare everyone else for you.' He chuckled before staring at the tree tops. 'That was the day we lost him.'

'I can't remember him...' Laria admitted. 'But I feel a connection to him.' Zanobi found himself stopping when he noticed a small creek concealed in the trees. 'Why are you telling me this?'

There was a fallen log within the forest and Zanobi took the opportunity to sit. Laria joined him, looking down at her feet with the strands of her dark hair framing her round face. It would be a lie if Zanobi didn't think that it was rather an innocent face.

'Because you need to know the truth,' Zanobi declared seriously as he met her gaze. 'But I'll have you know, they believe in you. Your brother, the fallens, Tahani, Brodie, myself and even Leon believed that you will overcome this.'

The silence from Laria was haunting. He raised an eyebrow as Laria slowly nodded in acceptance to his words. She smiled and let out a soft mutter under her breath, too quiet for even his supernatural hearing to gather. But Zanobi knew it was only a short response to his confession. This girl was clearly Lucien's daughter; she had a lot more than his looks. She was passionate, loyal and determined.

After minutes of comfortable silence, Zanobi let out a heavy sigh. 'I suppose we should return,' he muttered as he pulled himself back to his feet. 'Just remember to be there for Brodie for when he needs you.'

'Yeah,' Laria agreed silently as she joined him.

They walked back to the estate with the same silence that they came in with, but it disappeared as soon as Laria recognised her human friends. Zanobi raised an eyebrow towards the pair of girls talking to each other with hushed words. The blonde he ignored, but there was something about the raven-haired female that was... rather odd.

As Laria went to her human friends, Zanobi took off his shades to watch them.

There was a part of Zanobi that wondered if Laria would've accepted the humans if she had been born a few decades earlier? Would she have accepted the humans as she did today? After all, Laria was an Alfero and the humans killed most of the Alfero family until there were a few remaining.

'Yer doing a good thing; helping her out.' Tahani's form slinked behind him, and Zanobi didn't move. She followed his gaze. 'That girl's a Rosa — that's probably why she looks familiar.'

Zanobi frowned in consideration. 'A late bloomer like Laria? Who are her parents?'

'Know nothing 'bout her,' Tahani confessed as she

watched the black-haired female. 'She hadn't been acting anything like me... she's defected.'

He raised an eyebrow. 'Kaeylin wasn't like you despite being your sister.'

Tahani's scowl only deepened. 'She was my baby sister so it's understandable for her to be as harmless as a butterfly. Rosa's are meant to be rowdy. That girl over there nothing of the sort, always staring at me as if I'm gonna haunt her nightmares.'

'Ah Tahani.' Zanobi chuckled with a light smile. 'What would I do without you?'

'Yer would be hopeless without me – just admit it, I make ya life far more exciting,' Tahani admitted with a cocky smirk and she wrapped an arm around her friend's shoulder. 'Anyhow – I know nothin' of her family.'

'You should find that out,' Zanobi suggested just as Tahani raised an eyebrow. 'We'll have a chat with the girl's guardian.' He stared back at the girl named Maya and she raised her head showing her bright blue eyes. When their gaze met, Zanobi knew that there was just something he had to know about her.

CHAPTER 13

Brodie couldn't take it. It was too much for him to deal with.

He sat by one of his armchairs with a deep expression, barely listening. Everyone kept laughing lightly and drinking to celebrate Leon's life but it only fuelled Brodie's rage. The shifter that got away with his father's death was probably mocking them right now.

'Sorry for your loss.' Brodie's rage ceased when he saw an unrecognisable human raise his hand to shake Brodie's.

'Thanks,' Brodie muttered, shaking the man's head to ignore his irritation and the stranger left for another to appear. Only this time, this stranger was a shifter that offered a kind smile.

There was something that got to Brodie about this shifter. His wavy brown hair was one thing, but his chestnut eyes struck his nose wrong. The man's face held a small beard, but it looked like he shaved occasionally.

'Leon Forte was a great man,' the shifter admitted softly and Brodie watched him uneasily. 'He was like a son to me; I wish I could do something about it.'

Then it hit Brodie. He felt his form freeze as it began to sink in and recognised this strange feeling, the deep voice and the look in the man's eyes. This man was the one that attacked Leon and killed him. Before Brodie's rage could shoot up, the enemy shifter grabbed Brodie's arm and smiled.

'You and I both know that alarming everyone is a bad idea

boy,' the shifter sneered. Killer or not, this guy had a point. There were too many humans that could be exposed to this.

'What the hell are you doing here?' Brodie snapped in a quiet voice.

'I'm visiting you Brodie Forte,' the man retorted darkly. 'I just want you to know that you aren't going to be the only one who's in this position. Just be wary that the thing that will change you is the one you care about most...' As he turned, Brodie saw that he was looking towards Laria, Jenna and Maya together. Brodie remained silent in his anger. 'For now, stay out of my path, because this bloodbath will not get any prettier.'

Brodie kept his glower aimed at the shifter, but he simply smiled and released Brodie's arm. The enemy took his silence as an agreement and dismissed himself. With that, the enemy headed out, leaving Brodie to glare at the shifter's back.

He felt anger stir in his chest, immediately wanting to punch the wall. The shifter was killing them off one by one, but Brodie couldn't do a thing about it. In annoyance, he turned away from the trio of his companions and forced himself out the back of the property. The sky was dark from the day's events with no stars showing themselves to the world. As soon as the cool air hit him, his eyes widened in recognition of Tara.

'Brodie,' the dux announced. 'Do you remember that thing you wanted us to look up?'

Brodie's eyes narrowed in recognition. 'I do.' After he regained consciousness from his father's final stunt, he found a code that was written with Leon's blood. Brodie had no idea on what it meant, but he was desperate to figure out the code. He pulled out a slip of paper and passed it to his aunt.

Tara accepted to paper and read it with a curious gaze. 'Are you sure it doesn't make sense to you?' She showed the paper and revealed the numbers on the slip.

$$2, 3, 1, 0, 9, 5$$

Brodie shook his head. 'No idea.'

After the silence settled on the duo, Tara quietly sighed and petted Brodie's shoulder. 'I'm heading home.' She softly whispered an apology. 'Be careful Brodie – I don't want to lose you too.'

'Understood,' Brodie replied. Tara was not a comforting type by nature, so it felt good to Brodie that she was starting to care.

As soon as she left, the energy seemed to sap Brodie's strength. Everything was just piling on him at the same time.

Why had his father kept the truth from him? Was his twin in Golden Cliff? What happened if his twin sister or brother was dead?

'I can't do this father...' Brodie admitted to himself, letting his body drop to the ground with pain in his chest. It hurt. He squeezed his eyes shut as he tried to shake the thoughts. 'You should've stayed alive Dad. I need you!' Clenching his fist, Brodie slammed it against the wet grass.

Deep down, Brodie would've sworn that he heard Leon's voice in the back of his mind. *Let it out my son, you must never bottle it up, Brodie.* That's when Brodie actually realised that he was completely alone in this world. His mysterious mother was dead, his father was dead, Tara had her own responsibilities to take care of and the single sibling didn't exist in his eyes.

Nothing could get worse – he had to let it out.

And that's what Brodie did.

The frustration went through his body as he let out a yell of distress. Anger was bubbling in his body, enough to make Brodie slam his fist against the ground again. It had done nothing, but Brodie could feel his energy waning as he cried out for help.

The only thing that stopped him was the sound of light footsteps. 'Brodie...'

He turned to see that Laria was staring after him with teary eyes. It wasn't Laria's fault that his father was gone. Despite his logical reasoning, a tiny voice reminded Brodie that his pain would vanish if he directed his anger at her.

As Laria crouched down to meet his gaze, Brodie looked up, his eyes filled with anguish. 'Laria...' They fell into a comfortable silence just by staring at each other, but Brodie had to look away. 'How do you do it?'

Laria understood his question, her chestnut eyes softened. 'I don't know,' she whispered and grabbed his arms to him to help him to his feet. 'I still have my brother and I have a feeling that it's got to do with me changing to the way of shifters. The reason why they are doing this is because they want us to bring suffering as the town did to them.' Her eyes flashed with a hint of determination. 'I want to prove to them I won't fall victim to their manipulation.'

Brodie stared back at her as if he had just found out what he wanted to do with life. His eyes roamed her face, recognising the same innocent face that used to smile childishly when they were kids.

'Don't you ever consider killing them?'

She looked back at him with surprise before stared at the cloudless sky. 'I do... but I'm stuck with this curse for a long time – I don't think I'm going to be denying it anytime soon.' Laria confessed softly and Brodie stared at the sky with her. 'I love staring at the sky with you.'

Brodie looked back down at her, and he noticed that she was looking back at him. 'Yeah... I do as well.' Their bodies were close, and Brodie felt the warmth of their contact.

They kept their eyes on each other and Brodie leaned in closer. 'Brodie...' Laria's whisper brushed his cheek but he was simply focused on the mirroring gaze that his friend had.

His best friend.

Yet, for some reason it didn't bother him.

Before Brodie could get any closer, someone shouted from inside and made them jump. He flinched away from Laria. Brodie's frown deepened on his face and he put his attention to the sky.

'I'm sorry.' Laria's apology surprised him but he didn't respond. She moved away and found a reason to distract herself. 'I've got to go home with Tahani since she drove here... I'll see you later Brodie.' Just as Laria turned away, Brodie stopped her for a moment.

'Don't be sorry,' Brodie muttered as he looked in her direction. As she left, Brodie found himself glad that nothing happened between them.

CHAPTER 14

The school bell screamed as Laria, Maya and Tahani returned to campus. Maya and Tahani were silent. Maya was trying to focus in a different spot, while Tahani observed her.

Laria felt awkward. Since both of the Rosa's didn't talk to each other, Laria was stuck in the middle. But then again, Tahani could always speak with Laria with mind communication.

Their previous subject was gym. Since Maya loved sports, it was obvious that she would play in any sort of activity and it was strange enough that Tahani loved the sports just as much as Maya did.

Maybe it was a Rosa thing.

When the bell screamed the second time, Maya checked her phone with a frown before groaning to herself. 'Sorry Laria but I have class now, I'll see you later.' She disappeared into the crowd of students.

'Thank bloody whoever is up there,' Tahani said as Maya left. 'That silence was so awkward, I was thinking of tripping the girl over but she sure is a Rosa with her attitude towards sports.'

'That's one thing I don't get,' Laria admitted and took notes from her bag. Since it was her last period of the day, she didn't have to worry about going to her locker to get them out. 'You say that Maya is part of the Rosa family, yet you had no idea she existed?'

'Yep,' Tahani agreed without hesitation. 'There are cases where the child is hidden from duxes, sometimes by being placed in their human side's homes. Don't know why. The Rosa's are out there, but there's also more of the Laurence and Forte families out there.'

'That's confusing,' Laria grumbled but her eyes raised when she saw Jason standing alone reading his notes. She smiled and strolled up to him. 'Jason!'

It appeared Jason's mind was elsewhere, before he flashed a boyish grin at her. 'You look well Laria.' If only he knew.

Before she could say anymore, Laria noticed the English teacher walk into the room. 'We should probably head inside.' Jason took his seat next to Laria as usual and Tahani remained in the spot by the back.

At first it had never occurred to Laria of why Tahani chose to sit away from everyone. But then Laria remembered that Tahani still hated humans. Whatever had happened to her in the past, Tahani had never forgiven the humans for it.

She wanted to know why. What could the people have done to deserve her hatred?

The class was steady; working on laptops to finish their essays. Occasionally, Laria looked at Jason's blank screen; it was almost as if he was too distracted to work. But Laria didn't say anything because she was no better.

Ever since Leon died four days ago, Laria's mind was elsewhere. Who was the shifter that was responsible for Leon's death? Only Brodie knew, but Laria couldn't ask him until he was better.

Then there was the situation with Brodie and her. They almost kissed. During their lives, Laria wondered if Brodie never chose to date anyone because he had feelings for her. However, he never gave any hint of it.

Laria told no one about this little problem she had on that

night. She was glad that nothing happened between them. They were friends and Laria wasn't interested in dating at the moment.

'Laria?'

Looking up to see that Jason had a warm smile, Laria couldn't help but relax in his presence.

'Sorry,' Laria apologised and went back to her work. 'I just... spaced out.'

'Well it looks like none of us are going to finish it,' Jason chuckled in reference to the unfinished essays. 'How about get this over with this afternoon? I feel like we haven't spoken in a while and it looks like we need help.'

'That sounds great,' Laria responded and she grinned. 'I really look forward to it.' She suddenly paused, recalling the fact that Tahani was still in the same room. When Laria turned, she saw that the dux suddenly scowled in Laria's direction.

'Yer going with the human?'

Laria narrowed her eyes. *'Tahani whether I'm a shifter or not, I have to get through my human life.'*

A grumble of annoyance escaped Tahani's lips. *'Fine. Whatever – I'm gonna head to the pits tonight so I can blow off some steam.'* She leaned in her seat and packed her equipment up, which probably meant that it was time to go.

'Make sure you finish that essay,' Laria retorted with a scowl and the bell suddenly rang to announce that school was finished for the day. With a snort, Tahani stood up and sent a smirk.

'And make sure ya actually finish that paper off – those bloody pretty, blue eyes happen to distract ya from finishing off anything nowadays.'

Finally catching on with what Tahani had meant, Laria suddenly halted in her tracks and glowered at the dux with annoyance. Did Tahani think that she was talking to Jason because she had some sort of feelings for him?

Before Laria could snap at Tahani, the dux hummed innocently and walked out of the room to avoid Laria's rant. As soon as she saw Jason's puzzled expression, Laria straightened up and quickly packed up her things, pretending that she wasn't having a silent conversation with Tahani.

'Are you alright there?' Jason wondered, smiling when Laria spared her neighbour a glance him with a light chuckle. Even though everything was messed up, Laria found it rather amusing that she was able to stay sane. He joined in with the chuckling without thinking. 'I'm sorry,' Jason held in the rest of his laugh but kept his boyish grin. 'I can't help but laugh whenever someone laughs.'

'I understand,' Laria mentioned with a mirroring smile.

Brodie was the same.

'So we head to the public library?' Jason asked curiously when she finished packing.

'Definitely,' Laria answered and forced a smirk. 'My job is to take you to Golden Cliff's decent library.'

***

It was the first time he'd been in the public library. It was a tall building with countless stacks of unrecognisable books. There were large shelves filled with books and rows of computers at one end of the room.

'Alright then,' Laria decided as she placed her bag on the table. He followed her actions, placing his bag to let the notebooks fall out. 'I'm going to get started with it.'

She sat down to begin her typing, losing all of her attention on him. Jason found himself going towards the shelves to find the books that he needed for his essay but something else got his attention.

When he returned with a book, Laria's eyes flashed towards it in his hands and raised an eyebrow in confusion. 'I thought you were here to do an essay about Shakespeare not about old stories in our town.' Jason looked down to see an old book on the Navajo tribe.

'Well...' Jason looked back at Laria with a sheepish grin. He couldn't tell her about the shifters – when Seth told him everything, Jason was trusted that he wouldn't tell another human. For the first time during the month, Jason wanted to open up.

He had only one friend who knew, but the only friend that knew wouldn't understand. Laria had lost her mother. She would've shared his pain, but until Seth figured out why Mae was murdered in the first place, no one else was allowed to know.

At the thoughts of the man with the dancing flames, Jason felt his fist clench before he remembered where he was. 'I just want to read this book.'

'Alright then,' Laria muttered with a smile to dismiss the thoughts. 'I'm not going to force you to work, but you better be careful.' She gave herself a light-hearted chuckle. 'You'll get sucked into it because it's so interesting.'

Seeing Laria chuckle made Jason smile. He wasn't exactly lying when he admitted that seeing someone else laugh made him laugh. It had always been a habit of his.

'I won't get sucked into it,' Jason promised as he met her chestnut eyes. 'I know that you'll pull me out of it, because that's what friends do.'

'It is what friends do,' Laria agreed and went back to typing on her laptop. 'I'll bring you out of any demonic trance.'

As she went to work, Jason skimmed through the pages and gently stroked the paper. It was a book that was at least a century old. His eyes flashed momentarily to see the book's author and widened his eyes in recognition. 'This was written by one of your ancestors.'

Laria snapped her attention to Jason with a deep frown. 'Huh?' She leaned forward to see the author's name. 'Well, well... it looks like my great gramps was famous – bless the guy's soul.'

'Well, let's see what dear old William has to say.' Jason read through the page and he suddenly stopped. Now he knew what Laria had meant by sucking him in, but she was already back on the laptop to finish off her work. He was barely reading half the page and it was detailing that the rectocs trained the shifters to kill which led to their revelation of their kind. He quickly skimmed to the earlier pages and saw the original story of how they were born.

Four tribes.

Four sacrifices.

Four families.

Jason looked up to stare at Laria, who was busy with her work. Was it possible that her and her family were shifters? It seemed impossible, Seth would've told him if he was hanging out with shifters but then again, Maya and Brodie were a part of the list of families too. Were they shifters as well?

Instead of asking, Jason looked down to read more and something seemed to jump out of the text. There was a term that he had heard once or twice when Seth was telling him about the shifter. Something about late bloomers, they were shifters that had yet to reveal their true abilities –Seth had reminded him they were out there.

So maybe the reason why Seth hadn't told him was because Laria was a late bloomer like the book stated? Now he felt like a complete idiot for over reacting. Besides, it wasn't exactly bad idea if Laria was a shape shifter. He would've been able to open up a bit about his secrets.

Deciding that he would read the book later, Jason took out his laptop and began to finish off the work that was due by the end of the week. They were able to quietly work without distractions. Laria finished first, but it didn't take long for Jason to finish as well.

'So are you burrowing that?' Laria wondered, looking towards the ancient book that Jason still had sitting on the table. He smiled as he picked the book up gently, giving a quick observation to the condition of the book.

'Yeah, it seems that I've gotten too sucked in for even you to help me,' Jason joked, his smile disappearing when Laria's face seemed distant. 'Are you alright?'

'Yeah... sorry,' Laria apologised and brushed some of her hair behind her ear. 'You remind me of someone.'

'You look like you're going through more than just problems with Brodie,' Jason whispered and Laria's eyes narrowed sharply.

'It's not about Brodie.' Laria's tone had a hint of annoyance. 'As you probably know, Brodie and I have been best friends for as long as I can remember so I bonded with his dad since I didn't have one.'

'You lost your father too?' The sudden question made Laria look back at him with a hint of vulnerability and confusion. Jason realised what he had said. There was no point in keeping it a secret from her anymore. 'When I was born... my dad left me and... my mother... I know nothing about my father.'

'We're in the same boat then,' Laria whispered gently. 'Brodie's dad died only recently... and you remind me of him.'

Now Jason had a reason to feel sympathetic. 'What was his name?'

Laria's eyes flashed with uncertainty but she spoke up, 'Leon...'

Jason recognised the name instantly. It was meant to be one of the few people that Jason was supposed to find after reading the letter, but the letter remained unread.

He stood up from his seat to hold a hand out for her. She stared back at him as if he had done the most reckless thing in his life. 'If it means anything, I wish to apologise for everything that has happened to you. I...' His voice died down when he couldn't finish his sentence.

Laria took his hand and allowed herself to stand up with him. 'Thank you, Jason.' She pulled her hand away when the phone in her pocket buzzed. Laria took the phone out and read it. 'I guess we should go...'

Jason shook out of his trance and nodded in agreement. 'I'll walk you back to your house.'

'Oh no,' Laria dismissed her words with a smile. 'I stay with my godfather. He'll pick me up. Let's go to your house and I'll let him know where to pick me up from.'

Jason paused when he realised that no one knew about his conditions with Seth. It had been a few days since he went to Mae's house. It was like a reminder that Mae had died and Jason couldn't do anything to save her.

'Sure...'

Laria frowned. 'Is something wrong?'

He looked back to dismiss his pain. 'Nothing's wrong... I promise you.' It appeared that Laria took the answer and Jason went to scan his new interest. As soon as he placed it on the desk, the elderly librarian smiled lightly and took the book. When she asked for Jason's student card, he passed it in return.

Laria came from behind Jason and grabbed his arm. 'You ready?' Her laptop was back in her bag over her shoulder.

'Yeah,' he muttered as he placed his borrowed book in his bag carefully. The last thing he wanted was to damage it. 'Let's go.'

The walk back to Mae's old house was quiet but Jason's mind was fixated on the book.

'Stop and wait a second Jason, there's something not right.' Laria's voice cut though Jason's thoughts. He stopped and listened out for something. It took him a moment to realise that they were almost at Mae's house; all they had to do was cross the street.

Jason turned to see that Laria's eyes were shut as if she was trying to focus. She inhaled slowly, and he felt his nerves set on edge.

With a frown, Jason opened his mouth to speak, 'Lari-'

'Crap!' Laria suddenly hissed, grabbing Jason's hand and with unnatural strength she hauled him to the nearby forest. 'Not now!'

'Wait, Laria, what are you-!' Jason tried talking her out of pulling his arm off, but his voice never gained her attention. She looked around the trees in distress.

As Jason ran, he was suddenly standing in Mae's house without Laria. 'Laria... What's going on?' He couldn't move his limbs and Laria was gone. Panic rose through his throat when he suddenly saw Mae's bloodied figure.

'Mum! What's going on?'

Mae didn't respond to his voice, but she moved her head towards the door at the sound of an annoyed curse from the entrance. Jason recognised the voice. He looked up to see an image of himself entering the room tripping over Mae's body.

That's when he realised that he was reliving a memory.

'Stop it...' Jason told himself, watching with panic as the memory unfolded. His eyes stung with tears when he saw the familiar envelope in Mae's hands as she weakly gave it to him. 'Please, stop it!' He felt frustrated when he still couldn't move.

When Edward entered the room, Jason felt the rage come back to him. *'Call me Edward.'* The man introduced himself with a sadistic sneer. *I was sent here to kill that woman behind you and then take you.'*

His eyes widened with rage and he shouted, 'Stop it!' No matter what, Jason couldn't get the thoughts out of his head.

'Does this make you angry? That you're unable to save her?'

Jason wanted to force his eyes away from the scene as he saw himself begging to let Mae go. Seeing her in pain once more reminded him of his failures. 'Please...'

'It's the thrill I enjoy, the screams of agony, the panic, the desperation,' Edward raised his other hand and Jason already knew what was coming next. He felt his insides twist as the same scene repeated itself. The pained screams from Mae made Jason fall, weak. *'The thrill of taking a life away with my bare hands.'*

Just as Jason couldn't go through anymore of the mental torture, he closed his eyes and tried to shut it off – the urge to find the man that ruined him. But as all the thoughts bubbled up, Jason saw the ones that stopped him.

He had to remember why he couldn't lose himself. Seth told him in the past that he needed to calm down. If he couldn't compose himself, then what good could he be to Mae? She wanted him to live a happy life.

She was the one that brought him to Golden Cliff, looking for a fresh start. On the night that they arrived, Mae took him out to Silver Roots to help him settle his nerves. It was the night when he crashed into Laria, spilling soda on her. His mother was the reason why Jason managed to finally find friends and possibly a home.

He needed to find out why he was the one that Edward was after.

'G... ba... ur fe...'

Jason paused at the familiar voice, he turned and desperately searched. 'I hear someone...'

'Sta... with ...e!'

He felt something stir in his chest before he shook his head. 'Laria?'

Jason!'

Pain shot through his head as Jason's eyelids lifted. Laria's distraught face was over his, patting his cheek gently as her eyes glistened. Whatever had happened just a moment ago, it took him out of the conscious world.

It took him a moment for his thoughts to come back to him. *Was she crying?*

'I won't leave you behind Jason!' she cried out, firmly patting his cheek now. He groaned at the pain but it was enough to make Laria widen her eyes. 'You're alright!' Another groan escaped his lips as Laria wrapped her arms around him.

Jason pushed himself up as soon as Laria let go of him to stand up. 'What happened?'

'We were running and you collapsed – but as long as you are alright.' Laria pulled him to his feet and stood in front of him with a stern stare. This different Laria stunned him; there were no signs of fear on her face as she looked around to search for something. As Jason tried to recover, Laria met a gaze with him and narrowed her eyes. 'There's something you need to know.'

'No need to say it love,' a deep British voice interrupted the duo and Laria glared in the direction of the new figure. As Jason felt his chest tighten with fear, he could tell that he was dealing with an enemy. The man that stood in front of them had short blonde hair. His blue eyes stalked them as if they were prey. He leaned on a thick trunked tree with dark intentions.

'Get behind me Laria,' Jason ordered fiercely as he shielded her. He couldn't see her reaction, his face remaining hard.

A devilish smile formed on the man's face as he witnessed

the scene play before him. 'That's cute,' he said before pushing himself off. 'The human has guts more than the shifter. I hate to tell you this sweetheart, but Jason already knows.'

As Laria sent an accusing look to Jason, he immediately backed up. The sudden change in her expression startled him. 'No, it's not like that. I only knew about Seth, I swear!'

'We'll talk about it later,' Laria decided as she turned her attention to the man. 'Who the hell are you and what do you want?'

The man offered a smile. 'We want to have fun. My name is Nick Forte.' Recognising the last name, Laria's look darkened. Jason stood helplessly.

'What the hell do you mean by 'we'?' Laria asked and no sooner, Jason noticed another figure above Nick staring down at them.

'Laria...' he breathed just as Laria looked in Jason's direction. 'Look up.' She followed his orders and stepped back to take in the view of the second man. Unlike Nick, this man had caramel hair and green eyes. He sat on the branch above Nick.

'Brad Forte,' the second man introduced. He didn't move from his spot. Laria threw an arm in front Jason to protect him.

'So you two are from the Forte family?' Laria questioned.

'*Not just them two, girl.*' The third voice was an accented woman. Jason turned to see a caramel haired woman with blue eyes enter the scene. One thing that stuck out was her bright red clothes and obvious red lips. 'My name is Charmi Forte.'

Before Jason could speak up, Laria's angry voice startled him. 'I won't let you lay a finger on him – I promise you that!'

'We'll see about that sweetheart,' Nick chuckled just as his eyes turned gold. This was the first time since Edward that Jason actually saw a fight between the shifters. Brad jumped down; Jason saw that Laria had a defensive stance.

As Nick sped towards Laria, the duo had a rough grapple. Laria looked like a professional fighter, attempting to flip the other shifter over her body. As Laria went with Nick, Jason realised that he was facing both Brad and Charmi.

Hadn't enough Forte's gotten to him?

Jason kept a stern face as he kept eyes trained on the pair against him. Charmi started to chuckle. She went to his face and stroked him. Naturally Jason would've moved away, but his limbs were completely frozen in shock.

'You are handsome for a boy,' she whispered gently as she leaned in to meet his eyes. 'But it doesn't change the fact that you're human.' Charmi's eyes darkened as a scowl formed in her pretty features. 'Why did he go after your family?'

Once again, Jason found himself staring at the scene of Mae's death. His eyes remained wide as he stared back at the familiar flames that burnt his mother.

'You are different Jason Amarel. There's always a special reason to why our leader chose your family of all human families,' Charmi said from behind him. He snapped his head to look back at the woman as she stared at the scene. 'My power as a Forte affects the subconscious mind – and I bring up the hidden memories that you try to block out. The death of your mother was the thing that you tried to hide... and it will eventually drive you insane.'

Instantly, Jason felt a sharp pain through his chest and he looked down to see Charmi's devious look. She pulled out the dagger from Jason's chest and kicked him into the ground.

As soon as he hit the floor, Jason suddenly returned to the current situation with Charmi and Brad. Jason let out a shaky sigh, checking to see if his chest had any blood spilling out. He looked back at the smiling woman and scowled.

'It wasn't me with the illusions, so you can stop glaring,'

Charmi stated innocently before she looked towards Brad with a smile. 'My little brother did it.' Jason joined staring at the silent male, whose eyes only turned gold in anticipation.

'It's nothing personal mate,' Brad said in a low voice before grabbing Jason's throat to lift him in the air. 'But I despise the weak.'

'Stop it!' Laria's voice overcame the mental screaming in the back of Jason's head. At first Jason saw that Laria had knocked Nick to the ground to observe the situation. Brad merely chuckled and tightened the hold that he had on Jason's throat. Jason's heart clenched as he saw the panic in her eyes – the panic for him.

But then, the pain was gone. Jason hit the ground and he reached for his bruised neck.

'Well then.' Nick pushed himself to his feet to look towards the duo. Jason couldn't see Laria as Brad blocked her. 'We managed to bring it out of its weak and pathetic shell. It looks like this is going to be fun.'

Charmi took a step back, however she had a comfortable smile on her face. 'I guess we did finish our orders.' Her eyes brightened up in pleasure and took another step back. 'Brothers, I will allow you to fight.'

As Laria lowered her arms, Jason noticed that her fingers had claws extending from their tips. He suppressed a chill of his spine and kept quiet as the males charged at her. Laria's movements were strangely different, before she looked like she had perfect control but now she attacked like a rabid animal.

She lashed out her clawed hands, attempting to attack the duo of shifters. Finally, Brad aimed a fist towards Laria but she caught it with one hand. It gave Nick time to strike from behind but Laria moved her head away to grab Nick's wrist.

However, the only thing that Jason paid attention to, was

the fact that Laria's amber eyes were glowing brightly, glinting with excitement. A few moments ago, Laria didn't have a smile... let alone a sadistic sneer of amusement as she held back the duo without struggle.

'You mutts think that you can take me on?' Laria spat as she sent Brad flying. As Brad crashed, Laria's amber eyes met with Nick's. 'And as for you...' With a flick of her wrist, a sickening crunch echoed through the forest.

Jason flinched at the sound of Nick's agonised screams. This wasn't Laria - it was impossible to believe that Laria would smile over snapping someone's wrist. Even Charmi's eyes suddenly turned serious as she watched the situation.

'Laria...' Jason spoke softly, watching as Brad recovered from his crash and Nick held on to his wrist protectively. Laria sneered as she took out both brothers when they tried to take her on once again. Even for someone around her age, Laria was easily taking out two middle aged men without breaking a sweat. This little knowledge he had on the shape shifters made him more in the dark than he assumed.

'How dare you?' Charmi's stern voice suddenly took over, making Jason widen his eyes to see that the woman was angered. 'You won't get away with this.' Laria's unique amber eyes met with Charmi's and she merely smiled in return.

'How dare I?' Laria mocked with a chuckle of amusement. Jason had heard her laugh previously, it was light hearted, but this laugh rather terrified him. It wasn't the same laugh that Laria had when they were talking – but a rather sinister sound. Charmi's eyes hardened and she suddenly threw herself at Laria, attempting to strike her without a second to pause. 'It really doesn't look like you have any chance against me.' Laria explained while she dodged each of the strikes.

As the fourth one came, Charmi's fist was caught by Laria and left the shifter completely opened. It quickly dawned on

Jason of her intentions which made him widen his eyes in realisation. The Laria he knew would never do this to another living being.

'Laria, no!'

She ignored his voice and her smile widened. 'I will kill for you Laria!' Laria spoke to herself and Jason hesitated. That wasn't Laria. She aimed her clawed hand towards Charmi's chest but then released the enemy and jumped back when the brothers entered the scene again.

Jason remained clueless. 'What's going on?'

Laria's eyes glowed in anticipation. 'I'll kill everyone…' She immediately stopped. When her breath was caught, Laria groaned in pain. Her growls were vicious, appearing more like a savage beast than a human as she held her head with her hands. 'Damn it.' Her eyes flashed furiously out in the distance and confused the audience. 'You will not take this from me!'

'It looks like she's fighting the bloodlust,' Brad said to Charmi, and Jason managed to overhear. He turned towards them and suddenly understood why Laria had been so different.

'I won't become like you,' Laria hissed to herself as her eyes darkened. After what seemed like an eternity of waiting, Laria stopped struggling and her eyes were hidden. At first Jason feared that Laria was still sinister, but as she lifted her head he sighed in relief to see the familiar chestnut eyes.

'Very well. We've done what we needed to do.' Charmi sneered towards Jason and noticed that he was watching them with a frown. Her scowl deepened and she turned away, 'Brad – kill the human; he's finished his part.'

Weren't they just saying that he was in this position for a reason? Jason's eyes widened with alarm as Brad turned towards Jason with a dark look in his eyes.

'Jason!' Laria tried moving, but she was cut off by Nick

shoving her. She yelped when she hit the ground and Nick laughed.

'You have to watch, love.'

Honestly, Jason didn't want to die. He wanted to survive so he could find Edward and destroy his life like his was destroyed. As Jason looked back at Laria, he saw the fear in her eyes – the fear for his life.

'Jason...' she breathed softly; her eyes were filled with distress. But Jason couldn't accept the fact he was going to die – he needed to live. Laria tried to get back up but Nick pressed his weight on her.

Nick chuckled in amusement, pushing his foot down with a sneer of excitement. 'You will hate us even more, which will bring your bloodlust to life – the stronger the hate, the less likely you will have any humanity.' As Jason looked back at Laria's struggle, he heard a strange voice in the back of his head that told him to fight.

But he didn't have to.

Just as Brad prepared a deadly strike, a familiar figure tackled him into the ground. Before Jason could recognise his saviour, Seth had appeared from behind Nick to throw him off Laria.

'We've arrived just on time it seems,' Seth muttered emotionlessly. Jason saw that the one who saved his skin was Brodie. But Brodie didn't pay any attention to Jason, keeping his hateful gaze focused on Brad.

'It looks like we meet the rest of the sorry group,' Charmi snickered and attempted to stand back but another man was standing behind her. She stopped and turned around to see a man with auburn hair who wore shades over his eyes.

'Zanobi Adkins.' The woman suddenly backed away from the man with a hint of fear and recognition.

As Jason went back towards Brodie, he saw that he was

glowering in fury. 'Tell me,' Brodie demanded as he held the shifter's collar. 'Who murdered my father?!' Brad looked back at Brodie but refused to answer so Brodie slammed the man into the ground. 'I asked you – who murdered my father, Leon Forte?'

Brad looked back at Brodie and spat. 'You're Leon Forte's son?' At the tone, Brodie snarled. 'How pathetic. It truly looks like you were more of a waste of space than your father was!' The shifter didn't get to say anymore, considering that Brodie had already put his hand through Brad's chest and pulled out his heart without another word.

It was Laria who suddenly gasped at the turn of events. Jason looked over to her, seeing that her eyes were filled with fear for her friend. He didn't like Brodie and he could tell that Brodie wasn't his biggest fan, however he had never thought that he was capable of killing another.

'Brad!' Charmi shouted, but she didn't move. Jason couldn't be sure if it was shock or in fear of being the next victim. Her shock dissolved to anger and her eyes flashed gold. 'I'll tear out your jugular and make you eat it!'

Without hesitation Brodie's eyes met back at Charmi's. 'Come try it – you won't be able to lay a finger on me!'

The woman laughed. 'It's funny how you and Laria have the same things to say! I wonder if I can make you eat those words like she ate them!'

'You are done for today,' Zanobi explained. Jason didn't recognise the stranger, but he really was in no position to question him. He'd saved their lives. 'Leave now while you all have your limbs intact.'

Charmi's hateful glare rivalled Brodie's but she said nothing and turned away. 'We're leaving, Nick.' Seth let Nick walk free, leaving the group alone. 'This is not the last of us, Forte – I don't care if the leader killed your father, I will be the one who kills you.'

Laria's exhausted voice interrupted them as she tried to get up. 'Wait, we shouldn't let them...' And with those last words Laria lost consciousness. Seth caught her before she hit the ground

'Laria!' Jason cried jumping up and running over to her without thinking. Judging by her exhausted expression, Jason could tell that the adrenaline had ceased when she regained control of herself.

'Brodie,' Zanobi said. 'Since you killed him, you deal with the body.'

Brodie grunted in annoyance but grabbed the body to drag it into the deeper part of the forest. Zanobi turned towards the remaining group, he approached Seth and took Laria out of his arms.

'We should get going,' Seth decided, turning to face Jason. Remembering everything that had just happened, Jason's eyes narrowed. For the first time since Jason had known about Seth's secret, he felt annoyed that he didn't know what shifters were capable of.

His scowl deepened as he met Seth's gaze. 'Yes – we should leave.' Not only that, he didn't want to spend any more time with complete strangers. He spared Laria a final glance before he followed Seth out of the forest with a heavy heart.

Jason wanted to find out everything.

CHAPTER 15

The silence that the boys had was uncomfortable. When they arrived, Seth's small house looked as it always did. It was just a building, just enough room for a small family and two parked cars in the driveway.

Throughout month, Jason was protected by Seth and his parents. Seth insisted that the majority of his family were shifters, even the cousins that he'd never met. Jason always thought it was strange, seeing that Seth's family was larger than the rest.

As they entered the house, Seth locked the door behind him. Without his parents in the house, he could speak freely. 'About Laria-'

'You have got to stop that mind reading stuff – it gets really annoying,' Jason growled. Seth's face remained neutral as Jason turned back to him. 'I have questions – let's start off with her then since we're on the subject! Why the heck didn't you tell me that Laria was one of you? Does this mean that Maya is one too?'

Seth's gaze hardened at the thoughts of her. 'Maya is not one of us,' Seth replied with a warning glare. 'However, the reason I did not inform you of Laria's status is because I was told not to tell you.'

'What do you mean?' Jason wondered, his anger replaced with confusion.

'Just as I said it,' Seth answered. 'My parents told me that

I wasn't allowed to speak about her to you. But I have a theory that since she is the last from the Alfero family that isn't in hiding, the shifters wanted her power which was why they attacked her. But even so – my parents forbade it. It's already tipping the scales that you know about the shifters – especially since we don't see your link with them...' The look in his eyes seemed to be silently considering the current events. 'I still find it strange. Why are they after you?'

With a sigh Jason brushed his hair back and sat on a chair. 'I don't know... I'm pretty sure Mae was... normal...'

Seth suddenly paused as if he had figured the missing clue all along. Just before Jason could continue speaking, Seth lifted his hand to silence him.

Immediately, Jason realised what he had said. 'Seth... no!' He stood up and approached him with a determined look in his eyes. 'Mae would never keep that from me – she would never be able to hide something like that from me.'

'Yet Laria's mother managed to hide the fact that she was a witch.' Seth retorted and silenced Jason. 'But that is not what I thought of.'

'Then what?' Jason demanded.

'Jason...' Seth's voice hardened. 'I think the enemies believed that your father... was the true descendant of one of the families.'

Suddenly, Jason felt his throat go dry. He instantly gulped, trying to find a reason to breathe other than the fact he needed oxygen. 'What does that mean Seth? I'm possibly a shifter just because my father possibly was?' In a rush, Jason's mind went back to the letter that Mae gave him on the day of her death.

It remained on his desk, unread to this day. He felt his fist clench in anger, recalling the memories of Mae's stories about his father that he'd never met. If he ever had a chance to encounter his father once again, Jason knew that he would never accept the man that abandoned him. Jason had lived nearly eighteen years without his father, happy that Mae was willing to take care of him.

'I believe that you already know the answer to that,' Seth replied after a moment of silence to calm Jason down. As Jason tried thinking of different possibilities, each of the pieces connected together. The story of the shifter slaughters, that the humans killed many of the true descendants and for the ones that lived ended up losing control. Edward had killed Mae to unlock Jason's bloodlust.

'Then what?' Jason was tempted to slam his fist on the desk. 'My only source to finding out about my damn father is gone – dead! I should've gone to Leon Forte while I had the chance.'

'While I do read minds, I do not know everything about the Forte family – I can see if I can ask Brodie if he has any cousins or uncles around your mother's age. Leon was killed because he had found out about the murders that had been going on, the same task that was given to my parents.'

If he had enough energy, Jason would've wondered why Seth's parents had been given such a task. 'You told me about the Beast and the murders... if your parents are up for the task...'

'Yes,' Seth finished for Jason with a look of slight anger in his eyes. 'My parents will be dying – we've all come to terms with it and as descendants, we die doing what is right.'

'Are you serious Seth?' Jason hissed, suddenly annoyed that Seth had both parents and dismissed them so easily. Seth knew nothing about what Jason had gone through when Mae died – it was the most horrific thing that he experienced.

'I understand Jason,' Seth spoke softly and turned away. 'But you already know it that my parents and myself aren't close. They barely connected with me and I was treated like I was alone to hone my abilities. While most kids were allowed to play, I had to stay away from everyone because I had a fear of the enemy using others to get to me.' He turned back to face Jason. 'Then I met Maya who tried to get my attention and she succeeded –I had to train, I had to watch her from afar so that no one hurt her. My parents know that their deaths will not result with my bloodlust and they're happy with what they've accomplished.'

Everyone knew that Seth was unusual. After all, he kept to himself most of the time with the exception of Maya who practically forced herself to be his friend. No one knew why Seth was so anti-social, why he chose to be by himself when he had the option of becoming friends. It had been because Seth wanted to protect the people – he knew that it was the right thing to do.

Some people had even called him selfish for coldly dismissing friends. But Jason believed that Seth was probably more selfless than he let on.

To comfort his friend, Jason placed his hand on Seth's shoulder and offered a nod with determination. 'It doesn't matter about that then – but I will be there for you, just like you will be there for me for when we find my father together.'

'We won't worry about your father Jason – it's clear that you want nothing to do with him and I respect that. After all, he lost his chance to know you,' Seth decided and pulled himself away. 'Now go get some rest, you've been through a lot.' Now that Seth reminded him, Jason's exhaustion did get to him. But still, Jason wanted to be there for his friend. Even so, his need to sleep felt much more powerful at the moment.

***

'Drink your tea slowly,' Brodie instructed as Laria recoiled in disgust at the burning taste on the back of her tongue. 'My father told me that the chamomile tea would do us both good in the future.'

'Right,' Her voice fell quiet at the mention of Leon and she rested the tea back on the table. She was back in the lounge room of the Forte estate, sitting comfortably on the couch as she recovered. Laria remembered waking up with many pains and a few plasters from the scratches. Her only conclusion was that Zanobi took her here with Brodie. Brodie was by her side since she woke up, but it was quiet.

It definitely bothered Laria, especially when she recognised a glass of whisky next to her tea.

Over two months ago, Laria and Brodie would often talk about nothing yet now Brodie had a hard time looking at her. It was a complete mystery to why Brodie had been acting this way towards her.

'I bet Jason was grateful that you saved his skin,' Laria said trying to bring up the topic. Brodie's eyes met with hers and for a moment, it flashed with irritation.

'It wasn't to save him,' Brodie hissed quietly as he took another gulp from his glass. 'The guy was an enemy and I killed him because that's what I needed to do.'

'But you realise that now you have someone that wants to kill you?' Laria suddenly reminded as Charmi's warning repeated in the back of her mind. 'I don't think it was a good idea.'

'Let the bitch try to kill me. I'll kill her before she can lay a finger on me,' Brodie replied as he finished his glass. As soon as he grabbed the bottle to refill his cup, Laria instantly snatched the glass to make the drink spill all over the table. His eyes hardened as he met the brunette's gaze again. 'Give it back Laria.'

'No,' Laria denied his request stubbornly. 'I know you've had too much to drink when you start to swear – but I've never seen you act like this when you're drunk.'

'Have you ever realised how annoying you are?' Brodie snapped, and Laria flinched. 'You are questioning if I made the right choice about killing someone. *An enemy.* If you're seriously questioning on why I killed him, then you should ask yourself if you're going to kill Edward.'

Suddenly, Laria's eyes narrowed in spite but she stood her ground. There was no way she was going to let him talk her down like this. 'Look, I know you're drunk but you're being insensitive about this-'

'Like hell I am – if anything I'm being bloody honest because other shifters are too scared to say anything in case you go crazy. Damn it, Laria!'

Without another second to hesitate, Laria flinched at the sound of smashed glass and she realised that Brodie had thrown the bottle into the wall behind her. He grabbed her and leaned close enough for Laria to cringe.

'You sound like a freaking hypocrite! Here you are, promising your own brother that you are going to kill Edward but you are telling me that I shouldn't kill someone that was about to kill *your* friend!'

'I am worried for your life Brodie! I'm grateful that you saved Jason's life but you put your own life in danger because of it!' Laria retorted. She shoved him roughly. 'Ever since Leon died you haven't been at school, you've been acting strange whenever you talk to me and all you've been doing is drinking. Seeing you kill that man out of rage made me scared that you aren't handling it as well as others assumed.'

'Get over it. I am a bloody shape shifter Laria! I kill! Zanobi kills! The Ungue Dux kills! Even Seth Laurence kills!' Brodie shouted and Laria felt herself stop as she stared back at him with distress in her eyes. She knew he was right. 'I have the bloodlust like you do and I kill like you will when you meet

Edward! So don't act like you are anything special just because you're the last Alfero! Let's face it Laria, the reason why Lesley is dead and Chris isn't here is because it's your fault that you acted like a naive brat who knew nothing about your own history.'

He stopped yelling, but his words were left hanging in the air. Silence loomed over them and Laria finally allowed the words to sink in. Was that what Brodie really thought of her? Both of them were panting with rage and Laria was tempted to punch him.

So she did, as hard as she could – so much for nerve settling tea.

Her fist collided with his nose, and it caught him off guard. He grunted as she knocked him off his feet to crash to the floor. She knew that if she hadn't received the training from Tahani then she would've broken her hand. Brodie held his position from the floor, holding his bloodied nose to glare at her.

No more words were spoken, but they were interrupted by a car horn which shattered their deathly silence. Laria couldn't be more grateful that her godfather had arrived. Brodie had gone too far for saying that she was a naive brat.

Neither of them said anything, too angry with another to acknowledge the other's existence. Without another word, Laria pushed herself past Brodie and grabbed her bags, placing the empty cup on the table that started the whole fight, before she exited the building to see the familiar Camaro.

Brodie wasn't going to get the last word and she wouldn't falter.

***

When Laria got in the car, she didn't feel like talking so Haroni let her be silent on the trip home. It didn't surprise him when she didn't talk. Haroni put the car into a park and watched as Laria get out of the car with a nod of acknowledgement.

At least she was accepting him.

He sighed gently at her actions and he followed along. As he entered the building, Tracy appeared with a cold look as she saw Laria.

'If you're hungry, there's food in the fridge,' Tracy informed before she took out her phone. 'If you two will excuse me, I have a call to make.'

'Hey Tracy?' Laria stopped the blonde from continuing her plans. When Haroni looked down at Laria, he noticed that it had been the first time she spoken since she saw him. 'Is Tahani here?'

At the thoughts of the dux, Tracy scowled up the stairs. 'That woman is upstairs; I think that she is on personal call from someone.' She returned to the phone and pulled it to her ear. 'As if I would know who.'

Haroni saw that Laria nodded to Tracy and rushed up the stairs without another word. As soon as they went to Tahani's door, Laria opened it without knocking and saw that she woman was on the ground with her knees up doing crunches.

'Hey,' Tahani said with a cheerful grin and dropped her legs. 'What's up Laria? Oh wait – let me guess, shifters ambushed ya and pretty blue eyes?'

'Zanobi told you,' Laria stated with a blank expression. Haroni raised an eyebrow and looked back at Tahani who simply shrugged with a lazy smile.

'Okay but there's something a bit more serious 'bout the fight,' Tahani informed. 'Mandati Dux told me that we will have to accelerate our plans – there's something you need to know 'bout, even if you don't end up developing them.'

Instantly, Haroni knew what the leader was talking about.

'As a shape shifter, ya got the transformation, the bloodlust and the powers,' Tahani explained in her strange way. 'Now, shifters have strange abilities.' She explained, 'Forte's have the special abilities of working on ya subconscious mind from deep secrets, instincts, hypnosis – all that creepy stuff.' Haroni looked to see that Laria's eyes suddenly hardened at the thoughts. 'Then there's the Laurence family and they're similar to Fortes but they are just the conscious mind - so mind control, memory erase.'

'So what do the Rosa family do?' Haroni asked from his position, which only made Tahani smirk as she lifted a single hand. Laria leaned forward with Haroni and when they saw her hand sheeting itself with ice, they backed away with shock.

Due to her ego being stroked, Tahani chuckled lightly and dismissed the ice forming on her hand. 'The Rosa family – they have elemental powers; my power, as ya can see, is ice.'

As Laria looked away with a hint of anger, Haroni could suddenly tell that it had to do with Edward. It was obvious after all – since Edward managed to burn down Lesley's home with her inside. So then it was clear that Edward was a part of the Rosa family.

'And what about... me?' Laria asked, looking back to see that Tahani lightly smirked. When she first came into the house, Haroni learnt that she enjoyed two things: fighting and smirking. Neither of the activities was approved by Tracy, but Haroni didn't seemed too bothered by it.

'The Alfero family are linked to life essence or *spiritual energy* – ya see, the rectocs that gave each of the shifters their abilities weren't the same rectocs so of course. When the rectocs passed their gifts, the shifters inherited their separate powers as well.'

'So are you going to help me with my power?' Laria wondered.

Tahani saw the confused expression from the Alfero and

patted her head. 'Yeah – but most of it has to do with ya... it's hard to explain but sometimes yer wake up feeling like ya had a nightmare.'

Laria's eyes went wide as soon as she realised what Tahani had said. 'You're telling me that my powers have to do with my nightmares?'

Again Tahani chuckled. 'Totally! Once ya learn ya power, it gets pretty decent and badass – oh yeah and ya finally access ya inner soul which is basically a part of those... nightmare things as ya have it.'

'Then I'll start beginning to tap into that tomorrow,' Laria decided with a smile on her face, the evidence of her internal suffering now disappearing. 'Thank you for letting me know Tahani – I'll be heading to bed now.' She left the room without another word, allowing Tahani and Haroni to be alone.

Haroni thought about the conversation between Tahani and Laria. 'Do you think you have what it takes? Doesn't unlocking the powers strengthen the bloodlust?'

'She'll be fine, Angeli,' Tahani dismissed his concern and turned away from him. Ever since meeting him, the woman had not bothered to call him by his given name – even being called by his surname seemed decent enough. 'She's meant to have bloodlust, no matter how much training any shape shifter gets, there's no erasing it.'

'I suppose I should trust you.' Haroni was about to leave but he exchanged a glance. 'I know this is strange but...' he smiled when Tahani raised a brow, 'would you want to accompany me for a drink?'

CHAPTER 16

'I see.' Zanobi held the phone to his ear as he drove his truck. 'Alright then Tahani – I've pulled up at the fallen's mansion now.'

He saw the door open and, much to his surprise, it was a blonde woman that stepped out. He recognised the cold eyes as she strolled up to his window. He knew Tracy well but he couldn't be sure if she knew him.

'Is there any reason why you're here Zanobi?' Tracy questioned pausing, when Zanobi met a stare with the woman. The look in her eyes was searching for something. 'If I recall, Laria had the day off her training to go see Maya.'

Bothered by her staring, a faint smile flashed over Zanobi's features. 'I am just waiting for Tahani. We have some errands.'

Before Tracy could say anything, a hand grabbed Tracy's shoulder. Relief flooded through Zanobi as Tahani made her face clear. 'Easy there, Ladas.' She woman stepped up, ignoring the scowl. 'Zanobi and I are just chilling.'

'Just like you and my foolish brother did last night?' Tracy retorted, shaking Tahani's hand off her shoulder. 'Spilling our expensive drinks as if you own the place.'

'Unless ya secretly a drinker, I doubt that they were gonna be used anyways,' Tahani admitted, which only made the fallen fall silent. Zanobi couldn't believe his ears. 'Also, last time I checked, the mansion is Haroni's – he just let's ya sleep there 'cause he pities ya.' The look on Tracy's face could freeze hell.

To prevent any fights, Zanobi cleared his throat and Tracy shot a glare towards him.

'I believe you can see yourself out.' The tone was colder than her as she turned to head back into the mansion. As she disappeared into the building, Zanobi snorted.

'I thought I would never see that,' Zanobi noted as Tahani took her seat in the car. 'She really hates you. I've never expected to see that with anyone.'

'Nah.' Tahani shrugged it off like it was nothing. 'She just hates the fact that I'm badass – everyone is simply jealous that they ain't me.'

Zanobi rolled his eyes as he put the shades over his eyes, starting up the car. 'For a woman that's about eight decades old, you sure act like you're ten.' He chuckled as Tahani's fist hit his shoulder. 'Alright then, subject changing... Where are we heading first?'

Tahani kept her window down and watched the roads. 'I guess we're heading to school – after all, Maya's details are probably all there.' When Zanobi started to drive, he felt the music from the radio ring in his ears.

'We're sneaking *into* school grounds – this doesn't sound like us,' Zanobi teased just as Tahani nodded in agreement.

'But since bitchy angeli ain't gonna be there, it's gonna be our only shot,' Tahani replied as Zanobi went through the gates to park at the familiar school grounds.

'So, did you find out anything about Maya while you were at school?' Zanobi wondered, looking over towards Tahani who shook her head.

'Nothing.' She scowled in annoyance. 'She hangs around Laria like she's a bloody shield from me – I swear she has no Rosa blood in her.'

'But didn't you say before that she enjoys the challenges?' Zanobi wondered, sparing a glance to the dux who shrugged to herself.

It was just too strange.

'Okay – park here, Zanobi,' Tahani instructed just as Zanobi followed her orders. He parked the car and took his seatbelt off, turning to see that Tahani had slipped on a pair of sunglasses.

They got out of the car and strolled to the main building. Since no one was at school, the duo knew that they had to break in. As if Tahani had read her companion's mind, she smirked and went to the closest windows to slide it open.

Zanobi's jaw dropped at the sight and Tahani laughed at his expression, 'Close ya mouth Zanobi – ya making a mess.' Tahani chuckled at his stunned expression and she pulled herself through the room before allowing Zanobi to climb through. He followed, keeping careful to prevent his fingerprints from touching the walls.

'How on earth did you do this?' Zanobi questioned.

'I've got a few friends that don't mind the extra cash,' Tahani replied with a smile as she led Zanobi through the rooms. He knew Tahani; she was a thrill loving maniac.

'You threatened them, didn't you?'

Tahani sighed in defeat and turned back to her companion with a sheepish grin. 'Okay Zanobi, yer got me – I scared the janitor into leaving the window open.'

When Zanobi headed to the familiar office that belonged to Tracy, he felt himself stiffen up. She was ready to cut him in half just because he had pulled up in the drive way, Zanobi couldn't imagine what would happen if Tracy found out that he was snooping in her office with Tahani. Hopefully she wouldn't notice anyone had gone through her files.

Tahani tried opening the door but she found it locked. 'Damn it... that bloody bitch knew that we were gonna come in here,' she hissed which only made Zanobi cross his arms over his chest.

'Either that – or she's protecting the student files,' Zanobi enlightened but Tahani wasn't paying attention to him. Her midnight eyes were focused on the doorknob, but it only took a moment until ice sheeted over the metal and shattered into tiny shards under her hand. Zanobi yelped at the action, seeing Tahani easily push the door opened with a cocky smirk on her lips. 'Tahani – we aren't meant to make it look obvious!'

'Zanobi calm down,' Tahani responded lazily as she stepped inside. 'She will find out by the time she comes in here anyways – the angels can feel our presence like we can sense theirs.' She went through the drawers, picking up a tiny key with a smile. 'These files are gonna give us the info that we need to learn about Maya.' As the dux turned to the cabinet behind the desk, she searched through the files and left Zanobi to look at her desk.

'Alright then.' He looked at the tidy desk before something caught his eyes. Zanobi picked up a page that looked like it was torn from an ancient journal. He frowned when he realised that the page was fragile and even the handwriting was faded.

'Wat'cha looking at?' Tahani wondered. He skimmed through the faded script, cursing the lighting for making it harder for him to read.

'It appears to be a letter from Abeytu.' Zanobi felt himself shake the cool feeling that chilled down at his back. He knew the name too well. 'No way... It's hard to think that she would've kept such a thing.'

The dux raised an eyebrow but went back to going through the cabinet. 'That's the first Alfero shape shifter ain't it?'

'Yes,' Zanobi said and he put the letter back in the desk. 'I don't think that I should've touched it.'

'It's fine – she's only got a bark with no bite.' Tahani dismissed Zanobi's concern as pulled out a single file.

'Anyways, I found Maya next to my file and her legal guardian is...' She trailed off, using her finger to find the name. 'Adelle Cadmen? Impossible.'

He saw the shock in Tahani. 'You know this Adelle?'

'Yeah.' Tahani placed the file on the desk to get out her phone. She busily wrote the details on the device. 'She's a human that was at the ceremony of the treaty. She was only a kid then but she'd know 'bout Maya's family secret.'

'Do you think she took Maya in?'

Tahani shook her head in dismissal. 'I don't know – but I heard that she had a son with a bit of a troubling reputation, so I will look up police records on the guy.' As she silently plotted, Zanobi took the files himself and had a quick scan on her details. Maya did have the Rosa traits in her – according to the reporting she excelled in anything physical and failed in the theory. Teachers even commented that the girl was loud and always challenging the boys for a race.

'First a school and now we're breaking into a police station?' Zanobi smiled when Tahani winked in his direction. He placed the files back and locked it up. 'Very well – let's just hope that Venatione Dux doesn't skin us alive.'

'If Nadia gets cranky I'll just make some ice on the floor so she slips on it.' It probably wouldn't fix their situation. If anything it would make it worse. Zanobi sighed to himself again – it took him years to reach his rank as a deputy, he didn't want it to crumble after taking over eighty years to getting it.

***

'...Seeing you kill that man out of rage made me scared that you aren't handling it as well as others assumed.'

The words never left Brodie's mind as the day wore on. Now that Leon was dead, Laria had been acting like she had cared about him all along when it was the first time she had seen him since Lesley's death.

Brodie's hazel eyes darkened as he tightened the grip on the glass, feeling it crack under pressure. No matter what he tried to do, tried to think, Brodie couldn't help but realise that he had said cruel words to Laria.

'Damn it,' he cursed, hurling the glass at the wall with full strength. As the glass collided with the surface, he felt anger rush through his system. 'Why am I so angry at you Laria?' Silence met his answer and Brodie took a seat, leaning back on the couch to close his eyes. There was obviously a way for a distraction – to do his father's final wish.

Somewhere out there, there was a Forte that had the same blood as Brodie. There was only one person that could help the him out. Of course, the only person that could help needed a bit of convincing to assist. Brodie knew that it was a challenge that had proven difficult in the past.

He cleaned himself up to look suitable and left the estate to its own devices. As soon as he exited, Brodie cringed at the harsh light. Even though it had only been a day since he left his house, it felt like it had been longer.

Strolling to locate the house he wanted wasn't a problem and it wasn't far from his estate. Brodie ignored the stares from onlookers and knocked lightly on the door. He waited for the owner of the house to unlock the door but a figure appeared in his line of sight. It wasn't someone Brodie was expecting.

'What are you doing here?' Jason questioned with a scowl. Brodie refused to move from his spot.

'I'm not here for you Jason,' Brodie spat back meeting the glare. 'I'm looking for Seth. I have to ask him a question.'

'Does Laria know that you're here?' Jason asked, immediately changing the subject. Brodie didn't react well to this, remembering the pain in Laria's eyes as she tried to shake off the insults from him.

'No, Laria doesn't know that I'm here – actually I didn't expect you to be in a house with Seth.'

Jason crossed his arms over his chest and grumbled. Brodie had to admit – Jason had guts, but he was incredibly stupid for standing up to him. If given the chance, Brodie would end Jason like he had with Brad.

'Well, sorry to say it, but you really have no reason to be here.'

Brodie's reflexes were quick; he pulled Jason from the door and pinned him to the wall by his neck. His eyes met with Brodie's, wide with alarm as Brodie tightened his hold. There was a small voice in the back of Brodie's head that demanded for him to end Jason. End him, and Brodie's problems would disappear.

'I am drunk and I have little tolerance for you Jason – so it's either you tell me where Seth is or you'll regret not answering me,' Brodie hissed violently. He couldn't understand why Jason's presence annoyed him, but Jason certainly didn't make it better.

'That's enough, Brodie,' Seth ordered, exiting his house with a scowl to intervene with the duo. While Jason struggled in the grip, Brodie remained in his position until he turned back to face Seth's hard gaze.

Finally Brodie smirked in recognition and released Jason. His smile widened when he heard the thump and relentless coughing for air. Brodie saw the look of anger in Seth's eyes. 'About time you come out of that hiding hole of yours.'

'You will not go around attacking my guest, Brodie,' Seth explained in a neutral tone. 'What do you want?'

'You already know what I want, Seth,' Brodie replied and tried to ignore the fact that Jason stood up and went behind

Seth with a glare. 'You're going to help me get it.'

'Look at yourself Brodie,' the Seth snapped. 'You were not this person last week – in fact you have been like this ever since your father died.' Brodie felt his heart clench at the mention of his father.

'Are you going to help me find my twin or not?' Surprise flashed in Jason's expression, looking at Seth as if he was the guru to life.

'You have been saying ridiculous things to your friends, drinking, even threatening someone – I know that the old Brodie would've never harmed anyone over a comment.' Seth sighed after realising that Brodie's expression didn't falter. 'But we do need you to move on from this.' He sighed again and met Brodie's gaze. 'Very well... I will help you find your twin but you must give me time.'

The trio fell into a deadly silence and Brodie read their expressions. He didn't trust either of them, after all, Brodie had been lacking trust in pretty much anyone. Even Laria, who had been his friend for as long as he could remember, and yet Brodie shared none of the information with her. She was yet to know about his mysterious twin.

Judging the look on his face, Seth had read his thoughts without another word. 'You don't have to trust us Brodie – but I am the only chance you have to finding a single clue.'

'Start off by not going through my head,' Brodie hissed before he headed out. 'You two have a week to figure out anyone within Golden Cliff that has my birthday.'

Maybe seeing his twin would finally distract him from his vengeance with his father's murderer.

***

'Laria?'

Laria shook herself out of her daze to look back at Maya,

who had been sitting on her bed as she leaned on the wall. Since it was their day off school, Laria took this opportunity to hang out with her. She hadn't necessarily wanted to go hang out with Brodie since the incident, Jenna was already busy with her family and Laria still felt awful about letting Jason get hurt.

So that left Maya as the final candidate.

It was still strange to Laria that Maya was the same as her – she had yet to figure it out. In a way, Laria felt sorry for Maya. 'Sorry – I think I've been lacking in sleep as well – all I want to do right now is take a nap.'

'Looks like we're going to have insomnia night again.' Maya raised her hand and Laria clapped her hands with her companion. 'So... should we watch some movies so we eventually fall asleep?'

'Maybe,' Laria shrugged and she pushed herself to her feet. 'But I've got stuff to deal with at the moment – like older brothers and all that jazz.'

'Alright then,' Maya declared as she stood up. She turned to leave the small room behind. 'Maybe you should go see Chris – after all, you haven't seen him since your mum passed away. It would be good for you – you miss him, don't you?'

Laria silently followed Maya out of the room. Of course Laria missed him. It was Chris after all – he had always been the first person she thought of as she woke up each morning. However it was Chris – he wasn't like her. She may have gotten stronger within the time, but Laria was still frightened of her darker side.

There was no way Laria could let it happen again – who knew if one of her loved ones got in the way instead of the enemy? The conversation she had with Brodie rang in the back of her mind – eventually Laria was going to have to kill Edward... whether she liked it or not.

'It's complicated,' Laria said when she saw the curious expression from Maya. 'But maybe I could go to Cheyenne a bit... I heard there's a college there and I was considering applying for next year.'

'Then there's the plan...' Maya decided as she clapped her hands together. 'Go ask that Haroni guy to take you. He's a decent guy.'

There was nothing decent about the skirt chasing man, Laria thought.

CHAPTER 17

Laria knew she was in a dreamlike state when she found herself in the grassy plain, filled with the never-ending silence. It felt strange to not see Jason around, but she felt relieved that he wasn't a part of the nightmare.

'You really don't understand, do you?'

It was her amber eyed doppelganger. She felt her body tense and took an involuntary step back the second that the other figure advanced on her. This girl... this doppelganger was meant to be the source of her powers.

'Who are you?' Laria demanded, already annoyed. 'I know you aren't me. You're connected to me... but you sure as hell aren't me.'

The amber eyes that set the stranger apart was the only hint that she wasn't the real Laria. But it wasn't her... Laria knew that much. This counterpart was merely the opposite side of a coin.

'Such a pain,' the doppelganger finally replied with a sadistic sneer. 'You're right when you say that we're connected – but it's much deeper than that.' Slowly she brushed her hair back and Laria felt alarm tickle her spine. 'My name is Lux and I am the source of your power.'

'You're the bloodlust,' Laria stated rather than asked. She felt her muscles lock uncomfortably and she clenched her fists. Despite knowing what stood in front of her, Laria didn't feel like she knew anything about it. 'You've been trying to get me to break you out of your seal and now that...'

Laria couldn't even finish her statement. 'That's right Laria. The seal is already beginning to weaken the more you depend on me.' Lux snickered when Laria's throat tightened in denial. 'I am the bloodlust that you and your ancestors depend on – the shifters have accepted their fate of giving in... yet you resist this power...'

Images flashed in Laria's mind and her eyes flashed angrily as she remembered her most recent bloodlust attack. Memories of the shifter trio that went after Jason when Laria was desperately trying to protect him, rushed back to her.

The painful part of the memory was that she loved the idea of their misery. Laria still relished the satisfying moment when she snapped Nick's unfortunate wrist.

But it was because of Jason. When he screamed out her name, Laria felt the common sense hit her and she used the chance to fight back. Fortunately for Laria, she managed to break out of the bloodlust's grip before it consumed her.

She nearly failed her friend that day.

'You're the reason why I've been struggling,' Laria spat violently and fought the urge to end the bloodlust in front of her. She knew that if she did, she would be doing the one thing that Lux wanted. Lux on the other hand looked relaxed, with a hint of a mocking in her amber eyes.

'Correct, genius,' Lux retorted sarcastically before she chuckled to herself. 'I am the essence of our power, the reason why you're still alive to this day.' Sparing a gaze towards Laria, the doppelganger smiled. 'I speak the truth – don't you find amusement in having this power?'

'I nearly killed someone. It would've been your fault...' Laria's voice trembled. Ever since she crashed into Jason, Laria felt the desire to cause misery towards anyone who wronged her. 'Back when Jason had his first day and Sara-'

'You hate that girl,' Lux snarled coldly. 'Don't say that you haven't wanted to kill her because that's a lie. She made your life miserable growing up, then you act like I'm the monster because I'm whispering your darkest desires. Face it Laria, you want to cause misery.'

No, she didn't want to be that person. As Laria tried to move, she was shocked to realise that her body refused to budge. 'What did you do to me?' Laria questioned, stiffening when the woman took another step towards her.

Lux sneered in delight. 'Nothing I did, Laria – it's your fear whenever you hold back your true nature.' Laria's expression filled with an uneasy presence as Lux came too close to her.

'You want her to be as miserable as you were. Laria, you feed on the misery of others – that is how we thrive-!'

Something in Laria exploded and she felt her anger bubbling in her chest. 'Shut up!' Laria swung her fist with rage. The doppelganger was surprised by the hit and smacked into the ground. 'I've had enough of your crap.'

Lux didn't appear to be mad despite being on the ground. Laria's anger remained when it occurred to her that the strange woman was laughing at her.

'You're going to be one of "those" skin walkers,' Lux teased lightly recovering from her fall. The uneasiness returned to Laria as they met eyes again. 'Let me inform you that I will tear down every cage that you trap me in, make your instinct crave the misery that you place on others... but unless you lose your skin walker powers I will always escape.'

Laria remained silent for a moment, considering the warning from Lux. Even though she hated to admit it, Lux had already gained control of her more than once... and this bloodlust was closer than she originally assumed. Her training in controlling the bloodlust with Tahani had obviously tamed it down, but who knew how much damage it was actually doing?

Instead of commenting with fear like Lux would've wanted, Laria looked back up. 'Bring it on.'

'Well said, Mistress,' Lux replied with a sly grin. Laria's glare remained hard as the smile from the other woman's face only widened as if she was enjoying the hate.

'Wake up kiddo!'

Sensing another presence above her, Laria suddenly lifted her eyelids open to see Tahani's looming figure over her head. Laria let out a startled yelp.

'What the heck are you doing in my room?' Laria freaked out at the dux who chuckled lightly. 'I was finally learning about Lux!' Realisation dawned on Laria. It wasn't normal for her to remember her dreams – so why had it started now?

'It looks like ya've met the bloodlust,' Tahani replied as she pulled herself away from Laria. 'Anyways, get ready to head to Cheyenne.'

The frown deepened as the anger from earlier dispersed. 'Wait... what do you mean? Cheyenne?'

'Didn't ya speak with Haroni last night 'bout going to the big city?' she questioned with a frown. 'I overheard ya talking 'bout ya brother or something... It's weird that I haven't heard 'bout Chris in a while. Haroni sent me to go get ya stuff ready but I ain't no servant.'

'You know Chris?' Laria wondered, sparing a curious glance towards the dux. 'He would've told me that he knew someone like... yourself...'

'We don't actually know each other kiddo.' Tahani snorted at the thought and shook her head with a chuckle. 'I'm a dux – so it's kinda my job to know 'bout the mishaps of our extended life.' She clapped her hands together. 'But ya not gonna go there like that – get ready and Haroni will drive ya there.'

'Haroni...' Laria frowned in consideration, feeling a hint of guilt. Ever since she had met him, she had gone with her gut instinct and he had been nothing but kind to her. Even so, Laria still couldn't find any trust with Haroni. There was something that he was hiding. 'What about you? Aren't you coming along?'

'Nope,' Tahani replied as she neared the door and turned her head to look back at Laria. 'Zanobi and Haroni are the only ones that are going with ya – I can't leave my dux stuff behind.' When Tahani's figure disappeared behind the door, Laria fell back on the bed.

What a crazy morning.

***

'You're not busy are you Jason?' Jenna wondered, as Jason shoved his books in his locker. The past few days had been a lot to handle.

It was surprising to Jason that he didn't want to tear out his own hair in frustration. He looked in Seth's direction to see that he was talking to Maya. Seth's parents were the next targets of the Beast, but it wasn't only Seth's parents.

Maya was a target as well because Seth cared about her friendship and he couldn't push her away. Seth thought he was being selfish by hanging out with Maya casually like he usually did, but in reality, Jason knew that Seth needed a friend that would support him.

After losing focus on the pair, Jason grumbled to himself and he turned to see Jenna waiting patiently for his response. He sighed at the sight of her concerned stare, but he closed the locker door.

'What's wrong? I should be able to help.'

She nervously pulled a strand of blond behind her ear. 'Well Taro invited everyone to his bonfire – something he always does this time of year... so I was wondering if you can give me some tips.'

Jason raised an eyebrow as he observed the girl. 'Tips?'

Jenna's cheeks flushed pink at the thought. 'Well – the only thing I can think of to get Taro's attention is by making him jealous...'

It didn't take long for Jason to realise what Jenna's true intentions were. His eyes widened with revulsion and he felt himself back away from the madwoman. 'No, Jenna I don't think that's the greatest idea-'

'Why not?' Jenna protested with a pout as she got closer to him. She was close enough to touch him with her nose and it didn't sit well with Jason. His cheeks flushed with crimson shade at the thoughts of her getting any closer. 'We're gonna just be friends but we have to pretend that we're interested in each other!'

'No Jenna,' Jason stated with a stern glare. *What the hell did Jenna even see in Taro? The guy was an idiot and tried picking a fight with me for no good reason.* 'I'm already on thin ice with Brodie's patience by being friends with you guys –

She perked her head up. 'Don't worry about Brodie. He's been going through so much since his dad died – he has a lot on his plate right now. Just understand that Brodie isn't normally like this.'

If only she knew how he really acted.

Luckily for Jason, he was interrupted by a familiar face who appeared beside him with a smile. As soon as she appeared, Jason felt calmed by her mere presence.

'Heather,' Jason greeted, noticing that she flashed a kind smile in return.

'Hello Jason,' Heather replied before she looked over to Jenna and nodded to the blonde. 'It's nice to see you Jenna.'

'Good morning Heather,' Jenna said cheerfully before she paused and looked between the duo. 'I see now Jason...'

Before Jason could ask her intentions, she patted his shoulder and turned the opposite way. 'Alright then... I'll go with Brodie. I'll see you later.'

Jenna rushed off just as Jason turned to her. 'Hey, wait – and she's gone...' Jason sighed to look back at Heather who had simply giggled to herself. 'So anyways – how have you been? I haven't seen you around for a while.'

'Well... I was a bit busy with my sister,' Heather replied instantly and smiled to herself. 'She's lives out of the city and asked me to do a few errands...'

'I didn't know you had a sister,' Jason realised with a raised eyebrow. 'Are there any dark secrets you're hiding from me?'

The female had a pondering expression on her face before flashing a cheerful smile again. 'None that come to mind.' She took a moment of silence, allowing Jason to regain his thoughts before she added a soft question. 'Was she asking you to the bonfire?'

'Yeah.' Jason scratched the back of his head awkwardly. 'But it was more to impress Taro or make him jealous – something along those lines... But hey, it's something that I have to do as a friend.'

'It's to honour his lost brother,' Heather explained simply as Jason narrowed his eyes in concern. 'In a few days would be the anniversary of his elder brother's death... He died in military service.'

'That's harsh,' Jason admitted, frowning in concern. 'Do you often go?'

Heather brushed her hair back. 'Well, I go there to pay my respects. But this time I might have a reason to stay longer than I normally have to...' Jason blinked curiously at her words as she turned away from him. 'I have to get to class... alright?'

'O... kay?' Jason gave half a wave as Heather left him to his own devices, flinching suddenly when Seth clamped a hand on his shoulder. Seth had always been a quiet one

'You were talking with Heather?' Seth questioned, obviously too busy reading Jason's mind than actually talk about school stuff. 'Look, I'm not going to be my parents and tell you not to hang out with certain people... just be careful.'

'Why do I have to be careful around Heather?' Jason wondered, seeing that Seth's gaze remained stoic and calculating. With a slump of his shoulders, Jason looked at him. 'She's one of you guys too?'

'Heather is a witch from Cheyenne,' Seth explained before he shoved his hands in his pockets. 'But I say that because even witches have their reason to turn on humans... this world is filled with blood of the supernatural.'

Jason felt like banging his head on a stone wall. It was unfair; everyone in his life were the strong ones while he was frail and always under watch. He had to be careful around anyone that so much as spoke to him, regardless of being a human or a shape shifter.

Seth noticed his thoughts and removed his hand. 'Stop thinking like that... being a part of this is already bad enough. Now let's head to our next class.'

CHAPTER 18

Here she was, in the city of Cheyenne.

Cheyenne was an hour south from Golden Cliff; Laria always wondered what it was like travelling to the city on a train but never followed up with her curiosity. Ever since she was a little girl, Laria always wanted to travel.

She had to admit that Cheyenne itself was a big city. Golden Cliff was nothing compared to it – she didn't often see the tall buildings, the countless tourist attractions and the crowd. Many people were in the streets, performing fancy works in front of masses that only watched with eagerness.

'It looks like this is the first time you've been here,' Zanobi spoke up.

'Well, pretty much,' Laria answered awkwardly as she turned to face the other shape shifter. 'I've never left Golden Cliff with people I barely know.'

'Don't worry Laria,' Haroni interrupted with a smile. 'I will be here with you.'

'And that's exactly why I'm uneasy about this whole thing,' Laria muttered to her godfather with a scowl. Even though Haroni had gained a few points of her trust, Laria still felt uneasy around him.

Haroni didn't respond and kept driving; leaving her to once again take her attention to the buildings around her.

Her eyes followed the road with a curious gaze. Staring back at the city gave her a hint of ease, reminding her that despite that she had to live with a curse, she would still have the opportunities to explore the world.

Her thoughts turned glum when she remembered the dream. Judging Tahani's not so surprised actions meant that the bloodlust always had a name.

It felt real, staring back at the amber eyes that belonged to her doppelganger. Lux mentioned that she was the reason why Laria had felt the urge to hurt Sara back at school. So it was obvious that she was responsible for taking over her when the trio of shifters attempted to kill Jason. Laria couldn't help but wince to herself at the memories.

Those shifters had come to give her a scare. Had they done it because they knew that Laria would retaliate? Every time she remembered the story that Tahani told her, Laria couldn't help but feel frustrated.

I shouldn't think about this, Laria realised as she shook her head. She felt the car pull itself into a park, dispersing her thoughts. Chris was the reason why she came here, not to think about her problems.

'You seem to look better,' Zanobi mentioned once they got out of the car. Laria spared a glance towards the older shape shifter before she sighed to herself. He was always observant; it was one of the few things that Laria feared about him. She was glad that he wasn't against her though. 'Don't worry Laria, it will be alright.'

'Will it?' Laria wondered, looking back at him with a hint of concern in her features. In the corner of her eyes, she saw that Haroni beckoned them to follow him along the street. 'I know that I came here to visit my brother, but what happens if a shifter comes to attack us?'

'Believe it or not, you aren't the only protected one,' Zanobi reminded her as they followed Haroni into an apartment building. 'I'm sure that I, a fallen, and an Alfero descendant will be able to handle a few measly shifters.'

She slowly deflated in defeat. 'I know... but still... what happens if it isn't the enemies that we're meant to be watching out for?'

Hearing Laria's response, Zanobi halted his tracks and turned to Laria with a frown. 'Is there something that we should know about?' He flinched when Haroni interrupted the duo with a cleared throat.

'We're at the pub that we're meant to be in – Chris said he was coming here tonight,' Haroni announced with a smile on his face, gaining Laria's attention once again. She looked at the oversized building and found herself gulping down her nerves.

It looked like a place where the whole city came to eat, nevertheless Laria was nervous. Whatever she doubted had to stop, there was no turning back from this task now and she knew that. Even though it was her being selfish, but Laria really did want to see her brother.

Before Laria could speak, Zanobi's phone rang and he halted to see the caller. His gaze was hard. 'I'm sorry... but I must take this call. It's important.' He pressed the screen on his phone and put it up to his ear.

As Laria stared back at the shifter with worry coating her expression. She felt Haroni's hand grab her shoulder gently. Naturally, Laria would've seized up, so it surprised her when she didn't stiffen. 'Don't worry about him,' Haroni insisted with a smile. 'It's only a phone call.'

'Then let's eat,' Laria decided and she went along with her godfather into the building.

***

'Are you sure that we should be out here?' Jason wondered. The night had dropped down in temperature, giving those who walked through the town a chilly breeze. For the first time in his life, Jason was glad he'd brought his leather jacket along. 'You said that you were next on the list of losing your parents or Maya – if they find you with me...'

'It's alright Jason,' Seth replied. 'The shifters won't harm you as long as I can hear them.'

'It's not me that I'm worried about Seth,' Jason admitted with a deep frown. 'We've been out of the house for hours, searching through hospital records and even past residents yet we don't have a single clue.'

'Everything was erased,' Seth responded stonily and frowned. 'It's strange – like someone covered this Forte's tracks of his existence.'

Jason raised an eyebrow. 'Was it possible that Leon Forte pulled some strings? I mean, Brodie didn't know about his sibling until Leon told him. He may have done it in order to hide the kid from the other shifters.'

'Possibly – but due to this, the missing Forte may have fallen victim to the bloodlust,' Seth considered out loud. They fell into an awkward silence, but when Seth suddenly halted in his tracks, Jason only paused to stare back at his companion.

'Seth.' Jason kept the frown on his face. 'That look means that you're coming up with something.'

'There is a way to find the missing Forte,' Seth realised after his silent pause. As soon as he continued his path, Jason followed along obediently. 'However, it's a one in a million chance of success.'

'Seth, if it gets Brodie off our backs, then we have to take that chance,' Jason replied. 'He's getting more impatient by the second.'

Seth sighed softly to himself. 'I suppose you're right after all Jason.' When Jason's expression flashed with surprise, Seth turned to face him with a grave expression in his features once again.

'So,' Jason spoke softly, 'what is it?'

Seth's eyes met Jason's sharply. 'How much do you know about the Corvena?'

Jason blinked in response. 'I know that it was responsible of sealing the rectocs and that it was responsible for giving the shifters the abilities in the first place.'

'Interesting,' Seth said as he plucked out an object from his jeans' pocket and showed it off like a precious treasure. It was a small, round item wrapped in a cloth. Seth removed the cloth to reveal a small, red stone. 'It took four of the shifters to seal the rectocs, but it came with a price of the Corvena.'

The stone was a luminescent red, it almost appeared as if it was made of glass. It was no bigger than Seth's palm. Jason's eyes went to the stone, shuddering at the thought of its potential. His eyes widened at the glow. There was something about the stone that made it seem alive. It emitted a strange humming sound.

He wondered if Seth could hear it. 'Is this...?'

'The Corvena was split into four, and the true descendants watch over them.' Seth finished his explanation, 'As it split, each of the families were in charge of taking care of their stone. This is nothing more than a quarter of its true form.' Nothing but power emitted from the stone in Seth's hand. 'Jason – this is Verm; the stone of Corvena that was responsible for the Laurences' power.'

'Whoa.' Jason leaned forward. 'Why would you have it on you right now? Isn't it dangerous?'

'Shifters are a nifty bunch, but I am the guardian of Vern after my parents – that isn't why I brought up the topic.' He concealed the stone within his pockets as he explained, 'Leon would've been the previous guardian of the Forte stone, Rel, so naturally it was passed down to Brodie. Shape shifters and each of the stones are connected like threads. However, since

Rel is a part of the Fortes, it will only glow in the presence of another Forte just like Verm will only glow in a Laurence's presence.'

'I see.' Jason immediately understood why it was a long shot. Forte members were everywhere in Golden Cliff. 'We should do it anyway.'

'I knew you would say that,' Seth muttered with a small smile. 'Alright, I'll send a message to Brodie and...' He frowned and held his hand up to stop Jason from asking what was wrong.

Jason's frown deepened as he saw the deep look in Seth's eyes, before his eyes flashed yellow.

'My parents,' Seth interrupted Jason before he could even think about it. 'The scent of my parents... but I cannot hear their thoughts.' He rushed into an alley which left Jason gaping for a moment before he shook himself out of his daze.

'Seth, wait!' Jason exclaimed, following his companion with distress. Seth wasn't facing him, his body frozen in motion as he stared down at the mess before him. As Jason caught up, his eyes widened. 'I didn't...'

For some reason, Jason was surprised. It didn't matter that Seth already forewarned him that his parents were next on the death list, but seeing it made it real. They were both in a pool of their own blood. The recognisable faces of the Seth's parents were lifeless, their dull, dark eyes staring at the sky with surprise.

It took a lot for a Laurence to be surprised.

Jason wasn't able to react. It took him a moment to finally understand that Seth's parents were gone. They were as mysterious as Seth was, and they were kind. Now they were gone, just like that.

'Father, Mother...' Seth crouched down; his eyes remaining calm as his fingers lightly grazed their dead bodies.

Behind him, Jason placed a hand on Seth's shoulder as he attempted to comfort him. But Seth's voice suddenly startled him. 'This is ice...'

'Ice?' Jason pulled away, crouching next to Seth to observe the bodies. The sight and smell made him sick, but the wounds had light frost on them, as if the killer was trying to hide his tracks.

'Or her tracks,' Seth interrupted Jason's thoughts with a dark scowl. 'I know.' He turned and glowered behind him. 'You may as well come out of the shadows, coward,' Seth declared seriously. 'At least look at me in the eyes before you kill me because I'm not turning on anyone.'

Jason only turned in time to see that a figure was suddenly in front of Seth with a blunt object. Seth himself was alarmed by the speed, and the figure smacked him out before he could react. As soon as Jason heard a cold thud, he realised Seth was out. His eyes widened as the figure looked in his direction – it wasn't clear to see the facial features.

So, this was how it was going to end? It dawned on Jason that he really was going to die here. The last thing he saw was a pair of bright blue eyes before it went dark.

**

'Another shot for me, dear one.' Haroni smirked as the waitress filled the shot glass. Other people ignored their presence, minding their own business as Haroni and Laria sat together.

He took in the drink and slammed the cup on the table, sparing a glance towards Laria who showed no signs amusement.

'Lighten up Laria. Why do you always frown?'

'We've been here for hours and Zanobi still hasn't come back,' Laria replied, as she spared a glance over to the door.

'We should look for him – find out what's going on.' Just as Laria stood, the door opened and stopped her movements.

Christopher entered the building first, holding a woman's hand as he looked around to find the pair. He found them and dragged the woman with him, with Zanobi coming from behind with a blank expression. As they approached the table, Haroni finally recognised the woman by their side.

She had a petite body with olive skin and a smile in her young features. Her wavy, brown hair was in a low ponytail with hazel eyes hiding behind rectangular framed glasses. As her eyes met Haroni's, he flashed an all-knowing smile.

However, he forgot that Laria was with them. Since she was so quiet, Haroni didn't realise that she was running until it was too late. She went to tackle her own brother into a hug. Zanobi quietly strolled through, taking a seat next to Haroni.

Haroni smirked lightly. 'Where did you disappear off to?'

'I was talking with Tahani and she told me about our personal business.' Zanobi took a drink with a soft grunt and watched Laria laugh. 'I haven't seen her this happy ever... she must've missed him.'

'Christopher and Laria are the closest siblings that I know,' Haroni admitted with a smile. It was such a light-hearted feeling within him. As Laria spared a glance towards Haroni, he saw the hidden smile in her features – she was thanking him.

'I've seen a sibling bond just as powerful as this,' Zanobi confessed and gained the strange look from his drinking companion. 'Tahani and her younger sister... they stood by each other, it's probably why Tahani chooses to stand tall now.'

Haroni raised a brow as he turned towards Zanobi, the surprise slowly spreading across his face. 'I didn't know that Tahani had a sister.' It just proved how little Haroni knew about the her.

'It's not my story to tell,' Zanobi replied with a darkened expression. 'If she trusts you, she will share her story but considering you didn't even know the existence of her sister she probably won't trust you even if you were old and wrinkled.'

Now that wasn't a pretty image. Haroni never thought of himself turning wrinkly from old age. 'You know that would be at least another couple hundred years until I even get a line, right?'

'Exactly my point. In fact, the only reason why I knew was because I grew up with them – they think of me as an older brother.' Zanobi finished this drink when Laria came with the pair. Christopher offered a warm smile in greeting as Haroni raised his empty shot glass to the pair.

'Christopher Alfero and Liza Verdas, nice to see you again.'

CHAPTER 19

Brodie grumbled to himself, glaring at the couch of where Jason remained unconscious. Brodie tightened his grip on his glass of scotch and growled lowly.

Brodie didn't have any plans, but he was surprised when Tara came in the house with Seth and Jason. They were found unconscious in the middle of the alley, the same place where Seth's parents were found. At the moment Seth was resting in one of the rooms, and Brodie decided that he would keep a sharp eye on Jason.

Ever since Jason wormed his way into their shape shifter lives, Brodie had been nothing but suspicious of the other boy. Why on earth was *he* so damn special?

In frustration, Brodie finished his drink then placed the glass on the table beside him. That voice was back telling him that he should end Jason then and there. It would've been simple – no witnesses and Brodie could easily hide the evidence.

Even so, there was a tiny part of Brodie that questioned himself. Why did he have such a bad blood with Jason? He would've said because he put Laria at risk, but that was bull. There was something he was not reading correctly, and it was beginning to irritate him.

Turning away from Jason, Brodie rubbed his forehead to clear the migraine starting in his temples. He hadn't heard anything from Laria and he didn't blame her. If Brodie was in her shoes, he probably wouldn't be talking to him either.

She was another problem itself; Brodie feeling so angry with everything. Ever since his father's death, Brodie pushed everyone out of his life. Then Tara tried to console him, but Brodie ignored his aunt – only wishing for her visit when she had clues to figuring out the code that Leon had given him.

The only ones he didn't feel so annoyed over were Maya and Jenna, who remained his friends every time they met paths.

'Urgh...'

Brodie's thoughts were interrupted by Jason as he began to regain his consciousness. He snorted softly, taking his glass and leaning on an armchair with a glare.

'Where am I?' Jason's croaked voice wondered, before he reached up and clutched his skull with a wince of pain. 'Ow – why can't I remember what I did last night?' His grunt sounded rough, and he turned to see that he wasn't alone. 'Brodie...'

'Nice to see that you're awake,' Brodie spat quietly and brushed his scruffy hair back. 'Before you ask about your boyfriend slash bodyguard, he's sleeping upstairs.'

'You really are a dick.' Jason's eyes hardened as he admitted his opinion. 'Why did you save us?'

Brodie lazily shrugged. 'It looks like you *do* remember what happened last night.' He saw that Jason stared at the ground, his eyes filled with concentration. 'Besides it wasn't me who rescued you, my auntie gave a crap about you.'

Jason muttered gently, rubbing his eyes. 'I remember Seth telling me something.' His eyes squeezed shut to recall memories.

Brodie should've killed him while he had the damn chance.

Jason's eyes widened as he recalled a memory and turned to Brodie with a hidden determination. Now Brodie was the alarmed one, his brow furrowed in a confused line to glower at Jason.

'Your sibling's tracks have been completely hidden – we suspect that your father was the one responsible for it,' Jason confessed and Brodie felt the world go cold around him. 'Seth possibly found a way to find your twin.'

'Go on.'

'If we use your Corvena stone,' Jason explained in return. 'He told me that yours in particular would react to another Forte.'

'Good theory,' Brodie admitted while he raised his eyebrows at the consideration. Using Rel would most likely find his twin. 'Unfortunately, my father locked Rel in his chest and I respect his privacy.'

'What privacy? He's dead-'

Before Jason could say anymore, Brodie stood to his feet and his irritation was back. 'Say another word about my father and it will be the last thing you ever say.'

'You're right – I shouldn't speak like that... I'm sorry but... what happens if Leon hid that information for you?' A sympathetic expression appeared on the Jason's face, making Brodie frown in annoyance.

'It wouldn't matter – he has his past diaries, but it would never...' Brodie's eyes went wide as he filled the pieces. He hated the fact that Jason was the reason he figured it out. Without another word, Brodie stalked to his father's office.

'Wait up!'

Brodie scowled as Jason followed along. As he went to the large chest by his father's old desk, his eyes remained hard. *Forgive me father,* He told himself and suddenly opened the heavy chest lid. The dust floated in their direction. Jason coughed uncomfortably while Brodie found a familiar book, worn from the years.

'How did you know about that?' Jason asked, looking over the Forte's shoulder to see the journal.

'Does it matter?' Brodie retorted as he searched for a certain date through the pages. Finally his eyes recognised the similar date – October twenty-third.

The code was cracked. Brodie's date of birth – of course it was that damn simple – then September the fifth, which was his father's birthday. Brodie still couldn't understand what his father's birthday had to do with it, but if Leon wanted something for only Brodie to see then it had to be related to his date of birth. He noticed the next two pages glued together and carefully peeled the pages apart.

> Brodie – *if you are reading this, it means that I am dead. I wrote this the day after your birth, trusting you to guard Rel. Rel contains tremendous power on its own, just as Viri, Azu and Verm do. I kept it in a safe after sealing the rectocs.*
>
> *Please Brodie – keep it safe and never let anyone know about its location.*

'Well it looks like I've already screwed that up,' Brodie grumbled as he went behind the desk and found the familiar safe concealed. He heard Jason scurry through Leon's old trinkets, and Brodie promised himself that he would scold the idiot later. Once he pressed the final key, the safe unlocked automatically and Brodie opened the door.

It had been his first time seeing it but Rel was just like Brodie imagined – a small yellow stone glowing due to his presence. He dismissed his thoughts, grabbing the stone and he felt everything. He could hear, smell and even taste what every Forte was experiencing. However, it was only for a moment; Brodie got used to the presence of the stone and lifted it out of the safe.

Jason, who had been staring at a photo suddenly, glanced

at the stone. His blue eyes locked on the glowing rock. 'That's Rel?'

'Yes,' Brodie declared with a scowl. 'What are you looking at?'

Jason placed the photo back down in Brodie's view, stiffening upon recognition of the old photo. It was a pale woman with a warm smile on her face, her bright blue eyes gazing at the camera with wavy dark hair in a low ponytail.

Jason's eyes softened at the photo before he faced Brodie. 'That was your mother, right?' When Brodie lacked an answer and ignored him, Jason spoke up. 'She's pretty.'

Brodie snorted. 'It doesn't matter – I am only interested in looking for my sibling.' He jerked the stone away from Jason when he tried reaching for it. 'Don't touch Rel you idiot! You're just a human; direct contact could kill you with the power in your hands.'

'I didn't know that,' Jason admitted sheepishly. 'It was humming to me... the same with Verm.' Brodie didn't hear it. He shoved the thought aside and returned his attention to Rel.

Rel was his top priority. 'I swear it's like talking to a child.' He pulled a small cloth from his father's desk and wrapped Rel in it. Even concealed within the cloth, the yellow stone kept glowing. But it was strange; from the stories that his father told him, the stone wouldn't glow if it was concealed.

Maybe Brodie just pictured it differently. 'So this is how the rectocs gave the shifters their powers?'

Exactly. Now if only he was smarter during the rest of the day. 'My family's rectoc – Vindi is in here and she can force her powers into you without effort. She could possess your body and you would be nothing but an empty stone.'

Yet Brodie didn't mention another important factor. If a late bloomer came in contact with the stone, then it would merely awaken their abilities. Jason looked like he was about to say something but he was interrupted.

'So you'll give us the stone?'

Brodie and Jason stopped, turning to see that Seth was standing by the entrance. His dark eyes went down to the stone as he recognised it instantly.

'I see.' Seth must've read his mind again. Annoyance crossed Brodie's face as Seth approached him, shoving his hand in his pockets to fish for something. 'I know that this is risky, but I will return the favour for you.' When Seth took the item out, he placed a small red stone in Brodie's hand and took Rel in return.

'Wait,' Brodie realised what Seth just did. 'Why are you giving me Verm?'

'Believe it or not Brodie, but you trust us enough to give us Rel.' Seth replied immediately and took the wrapped stone away from Brodie. 'And if I were to be attacked, then the enemy would have two of them which would be bad for us.' As soon as it left Brodie's hands, the bright glow dimmed down to a light flicker. 'At least I know that Verm will be safe.'

Rel shouldn't have been glowing as much in Seth's presence; yet it was. However Brodie did know that it could glow due to the presence of more than one Forte but there was only him, Seth and...

Brodie suddenly cursed in his head. His eyes turned hard as he clenched his jaw in fury. Silently, he snapped, 'If you would so kindly get out – I have things to do.' In the corner of Brodie's eyes, he saw that Seth was staring at him. 'And stop reading my mind Seth!'

'Let's go Jason,' Seth grunted and turned away. In a fit of anger, Brodie clenched his fists.

'You're not going to tell him?' Seth wondered telepathically and Brodie scowled. Stupid mind readers and their mind tricks – they always stuck their nose in places they don't belong.

'No – don't say a damn thing either. I will not believe it until there's no other option.'

Due to his hearing, Brodie heard them exit the building. He eyed the photo again, staring at his mother's image. Now that he thought about it, the woman did look like him – they had matching eyes and even the same hair colour.

Out of all damn human beings on earth, why did Brodie have to be the brother of Jason Amarel? It all became clear. Shifters tried attacking him, the familiar stern looks that once belonged to his father.

He should've killed him while he had the damn chance.

***

Laria was glad that she finally met Liza. Liza was naturally relaxed, and she was a witch who surprisingly didn't care that Chris was an Alfero.

'So anyways,' Liza said showing Laria into her apartment, 'Chris tells me that you're trying to access your powers.' Haroni, Chris and Zanobi insisted that they needed to do something, and they left Laria alone with the witch.

'Yeah,' Laria mumbled, playing with her hair and ignoring the intelligent stare from the stranger.

Laria looked around the sparsely furnished room and took a seat on the closest armchair to her. Liza turned to face her, but her frown formed when she noticed something. 'You left the door open,' the witch said and flicked her hand to make the door close.

Witches were... pretty much the same thing she had been seeing on television. Laria didn't comment on her view on witches, as Liza brushed back her dark hair and let out a lazy huff

'Sorry...' Laria sheepishly returned and Liza gave her a simple shrug to dismiss it.

'Don't worry about it – you didn't kill anyone.' The witch pulled out an old book from the shelf, studying its aged cover before bringing it closer to Laria. 'As for powers – I can't really teach you how to use them since we're two different species.'

'So what? Do I have to keep dreaming about them until I accidentally sneeze out extra energy or something?'

Liza snorted at Laria's attempt at humour. 'It doesn't really work like that.' She took a seat on a mat on the other side of the room. 'Powers that you access are powers originating from the rectocs.'

'The rectocs?' Laria knew this information already, but she was still confused over the rectocs.

'Yes, but they're still alive inside you,' Liza explained curtly. 'They are alive as a part of the bloodlust – your instincts that your ancestors took in.'

Laria stared in silence.

'My point is,' Liza's voice cut Laria's thoughts as she plucked a feather from the mat she sat on. Laria forced a frown as Liza lifted the black feather from her hand without any physical contact. 'The more you connect with your bloodlust, the more you're likely to be able to access your power. I can tell your relationship between shifter and bloodlust is very rocky but it's the inner connection with your power.'

'So I'm stuck with Lux either way?' The flash of amber eyes spooked her, and it didn't help that she felt something stir within her.

'I heard this saying from my mum a long time ago,' Liza reminded before she lowered the feather. 'Magic always comes with a price – you have to be willing to step into the dark boundaries in order to tame the darkness. "Lux" as you put it – will most likely consume you with the need of misery unless you learn how to control the bloodlust.'

'How did you know about her constant talk of misery?' Laria wondered, stiffening when she noticed that Liza's gaze turned serious.

'Each of the rectocs signifies reasons to kill...' Liza explained and Laria felt her eyes grow wide. 'Alferos are associated with a rectoc named Perio; he enjoyed causing misery as he killed.'

Instantly, Laria felt that she knew that name despite never hearing it. Perio. As she heard his name spoken, the presence of Lux began to unsettle in the back of her mind.

'It's alright Laria.' Liza's voice took Laria out of her momentary trance. 'He's been sealed up along with the others for roughly sixty-five years. No one is stupid enough to revive him, not even the shifters that are after you.'

'That's comforting,' Laria replied sarcastically and she tried to settle again.

'Anyways – back to my point.' Liza clicked her fingers and the curtains closed around them, darkening the area around them. 'It's your connection with the bloodlust; the stronger your bond is – whether its hate, love or whatever – the more likely you'll be able to access it.'

'I understand.' She felt her breath leave her and she closed her eyes. She needed to relax her body as if she wanted to meditate.

Soon, Laria heard her own heartbeat and found herself standing in the same place that she stood in the dream. Slowly she opened her eyes to look around her. Her eyes scanned the field, but she froze instinctively when she recognised Lux standing in front of her.

'Welcome back Mistress.'

Suddenly Laria felt like she was zapped and she jolted from her seated position. Liza flinched from Laria's gasping and she bounced to her feet with a concern frown.

'Did I fall asleep?'

'No – you used your connection to put yourself in there,' Liza replied honestly. Laria felt her breath fall back into pace as the witch grabbed a glass of water to pass it to Laria. She reached out for it, taking it gratefully and sculled the drink with greed.

She finished the drink and the memories of horror flashed her mind. The memories were finally coming back to her – fire had nothing to do with it. 'It felt like it was nothing...'

'Don't put yourself through too much,' Liza advised and took the cup back. 'Having just that small connection is a start and you will be able to tolerate your bloodlust. Soon your powers will unveil themselves.'

'I have a question,' Laria confessed, which only made the witch smirk.

'And I have an answer.'

'Your last name...' Liza's expression turned serious and Laria returned the gaze. 'Haroni called you a Verdas... which means Heather from Golden Cliff...'

'Right.' Liza suddenly looked uncomfortable. 'That would only mean that you have acquainted yourself with my little sister.'

Laria's eyes widened. 'Heather's your sister?' No wonder they looked similar.

Surprisingly, Liza didn't show any sadness as she spoke. 'Like me she has the barrier magic to stay in Golden Cliff to protect the humans. She had a mission in particular that was set by the Mandati Dux himself a few months ago.'

'Takon set a mission for Heather?'

'Yes,' Liza explained with a serious expression. 'There was a shape shifter hybrid that she was meant to protect – to use her abilities to cover him. I don't even know who he is but she is meant to keep a barrier on him to make other shifters leave him be.' Laria knew well that Lesley tried to keep her out of this life, but it didn't work.

When the duo fell quiet, a single knock broke their silence and they pulled apart.

'Anyways, enough about that.' Liza spared a smile and went to the door. As soon as she opened it, she saw Chris enter with an elderly man. Chris spared Laria a smile, and she turned to see that this man was greeting Liza with a blunt manner.

'It feels like someone stole your youth Liza,' the man grunted as his misty white eyes went over to Laria who flinched upon his gaze. It didn't have to take a genius for her to figure out that the man was blind in both eyes. 'I don't actually believe it... we have Alferos in my presence.' As he limped in Laria's direction, she showed off a confused frown.

How on earth did he know who she was?

'Don't give me that expression child,' the man grumbled. 'I may be blind and old, but like you I am an Alfero – Henry Alfero. My abilities are my sight now.'

Laria's eyes widened slightly as it dawned on her. She voiced out her thoughts. 'Why would they say I'm the last?'

'Technically you are the last shifter with Alfero powers. Your connection with Abeytu is powerful – the representative of fire and the leader that was sought out to be,' Henry explained before he took a seat on the leather armchair. 'I'm pretty much useless 'cause I'm blind.'

'Henry,' Chris spoke up to approach the man. 'You know why you're here right?'

An irritated grunt escaped the man. 'Yes, I do.' The stare from the blind gaze felt foreign – especially since he shouldn't be able to see her.

'What's going on?' Laria wondered, following the elder's example by taking a seat on the couch on the opposite side to him. Her body sank in the cushions as she got comfortable, while Liza went to get tea from the kitchen.

'Christopher told me that you lack the knowledge of why you mistrust the fallen.' Henry explained and Laria spared a glance towards her brother with surprise. Chris gave her an encouraging nod, letting Laria look back at the old man with a hint of wariness. 'I'm here to tell you why you fear him as you do.' Him meaning Haroni.

'It's alright,' Chris encouraged and left the room to join Liza.

Finally Henry sighed in exhaustion. 'You know how the skin walker kind began, correct? The tribe made a deal with the rectocs to save them from plagues and they accepted in return for four human sacrifices.'

'Yes,' Laria replied automatically, surprised over her own tone of voice.

'Their names were Abeytu, Ooljee, Yiska and Ahiga – over nine hundred years ago, they became the first skin walkers. Given the power to mindlessly kill like the rectocs and that's exactly what the rectocs succeeded in. But nature tried to restore the balance so in return, they sent the angels.'

Laria didn't respond as she tried imagining such a time when the angels and rectocs would fight. How much blood was spilled in order to fix what was wrong?

'The skin walkers and the angels fought for decades, trying to outmanoeuvre the other but it changed when Abeytu was severely wounded and encountered an angel. Much to his own surprise, the angel did not go through with killing him... instead she helped him and made sure he was alright. This surprised him greatly, despite being his enemy – he saw her as a kind-hearted woman.'

Laria kept quiet, her eyes on the blind man as she filled with interest. Her great ancestor had a heart like a good leader.

'Life remained the same after that. The skin walkers and angels killed each other but one day Abeytu found himself against the angel once again. Since he was in debt to her, he was willing to help her. He was curious to why she saw goodness in him. The angel told him that she saw in him something human that was only manipulated by the rectocs themselves.'

In the back of Laria's mind, Laria wondered about the woman that risked herself just to save Abeytu. If they had met in different circumstances then they would've never endured struggle.

'Soon enough, they fell in love.'

Laria found herself choking on her own spit.

'Their love was forbidden, but they didn't back down from the obstacles. No one could stop them from being them, however all good things came to an end when the angel's brother found out.'

Finally, Laria realised who they were talking about. 'Are you telling me that Tracy was the one that fell in love with Abeytu?' Tracy of all people managed to fall in love. It was one of those things that didn't sit well with Laria. In her head, Tracy could never fall for someone, let alone a shape shifter.

'Yes, Tracy Ladas was once a kind woman but as Haroni found out, their secret was exposed immediately. Haroni was forced to execute Abeytu. He refused at first, angry that he was ordered to, yet he was tricked into executing the man. They were both punished to live in this world for the rest of their days. Tracy was betrayed by her brother for not putting up with a fight to protect the man she loved and Haroni was betrayed by his sister for falling in love.'

'What about the other shifters?'

'The angels disappeared shortly afterwards – they fled from Utah and separated into other tribes. In the end, the skin walkers took Abeytu as an example and began to regain their humanity before putting the rectocs down for good.'

'With the Corvena right?'

'A powerful weapon, that Corvena,' Henry explained gruffly, scratching his head. 'Its origins are unknown but it has the power to seal off the four rectocs. They are trapped within the stones; they can never be released unless the four stones unite with four deaths, four lives and a Uniter.'

This was the first time Laria heard it. 'A Uniter?'

'A gifted individual who gives enough impact towards the true descendants for them to come together. The last one that was seen was over a hundred years ago, but when the rectocs were sealed; Lucien Alfero was the one who used the previous Uniter's memory to save everyone.'

Laria looked at her hands, thinking about her father. He was a hero after all. Was that meant to be her legacy? To use the Uniter's memory to stop their future enemies?

She decided to talk to Tahani about it later. 'Thank you for telling me this Henry... I feel closer to my heritage now.' And she did. Now she understood why she feared Haroni – it had been her instincts that feared Haroni would kill her as he did to Abeytu.

'Letting you in on the story should've given you a new purpose to why there's so many enemies. It was fear that brought them into this world, and maybe it would be the bravery that can settle their monstrous bloodlust-'

The door suddenly swung open and Laria jumped as Zanobi entered with Haroni. Both men had their eyes narrowed; Zanobi's gaze looked like it was filled with a hidden anger.

'Laria,' Haroni said seriously and Laria met his gaze without hesitation. 'The Beast has struck again, and we know who it is.'

'Who?' Her gaze went to Zanobi, who didn't look any happier.

***

'What are we doing here?' Jason asked Seth, whose eyes remained on the house. Not once had Seth bothered to look at the sacred stone in his pocket.

'Maya lives here,' Seth replied gravely. 'And ever since Tahani has been at our school – she's been trying to figure out Maya.' As they reached the porch, Seth knocked on the door swiftly and waited for someone to answer the door.

Maya was the one to answer. Something Jason noticed was that Maya didn't keep the door wide open. 'Jason, Seth, what are you guys doing here?'

'Have you seen Tahani recently?' Seth asked, looking straight at her stunned expression.

'N-no...' She had a tough expression, but Jason was sceptical. He could tell that Maya was usually a good liar, but it was pointless when the one she lied to was a mind reader. Seth's dark eyes hardened and he pushed the door open with ease, much to Maya's displeasure.

'Hey!' Maya snapped, trying to fight back as Seth entered the house. Jason followed and paused when he saw Tahani glowering at an elderly lady against the wall. Slowly the dux turned back and shot a glare towards Maya. 'Seth don't-! She's been in here demanding answers from my grandmother and she won't leave until she's gotten stupid answers about some Rosa that we don't know anything about.'

'Ya had one job Maya and that was to keep others out of this,' Tahani growled before she turned to Seth. 'What's up Seth? Ya wanna take Maya away, go ahead – I just want to talk to Adelle.'

'I'm here to see you actually Ungue Dux,' Seth announced

and it stopped Tahani as she faced Seth once again.

'Fine,' the dux hissed, dropping the lady. 'What do ya wanna know? I can pretty much let ya know of what foods I eat. Or is it perhaps the shampoo I use?'

'Seth.' Maya looked on with a frown of confusion on her face. Even though she was confused with the conflict, Jason could see the hate in her eyes for the other woman. Adelle was still by the wall, her blue eyes hard. 'What are you talking about?'

'Exactly as the kid said it,' Tahani added.

'Don't act so innocent – it pisses me off.' Seth stepped in angrily and ignored Maya. 'You murdered my parents; you're the reason why Leon Forte is dead and you killed countless people recently. You're the Beast.'

Tahani's smirk was gone and replaced with a glare. 'I told ya,' she said, 'I have no idea what ya talking 'bout. I was at the pits til ten then...' Her features were filled with confusion. 'What the hell? Why can't I remember anything?'

No sooner than she said the words out loud, there was another loud knock on the door. Everyone turned to the door with surprise at the insistent knocking.

Tahani Rosa! It was Sherriff Nadia Cyler that was knocking and Maya automatically dropped the phone that she used to dial the police. Tahani noticed the phone on the ground and cursed. *I know you're in there! We have a warrant!*

'Are you saying that you don't remember?' Jason suddenly turned to Tahani who glowered at Jason in return. 'But we saw you last night,' he argued back. 'You knocked us out as soon as we figured out that you're the mole!'

'I hate humans and I want nothing to do with them but, I'm not the damn traitor to this town,' Tahani snapped. When she heard another knock from the door, she let out another curse. 'I need to get outta here-!' The door slammed open as

Nadia kicked against it in with ease.

Seth wrapped his arms around Maya as a team of police surrounded Tahani and pointed their guns at the dux. Adelle let out a startled yelp, her eyes wide. Jason stood by the elder's side with a serious gaze. He wasn't going to leave an old lady to face the woman that could've killed Laria.

Being surrounded by the people, Tahani surprisingly didn't fight back. Much to Jason's surprise, she lifted her hands in surrender. Her eyes narrowed when Nadia stepped forward.

'Tahani Rosa,' Nadia repeated as she stood in front of the dux. She revealed the cuffs and with a click she confined Tahani's wrists. 'You are under arrest for murder – you have the right to remain silent. Anything you say can and will be used against you in a court of law. You have the right to speak to an attorney, and to have an attorney present during any questioning. If you cannot afford a lawyer, one will be provided for you at government expense.'

Slowly the sheriff took Tahani out of the house with the police following along silently. Seth released Maya as soon as most of the police left the house.

One of the officers stopped to glance at the group. 'Do you guys mind answering some questions?'

Adelle, Maya and Seth agreed to answer the questions instantly but Jason looked outside to see that Tahani was forced in the backseat of the car. As she spared a final look towards Jason, he turned to the officer.

'No,' Jason muttered, 'I don't mind.'

CHAPTER 20

'You've got to let me in,' Laria demanded fiercely, slamming her hands on the desk in front of the receptionist. 'Tahani's my friend —she wouldn't kill for no reason.'

'Look, even if I wanted to let you have a chat, I can't. Miss Rosa is being questioned and without Sheriff Cyler's permission, no one is allowed to speak with her.'

As soon as Zanobi told Laria that Tahani was accused of being the Beast, the small group drove all the way back from Cheyenne to Golden Cliff.

'Well, I don't believe she's the murderer,' Laria stated in determination. 'Just give me five minutes to prove that she didn't kill anyone. I trust her.' She paused to herself when she let the words slip out of her mouth.

'You don't need proof. Tahani Rosa has always been a killer that uses her bloodlust as a thrill.' Nadia's form materialised from her office as she calmly approached Laria. It seemed that the dux remembered Laria's face as well. 'The recent victims, Ross and Mindy Laurence, had been stabbed by a long weapon made of ice. And we have witnesses saying that it was her attacking them before she knocked them out.'

'Alright then, Sheriff,' Laria challenged with a scowl. 'If she was to really kill someone then why would she knock the witnesses out and not kill them too?'

Yet it looked like Laria's determination didn't faze Nadia. 'These witnesses are Jason Amarel and Seth Laurence.'

'Surely there's an explanation.' Laria didn't want to believe that Seth and Jason were attacked by Tahani. 'Maybe it was Edward. He would've done something to frame Tahani!'

'Edward has not been around since he attacked Jason and murdered his mother.'

Laria's eyes went wide. 'Jason lost his mother?' *And why would Edward target Jason in particular?* she thought to herself.

All of a sudden the lady at the reception desk looked nervous. 'Sheriff, is it wise to tell her details about the witnesses?'

'It's alright Carla.' Nadia didn't spare a glance at the other woman. 'Laria knows them both and probably believes me now that her two companions are key witnesses.'

While it was true that Seth was a true descendant, Laria had still yet to figure out Jason's situation. Why wouldn't he have told her? After it felt like forever of thinking about it, Laria looked up keeping her determination.

Her gaze hardened as she stepped towards the cold sheriff. This woman was nothing compared to Tracy. 'I'm not leaving here until I see Tahani. You can lock me up or kick me out but I'm seeing her,' and she telepathically added, *My Magister.*

Nadia remained harshly glaring at Laria, until she eventually backed down. The woman pulled the keys out of her pockets and beckoned Laria to follow.

Laria tried to not show her excitement as she followed Nadia to the small cell. When they got there she almost widened her eyes in shock at the scene before them. Tahani was sitting on her cell's bed, leaning against the wall.

'The Ungue Dux tried to attack one of my men when he questioned her, so we won't let anyone within the cell,' Nadia explained curtly, gaining Tahani's attention.

'Laria?'

Laria felt gratitude blossom as she reached the cell.

'Tahani, I've been worried.'

'Don't try any funny business, Alfero,' Nadia warned with a growl. 'You have three minutes. You better start talking.' As she turned away and left the two on their own, Tahani snickered.

'What a bitch.' Tahani voiced Laria's thoughts before she'd stepped close to the bars. 'Even though I'm probably dead in a week or so, then have my guts experimented on by Jyle the mad scientist, I still think she's not gonna get that stick out of her ass.'

'Tahani, I can get you out,' Laria promised as she gripped the bars. 'I know you're innocent – you don't kill without reason.' When she didn't hear a reassuring response, Laria looked up and frowned at her friend. 'Tahani?'

'Look – I'm not as innocent as yer think, while I'm glad for the support, I don't actually think I'm gonna be proven innocent with this case. Nadia now has every reason to finish me off – the only reason why they haven't, is because they think I know something 'bout the enemy's next attack.'

'But did you kill them?' Laria asked desperately, clutching on the bars.

'What? No! Of course not!' Tahani's face morphed into one of confusion. 'But then again... I can't remember.' In frustration Tahani grabbed her messy hair and growled. 'Argh! This is confusing; I've never experienced this before.'

'Then it wasn't you,' Laria defended proudly as the hope restored in her eyes. 'It was probably your bloodlust. I know that you would never kill-'

'Laria,' Tahani interrupted sternly, 'Whenever I let Sangri out I remember every detail; from their blood to my thrill.' She sighed again and her eyes turned serious. 'Look... I know ya wanna prove that I'm good but let's be honest. I've killed my share of humans in the past... I couldn't protect my own sister from the damn monster that murdered her...'

'But Tahani,' Laria replied softly and she ignored the stinging sensation in her eyes. 'I can't lose you either... I've lost my mother, my best friend...'

'Ya gonna have to,' Tahani admitted as her eyes hardened. 'At least do me a favour – just for me, please.' When Laria looked up to see her friend she felt the mental pain stab her heart. 'Ya gotta protect Maya Rosa and Azu.'

'Azu? And I thought you hated Maya.'

Tahani chuckled dryly. 'There's a bunch of things that yer don't know 'bout me. Like how my sister had a child with a human.... and turned out to be yer friend Maya Rosa.'

'Wait.' Laria's eyes went wide as she realised it. 'Maya's your niece?' The Tahani let out a weak chuckle as Laria figured it out.

'Twenty years ago, my sister Kaeylin and I had a falling out because she fell in love with a human. Me being me, I got angry and we didn't speak to each other – she died ten years later and I pushed my limits to become a dux in order to avenge her death.'

Laria was still shocked that her friend was closely related to another. 'So how did you find out about Maya?'

'Adelle Cadmen – Maya's grandmother had a son, he was Maya's father. I knew that Azu would be within the building and I asked for it, but I got bloody arrested before I could get it.' Her eyes turned serious once she met a stare with Laria again.

'Tahani...' Laria's words died in her throat. She didn't know how to process the new information in front of her. If Maya was truly Tahani's niece, then it meant that it was Tahani's sister who died in the fire.

'So I beg of ya Laria,' Tahani demanded hoarsely. 'Not as my pupil but as a friend, yer have to find Azu and protect

Maya – no matter what.'

The Alfero found herself lacking a response. 'Tahani... I'm not sure if I can without you... I still don't have any control over my powers or my bloodlust...'

'Ya've got it Little Ria,' Tahani promised with a smile. It wasn't her usual smirk but a true smile that managed to bring up Laria's own. 'I promise that I'll try my best in getting myself out of this situation.'

Laria's gaze turned serious. 'I won't swear to you that I will protect Maya, because I would've done that regardless – but I promise that I will find Azu and keep it safe for you.'

'Time's up,' Nadia announced, stepping in the room to grab Laria's arm. 'Let's go.'

Laria didn't protest when she saw Tahani nod encouragingly. *'And make sure ya find the real traitor... for both our sakes.'*

'I will,' Laria swore under her breath, sparing one final look at Tahani before she was taken out of the room.

***

Sparing a wave towards Heather, Brodie closed his locker and leaned his head against it with a grunt of irritation. Maybe he should've stayed home. But on the bright side, there was no nagging Jason and Seth tailing him.

Brodie'd had enough of them for one day – it was bad enough that he would eventually have to tell Jason the truth. He clenched his jaw and let out a long sigh as he stared at the metal door.

'Brodie!'

Ignoring the voice, he let his lids close and tried to sense if Jason was around. But then again, it was in the middle of the day and Brodie had been avoiding most of his friends.

'Hello?'

As soon as he felt a pair of warm arms wrap around him, Brodie froze from the contact. He relied on the perfumed scent to tell who it was. Slowly Brodie turned to offer a smile of gratitude that she was around. 'Jenna.'

Jenna's eyebrows drew together as her eyes narrowed. 'Don't you dare *Jenna*' me!' She snapped and placed her hands on her hips in concern. 'I've been worried sick about you for days and I've been trying to call you but you never answered!'

'I'm sorry for worrying you Jenna.' Brodie turned as she let go. 'Sorry I haven't been around. I've been going through my father's things but I think I need a break; I'm sick of being in my house.'

'I have an idea to get rid of your inner stress,' she announced with a grin. 'We can go to Taro's party tonight – everyone should be there.' Brodie blinked in sudden realisation that it was *that* day once again. Personally, Brodie didn't like Taro since the guy was a jerk to his friends, but Brodie was willing to go for her.

'Sure – I guess it wouldn't be the worst thing in the world to be stuck with a girl crushing on the most moronic guy on earth,' he replied with a smile and Jenna lightly swatted his chest.

'Thanks Brodie.' Jenna offered her widest smile before she frowned. 'I mean, I haven't seen Maya since I heard about the Tahani drama, and Laria was meant to be here by now. You're the only one left!'

'I'm glad that I could of service to you milady,' Brodie faked an accent and smiled when he heard Jenna's laugh once again. It reminded Brodie that he was still sane, despite everything he went through.

Brodie's smile dropped when he lifted his gaze and recognised the figure approaching them. Jenna's confusion filled her eyes and she turned to see the Mandati Dux stroll towards them.

'Good day Brodie, it's been a while since I've seen you here,' Takon reminded as Brodie stared on grudgingly. 'May I speak to you in private about something important?'

Brodie was about to refuse, but Jenna pulled herself away and flashed a grin. 'You can talk,' she said and held her bag. 'I need to get to History to get some notes for Laria to catch up on! I'm pretty sure she was meant to be back today...' Jenna turned away to briskly walk back to her class, leaving the two shifters alone.

Brodie didn't appreciate it one bit. He glared at Takon. 'Mandati Dux, what's wrong now?'

'Not in here,' Takon decided and led Brodie to his office. Once they were behind concealed doors, Takon brushed his hair back and groaned. 'I'm sure you've heard by now that Tahani is the traitor and I would like to personally apologise-'

'Don't apologise for my father until you know the truth,' Brodie snapped with a dark glare. Takon was suddenly stunned into silence as he continued. 'The day my father died, the killer knew my own movements and had a counter for it – heck he even came to my father's wake.'

'Your father's murderer came to your house?'

So much for keeping that a secret, yet Brodie didn't care. 'My dad would've known about the Ungue Dux and called Laria the second he figured it out, who was with Tahani every day. The fact that he didn't means that the traitor planned for this to happen.'

Before Brodie could continue his rant, Takon already spoke up to defend his case. Of course, Takon wouldn't be the Mandati Dux if he didn't have a counter. 'Jason Amarel and Seth Laurence both saw her – and the victims had ice on them-'

'Who knows what they saw?' Brodie dismissed the recent pair. 'Did the previous victims have ice on them? I sincerely doubt it.'

'Your father knew who the Beast was,' Takon said with a serious gaze. 'If you believe that it's not Tahani, then you're going to have to get proof. But if you can't find anything we are going to punish her.'

'I understand. We have a deal.' Brodie strolled out of the office and brushed his hair back in frustration. Now he had to discover the final clue to finding out who the killer was but the only way he could figure it out was if he went in *there*.

CHAPTER 21

Sitting on an old bench, Jason held his plastic cup and observed the scene with a critical gaze. Everyone was cheering, drinking or hooking up beside the large fire in the centre of the park.

Jason took a drink, finding a strange sense of relief in the taste of beer before he went back to watching the fire. They didn't go to school that day, answering any of the questions that the officer asked as detailed as they could. Jason told his story, but something seemed off

Why would she head to Maya's house of all places? And why was she so confused when she tried to remember the attack the night before? Then there was the issue with Brodie's twin that they had yet to find. At least they had Rel now – they could probably try finding the twin sooner if Seth brought the rock with him.

'You look extremely depressed.' The voice made Jason glad that he came to the party. He lifted his head to see that Heather had come. 'And it looks like the dark colours are your theme this time.'

Jason looked down at his clothes. His black button up shirt was uneven, and Jason would've sworn that the black jeans weren't even his.

He sheepishly smiled and scratched the back of his head. 'Honestly I had no idea what to wear to a bonfire in honour of the deceased.' As Heather offered a smile, Jason thought back to Seth's warning about trusting others.

'Hey,' she whispered and took a seat beside Jason. 'Is something wrong Jason?'

'Why do you talk to me?'

The question seemed to surprise Heather. 'I don't know what you're talking about.' She frowned at him. 'Do I need a reason to talk to you?'

'No. No one needs a reason to speak with little old me,' Jason responded with a light shrug. The look on Heather's face indicated that she didn't understand. 'I just want to know why you would talk to me; a mere human while you probably have other witch friends.'

Heather seemed surprisingly quiet and she turned away from Jason. 'You know about that?' Her voice appeared frail – like she was about to lose the most important thing to her.

'Yeah – being friends with Seth has its perks such as true information, first hand,' Jason admitted, sparing a glance towards his friend in the distance before he turned to Heather. 'Look, Heather, I honestly don't care that you're a witch – I just want to know why you care about me.'

'At first I didn't – you were nothing but a stranger to me. But then I got a mission from the Mandati Dux himself,' Heather replied softly, and Jason frowned. 'I have the ability to cloak another with a human presence – in other words... yours.'

Jason found himself slowly processing the information. 'So it's true then?' he asked, tightening the hold he had on the cup. 'My father really was a shifter?'

'I don't know him, if that's what you're thinking,' Heather said. 'I'm sorry – I'm a horrible person. I pretended to be comforting after your mother's death... but then, as I spent time with you, I found myself actually liking you more than a friend.'

Jason felt like he should be angry – heck, no one had ever pretended to be his friend like that but for some reason, he couldn't. He knew that Heather done what she had to do.

Instead, Jason smiled and leaned forward, gently pecking the girl's cheeks. He loosened his hold on the cup, dismissing the hidden anger like it was nothing. Heather looked surprised.

'I don't care,' Jason admitted with a smile. 'As far as I'm concerned – I'm a human and you're an amazing witch that wants to protect me.' He slowly shrugged at his thoughts and continued. 'It's sort of pride wounding, but Heather, I've come to care about you as well.'

Heather looked at him; a smile formed on her lips and she leaned closer to Jason. 'I know you will find out everything, Jason – it's only a matter of time.' When Jason wrapped an arm around her, his blue eyes went back to the flames and didn't fight the smile on his face.

***

'Brodie, you have to dance with me!' Jenna begged, forcing Brodie's arms to move while he laughed at her attempts. Slowly she was beginning to show her frustration. 'You promised that you would dance with me and at least have fun.'

'Do I really have to? It kinda makes me move and I really don't feel like-' Brodie feigned a whine and let out a soft grunt as Jenna hit his chest. She paused for a moment, before she looked down at his abdomen.

She lifted the bottom of his shirt and suddenly gasped. 'Wow!' Jenna exclaimed as Brodie pulled the shirt back down in embarrassment. 'You could grate cheese on that thing! I never knew that you had a six-pack.'

'Training,' Brodie replied simply as the heat left his cheeks. As a shifter, Brodie was meant to be training constantly since he never knew when the enemies would come. Even in his recent state, Brodie spent some time trying to hone his skills. 'Ever since I was five my dad and I use to do Muay Thai pretty much every day.' His mood dropped and he felt a reassuring squeeze on his own hands.

'You're a wonderful person Brodie,' Jenna admitted. Brodie kept still as Jenna once again hit his chest to get his attention. 'I bet you that your father would be extremely proud of you for getting through this.'

If only she knew, Brodie thought as his mind went back to Laria.

Jenna flashed him a cheerful grin and grabbed his hands once again. Brodie almost rolled his eyes with laughter. 'As your fake girlfriend – it is your job to treat me like a princess! Now dance with me like you mean it.'

'Nah,' Brodie said, lifting her up by the waist and spun her in the air. Naturally Jenna shrieked out and tightened her hold. 'If I ever had a girlfriend – or someone special, I would treat her better than I would a princess.'

'Jeez,' Jenna muttered once she relaxed, keeping close. 'Here I thought that you would be doing this to Laria before you were doing this to me.'

Brodie raised an eyebrow in confusion. 'Come again?'

Realising what she said, Jenna tried to dismiss it with a shake of her head. 'It's not important – it's just before her mum died, you two were so close and now you two are barely on speaking terms.' She suddenly realised what she said. 'What I mean is that-'

Brodie suddenly stiffened when he felt Taro's hand on his shoulder and he jerked back with Jenna in his arms. Jenna looked on in confusion when Taro glared at Brodie from his position.

'Mind if I cut in?' Taro wondered, sparing a glance at Jenna who suddenly looked eager. Seeing this reaction made Brodie step back. 'Go ahead Jenna.' Jenna almost gave Brodie a look, but she immediately went with Taro and began dancing with him. Brodie went to the edge of the party and listened in on the conversation that they had.

It seemed at the moment they were making small talk. In the corner of his eye, he saw a familiar face staring back at the fire with unease and Brodie made his way to her. Once she realised he was approaching her, Laria suddenly turned to him with an awkward expression.

'Hey,' she began bluntly.

'I'm sorry,' Brodie muttered as he shoved his hands in his pockets. 'I shouldn't have said those things.'

After a moment, Laria sighed, shaking her head and as she went back to staring at the flames. 'No problem, it's behind us now.'

Brodie considered an idea – a distraction. 'I need to tell you something about my dad.' Finally, he reminded himself that he needed to go through with this. Laria was his friend after all. 'I have a brother.'

'A brother?' Laria widened her eyes. 'How did I not know about him?'

'Because I just found out that he was my twin,' Brodie answered the question and looked in the direction of Jason. 'And it's Jason Amarel.'

'Jason?' Laria suddenly looked in Jason's direction with shock.

'It's true,' Brodie spoke harshly as he thought of it. 'I gave Rel to Seth but it was reacting the way it would've when it had more than one Forte in its presence.

'But didn't he have his mother? Jason didn't know his father – that would make sense, but Jason had a mother. She died recently, and Leon did say that she's been dead since...'

Laria's eyes came to an understanding; an understanding that Brodie didn't like to think. 'Brodie, you don't think...?'

Brodie didn't know if he could reply to it. He knew exactly what she was thinking. 'Laria...' A shout interrupted the pair and they turned to see someone on Jenna.

'You bitch!' Sara snapped, trying to claw Jenna's face. 'First you go slutting yourself to Brodie and now to my boyfriend?!' Jenna fought back in protest, her eyes filled with pain as a red mark formed on her cheek.

The rest of the party watched the two girls fight. Brodie and Laria raced their way over, shoving past the crowd of people to reach the fighting pair.

However Laria beat him to the punch by literally shouting out his inner thoughts. 'What the hell is wrong with all of you?' She grabbed Sara and pulled her into an arm lock.

A random student called out. 'You should've let them fight! It's not every day we see babes have a catfight!'

Brodie glared at the one that spoke, and he didn't even hesitate in hitting him. It was Brodie's intention to give him a broken nose, but he held back on his blow. As soon as the drunk guy dropped to the ground and groaned in pain, Brodie's eyes hardened.

'Now, all of you get back to the party,' he commanded and turned back to Jenna immediately. He lifted his hand to help her up and she gladly accepted. Her back was covered in dirt and her hair was a bit messy, but she looked alright. 'Sorry that the bitch got to you.'

Obviously Sara heard him. 'Screw you Brodie. Oh wait... I wouldn't want to wish that on any girl that exists. Not even whore bag over there.' Laria almost looked ready to snap but instead she let Sara go with a scowl and she snorted at the pair. 'Maybe you two should ask what she did before you go jumping into conclusions.' It wasn't long until Sara stormed off and Taro, who had been completely silent, suddenly snapped out of his daze and went after her with a yell.

Brodie narrowed his eyes at Jenna. 'What is she talking about?' He knew that Jenna liked Taro, but he wasn't sure what she would've done to get him. 'What did you do?'

Jenna nursed her face and Brodie would've sworn that it was the first time that she had true anger directed at him. 'She doesn't get it! We were talking then he started acting all weird. I tried pulling away from Taro, then he totally kissed me like he was like in a trance!'

Brodie frowned. 'Why would he do that?'

It looked like he gave the wrong response, judging from the anger increasing. 'Are you saying that I'm not good enough?' *How did she jump to that conclusion?* 'I like Taro, and he deserves better than someone like Sara,' Jenna snapped and shoved him out of the way. She spared a glance towards Laria. 'Careful Ria, he's back to being an asshole.' Without another word, she stormed off in another direction and left Brodie alone with Laria.

'What just happened?' Brodie asked, before he turned and saw Laria's petrified expression. He looked back at the flames and it quickly dawned on him. 'Come on Laria,' Brodie urged to get her out of the range of her fear.

'Thank you.' Her voice was weak in his head, and Brodie only pressed on without another word.

As soon as they were a short distance away, Laria let out a shaky sigh and she dropped to her knees. Brodie crouched down beside her, his eyes hard and filled with worry. 'Are you feeling better?'

She numbly nodded and Brodie relaxed. It was a good thing that he had his friendship fixed, but now he had to see why Jenna was so mad. Before either of them could talk out loud, they paused when they both heard a phone vibrate. Laria frowned as she checked her phone and answered the call.

'Hello, who is this?'

'I have a confession to make Laria.' From what Brodie could hear, it was someone that he didn't know. Laria's eyes suddenly turned serious as she regained the strength to stand up. *'I'm very bored.'*

'Edward,' Laria's spat. Brodie followed Laria's actions with a scowl and he noticed her eyes glow amber. It was a dangerous thing to look at; but he could've sworn that he'd seen them before. 'You have a lot of nerve calling me.'

'And you have a lot of nerve, Laria,' Edward retorted harmlessly. *'You and Brodie Forte both have a lot of nerve trying to threaten me while leaving your human friends scattered all over the place.'* It suddenly dawned on Brodie that Edward was actually near them.

'Jenna,' Brodie gasped, sparing a glance to Laria who nodded in agreement.

Without another word, he left Laria on her own and charged back through the crowd, trying to locate Jenna by following her scent. It didn't help that there were people in the way. He let out a yell of frustration.

CHAPTER 22

Brodie was glad once he was free from the crowd. His relief flushed through him and he hurried towards Jenna to grab her.

She was startled, letting out a yelp before she turned to recognise him, then jerking herself away from him.

'What do you want?' she asked.

'Look, I would explain it if I could,' Brodie stated as he suddenly grabbed her. 'I'm sorry for what I said.' He really was clueless about this stuff. He recognised the sound of a car pulling up in the park; Brodie thanked his luck. 'You need to go.'

Even though Jenna was safe, it didn't mean that Maya wasn't. Jenna frowned. 'What are you talking about Brodie?' But he didn't give her time to explain. The car pulled up, revealing Jenna's father and Brodie flashed the man a smile.

'Hey, Clark.' Brodie faked a smile and petted Jenna's back. Jenna scowled at him before she took her seat in the car. 'It was pretty dark out so I decided to escort Jenna out myself.'

'You're a good lad, Brodie,' Clark replied as he spared the boy a grin. 'You're always watching out for my baby girl.'

Her anger at Brodie now disappeared, due to her newfound embarrassment from her father. 'Dad! You have more than just me now you know!' Her cheeks had flushed bright red.

'Alright, thank you again, Brodie, for taking care of her.' Brodie closed the door for Jenna as she stared at the window with confusion. Maybe she was trying to figure out why Brodie had lied – but Brodie knew that it wasn't the time. As long as she was safe, Brodie knew that he could work much harder.

As the car drove off, Brodie turned away and tried searching for Maya. He raced through the party; they still seemed to be a bit oblivious to the fact that a madman was around.

'Brodie? What's going on?'

At the sound of his name, Brodie turned to see that Maya was staring back at him as if she was waiting for some sort of explanation. Yet Brodie once again felt relief flood back into his chest as he realised Maya was safe as well.

If Jenna was alright, along with Maya... then who could've it been?

'Brodie? Don't space out on me.' Maya clicked her fingers in front of him. He flinched at her actions and shook his head, 'Laria said that I should be with Seth or something. Do you know what she meant?'

Suddenly Brodie realised what was wrong. 'Wait, Seth isn't with you?'

'No – he said he went to get a drink and he hasn't been back. Then Laria came over and asked me where Seth was.' She looked around them to see any signs of him before gazing back at Brodie. 'Should I be worried that he still isn't back?'

'No.' Brodie offered a smile and he sighed when he saw Laria looking for them. She still had the phone in her ear, so it meant that she was listening to Edward and trying to distract him. 'Just stay with Laria right now – I've got to run.' As Laria came closer, Brodie spared her a glance. *I'm going to find Seth – just stay by Maya's side.'*

Brodie felt grateful when he saw a returning nod. He darted into the trees away from the humans. When even he couldn't see, he stripped off his clothes and left them in a pile.

The crack beneath his bones made Brodie growl in agony, but he allowed it to continue. It felt so painful for such a fast transformation, but when fur sprouted all through his body and he expanded into his cheetah form, Brodie knew that it was over. Now, as a large feline, Brodie was able to see better in the night and focused his attention on the scents around him.

Brodie quickly raced within the trees, trying to conceal his form in case a drunk human stumbled upon him. At least they would've assumed that it was the beer in their system and not an actual cheetah, but Brodie still remained cautious.

'Seth? Where are you?' His throat rumbled unnaturally as he raced throughout the trees. Brodie's desperation grew; there was still no sign of Seth.

However, he got something else. A scent filled Brodie's nostrils. The trail smelled like smoke. He followed the trail silently, but when he saw a tall figure with crimson eyes, Brodie knew for sure it was Edward.

'Edward,' Brodie growled and made himself visible.

Edward wasn't surprised. *'Do you really think revealing yourself in front of school girls is a good idea Brodie?'* Before Brodie could question, Edward kicked a second figure over – one that Brodie didn't notice before.

'Sara.' Brodie saw the sudden fear in the girl's eyes.

'What's that?!' she cried, still trying to identify Brodie in the dark.

'Well I hate to break it to you, but this was merely a distraction.' With an instant swipe, Edward hit the back of Sara's head and knocked her out. Brodie didn't hesitate. He leapt at the shifter, but a sharp pain went through his shoulder. The sound of a gunshot came first, then Brodie felt the rippling pain. His body dropped to the ground, automatically

shifting back into his human form with agony.

Edward lowered the pistol with a smile. 'Now I would kill you, but I have other things to do.' Brodie tried getting back to his feet but Edward was already in front of him, kicking out his foot to meet his face

'Laria... will get you for this...' Brodie hissed, glaring at Edward. He didn't want Edward to get away with all that he had done. With the taste of blood in his mouth, Brodie groaned threateningly as the pain extended from his shoulder to his arm. 'And I will kill the bastard that ended my father.'

With a scoff, Edward turned away from Brodie to dismiss him. 'By then – you would be far too deep Brodie. So I really do wish you luck on managing to get that far.' As he calmly strolled away from the scene with a chuckle, Brodie cursed his luck.

Before Brodie gave into his vengeful thoughts, he froze. 'Sara.' He ignored the pain in his shoulder and crawled to her, touching her head. His fingers grazed against warm liquid and Brodie knew that she was in trouble.

The pain was excruciating but Brodie lifted himself to his feet and picked Sara up as well. Her body appeared small and frail in his arms. However, friend or not, Brodie wouldn't let her die. He needed to call Tara; she would help him.

***

'Edward? Don't hang up!' Laria ordered angrily, tightening her hold on the device. Edward had encountered Brodie, and Laria could hear everything. The gunshot was loud enough for everyone to hear it, sending the drunk students into a panic. Laria panicked as Edward hung up the phone, she had to hope that Brodie was okay.

They had bigger problems to focus on.

All Laria could see was panic. The people ran in all

directions attempting to head to their parked cars for an escape. Laria managed to keep Maya still, even though she was beginning to stress and Laria lost sight of any familiar faces.

She wasn't sure how her other friends were, but she needed to get Maya out of Edward's range as soon as possible. She wasn't safe. Apparently Edward had more plans for his so-called game for tonight and he wasn't playing fair.

'Maya, let's go!' Laria finally got her to follow.

Cars began starting up to leave the place but most of the drivers were drunk and afraid. *Wait a second*, Laria thought and then she saw him. It was beyond her how fast he managed to appear before the cars. Staring at Edward was like a dream, he seemed calm in his position. *People were drunk – they were going to be driving with beer and there's going to be a lot of crashing.*

In return, she saw the smirk from Edward as he lifted his hand, creating the fire in his fingertips.

Everything came to a screeching stop the second she realised what Edward's intentions were. Laria attempted to grab Maya's arm and flee from the cars. Her eyes widened as she turned back to face Laria. Instead of thinking calmly, Maya tried to break out of the hold. 'Laria-!'

Laria refused to let go. 'Wait-!' The nearest car erupted into flames, making the other drivers race out of the car park in horror.

But it was already too late. It exploded.

It was deafening and powerful, throwing them both off their feet. Laria tried to focus her hearing, but all she could hear is a high pitch squeal. Her ears felt blocked and no other sounds registered in her head. It felt like she was watching the flames explode in a mute world. Laria tried calling out for Maya, but it was like her voice wouldn't work.

She lifted her eyes to see Maya, who wasn't moving. Laria's heart felt like it stopped beating, staring down at her dearest friend's limp body. No one else was meant to die, but Maya's body remained in front of her. Laria lost it. Even though she couldn't hear it, Laria could tell that she screamed out for Maya.

I will kill Edward... Laria snarled with promise, her eyes flashing amber. She wanted to cause him misery – Laria wanted to see Edward fear her before she ripped his heart out of his chest-

Something touched her.

Laria looked over and saw that Maya was still alive, staring at her with concern. Blood covered her forehead, but asides from the injury – she was okay. Despite the joy of Maya being alive, with sounds slowly coming to life around Laria, she was afraid for the people around her.

Then she finally heard them – the people screaming out in fear and panic. Cars were driving into the streets with loud screeches, and there were a few unmoving people on the ground.

'Now this is a lovely sight.' Edward's form came closer to them. Laria found her anger devouring her fear as she stood against the other shifter. 'Two nostalgic faces – one that refuses to give in to her desires and the other doesn't show for it.'

Maya shot a glare. 'Who the hell are you?'

Edward seemed to chuckle at Maya's fierce words. Even injured and bleeding, Maya never seemed to back down. 'Of course you wouldn't know me, Maya Rosa.' As he stepped closer, Laria automatically moved in front of her friend with a glare.

'Leave Maya out of this,' Laria snapped fiercely as her eyes glowed warningly. 'It's between you and me – so let's finish this.'

'You are clueless.' Edward stepped towards Laria, her

confidence wavering. He lifted a hand and allowed his flames to come to life within his fingers. 'All your friends have been a part of it – Maya Rosa, Brodie Forte, Seth Laurence, Jason Amarel and even that human friend, Jenna...'

Laria's eyes widened at the small fire, staring at it as if it was death itself, even for one so tiny. How could Laria fear such a tiny fire? Her limbs refused to move, she remained staring at the flame with fear in her eyes. What could she do?

The fear captured her heart. Just as Laria felt her heartbeat begin to race, she heard the familiar chuckle from the back of her mind. It was Lux.

Let me... It growled in temptation, almost persuasive. She had the urge to make the shifter scream out in agony as she ripped him apart. *I will kill him, make him scream out in misery – let his fear grow my strength.*

Back off! Laria thought fiercely, fighting off the demon from inside. *I won't let you out to harm anyone any time soon.*

She was so caught up in controlling her bloodlust that Laria didn't see Edward approach her. His flame free hand smacked her across the face and knocked her to the ground. As Edward made his way to Maya, she tried to desperately move away.

Of course, whether she was a human or a shifter – Laria knew that a Rosa was fearless.

'You are just like your mother – unafraid even when facing death in the eye. It's a trait that we share as Rosas,' Edward taunted as he stepped closer to her. Laria tried forcing herself up again, but her strength sapped away the second that Edward shot a few flames in her direction.

'You coward!' she snapped, her voice quaking with fear.

'I'm just doing my job,' Edward replied simply and pulled Maya to her knees by grabbing her collar.

'What the hell are you?' she spat at the shifter.

'Don't you know Maya?' The shifter leaned in. 'I'm the shifter that murdered your mother to awaken your powerful bloodlust and send your father packing.' Laria remained on the ground, her eyes suddenly wide. Edward was the cause of it...

Then that meant... that Edward was the one that killed Kaeylin, Tahani's sister.

'Of course – I needed to find Azu,' Edward continued and finally lifted Maya to her feet. She stood up against her will, her legs trembling under the pressure of her own weight. 'But maybe you know it.' He smiled and filled his free hand with flames again. 'Tell me – have you seen a blue rock that glows whenever you're nearby?'

'Screw you,' Maya snapped and spat in his face without hesitation.

He slowly sneered. 'Just like a true Rosa.' The shifter angrily shoved the tomboy back onto the ground. Maya grunted in pain as her body landed and Laria felt the anger lick at her spine like the fire she feared. Her friend was in trouble and she couldn't do anything because she was afraid.

But someone came.

A dark figure tackled Edward into the ground. Her relief spread through her chest as Laria smiled with gratitude. Maya on the other hand looked startled, her eyes wide with confusion before her voice worked again.

'Seth!'

Seth didn't pay any attention to Maya, he didn't even acknowledge her existence. As he attacked the shifter, Laria could practically feel the anger emanating from him. He landed blows on Edward and the sounds that he made from his attacks were brutal.

Hearing a voice, Laria turned to see that Jason was rushing towards them. There was a single car; a red sedan still waiting for them in the parking lot.

'No,' Laria protested as Jason tried to wrap his arms around her frame. He stopped the second he heard her protest. 'Help Maya first – I'm fine.' It was a lie.

Finally Jason managed to understand. He went to help Maya, lifting her off her feet. As Jason went to put her in the car, Laria kept her eyes on Seth as he yelled in agony when Edward got the upper hand.

Seth smacked into the ground and Edward pulled out his gun, making Laria panic. When she heard laughter, Laria saw that their enemy was laughing down at Seth.

The shifter's face was covered in his own blood yet all he did was laugh. 'It looks like you have it after all – I have to admit I never thought you would reveal your bloodlust,' Edward jeered and shot Seth's leg. Seth let out an agonised cry and reached down for his leg to stop the bleeding. 'I have a funny feeling that it has to do with Maya.'

Seth's glare turned into one filled with rage as his eyes flashed bright yellow. 'Touch one hair on her hair and I'll rip you apart!'

'I won't have to.' Edward lifted his gun and pointed the gun in the direction of the car. Realising what Edward's intentions were, Laria forced herself to her feet. The only way she could do this was if she was fast enough.

She had to step into the dark boundaries that led to the monster. *Lux!*

'A Rosa that doesn't turn is useless after all.' Edward prepared to fire, however Laria interrupted him. She stood in between him and Seth, grabbing his coated arm to direct the gunshot into the sky.

The shot was loud, and Edward didn't react. 'I won't let you hurt her!' Laria swore as her eyes glowed warningly. 'You better leave before I let the bloodlust loose and kill you.'

'Now... was that so hard?' He pulled away from Laria who glared in his direction. 'I'll keep in touch.' He turned away and Laria gritted her teeth to follow after him, but his form shifted into a mountain lion fleeing into the shadows. As Laria took a step forward, she felt her strength give way and she dropped down to her knees feeling her body shudder.

'Laria... you... used your bloodlust... didn't you?'

She looked up to see Seth wincing as he forced himself to sit up. His anger was gone.

When Laria didn't respond, Seth looked at the night sky with a gaze in his eyes. He sighed and said, 'I guess we have something in common.'

***

'All this time.' Maya's voice seemed to come to some sort of understanding as she listened to Laria's story of the shifters. Everything that Seth had told Jason, and that he'd read from the books was being told to Maya. Laria didn't leave out any details. 'I felt like there was a part of me that knew the truth... but maybe I was too afraid to admit it.'

'We don't know why you were a late bloomer...' Laria returned honestly and Jason felt himself pause in consideration. 'In fact, we haven't seen any signs of a shifter in you. You haven't snapped and you don't have the weird thoughts.'

Jason leaned on the wall of his room, overhearing the conversation. After Edward left, Jason managed to get them in Seth's car to drive them home. It was incredibly risky since he still didn't have his license but right now he didn't care.

After they got back to Seth's house, Jason treated Seth's bullet wound and left the two girls to have an important talk. It was strange that Maya didn't know about the shifters, but Jason slowly dismissed it and left his room to go check on Seth again.

Seth had an ugly bruise forming on his face and his thigh was wrapped in a bandage from the gunshot. In his hands, Rel was in its cloth. When Jason entered the room, Seth looked up with a serious gaze.

'Seth?' Jason was surprised when he refused to look back at him. After everything that happened, he was withdrawing himself. He knew what it meant. 'Come on Seth.'

Finally Seth did return his attention back to Jason. His dark eyes held no remorse for himself for the day's actions. It was Seth's idea to send Jason back to the house for the car. They didn't expect Edward to crash the party, but Seth immediately read Edward's thoughts and needed for Jason to back him up.

'Maya nearly died today,' he began with a grunt and Seth tightened the grip on Rel. Its yellow glow peeked through the hidden cloth and Jason ignored the faint hum ringing in his ears. 'If it wasn't for Laria...'

'If it wasn't for you, Maya would've died as well,' Jason interrupted. Seth refused to respond. Jason hated to see his friend in such a state. 'Look... I'm going to let the girls stay here for tonight – we've all been through a lot tonight.'

Seth didn't change expression, yet Jason could tell that he was impressed. 'If it wasn't for you, we would've been stuck out there to deal with the police.'

'Yeah, I've had enough of cops for one day and I'm sure you're sick of them too,' Jason replied with a sheepish grin. He went to the living room to see that Maya and Laria were sitting on opposite couches.

He flashed a smile towards Maya who seemed to show a look of understanding.

'You alright?' Jason asked, flinching when Laria turned to face him. Her face was covered in soot, much like Maya's but there was a small cut on her face. It was a tiny thing, but the scarlet colour stuck out like a sore thumb and made him uncomfortable.

'Yeah.' Laria's voice was soft and gentle.

It felt like Jason was under some sort of spell. He picked up the cloth from the bucket filled with blood stained water and squeezed the excess out of it.

Jason's eyes were filled with concentration as he raised his hand. 'Stay still for a sec – you forgot to clean up this scratch.' Once the cloth made contact with Laria's skin, she winced lightly as it stung her. 'Sorry,' he whispered. Jason moved slowly, focusing on his single action before he stared back into Laria's eyes.

It was Laria who pulled away, brushing her hair back. 'Thank you...' Jason placed the cloth back down and stared at the girls, trying to distract himself with a cleared throat.

'It's what friends do,' Jason replied with a small smirk.

'So Brodie called me earlier,' Laria said and Jason stiffened at the name. He didn't really want to know what Brodie did while their lives were in danger. 'He's got Sara to hospital and he's getting his wound treated while he's there. If anyone asks, Sara was drunk and hit her head on a glass bottle; Brodie was protecting Sara from a guy that was shooting at them. The sheriff is "chasing" the drunk as we speak.'

'I see,' Jason muttered under his breath, trying to avoid any sort of Brodie conversation. At least Sara was alright; maybe she would learn to not drink so much. 'Seth agreed with me to let you guys crash here for tonight because let's be honest – I can't drive us without getting caught.'

'Wait.' Maya suddenly looked over to Jason with a frown. 'Are you a shifter as well?'

Jason looked surprised that Maya asked him such a

forward question. 'No...' He lied simply and scratched the back of his head. 'I'm just a simple, plain human.'

Laria looked like she wanted to protest against the idea, but she shrugged it off. 'Jason's known about us for a while.' She quickly explained, before Jason flashed another smile. He was glad that he didn't put Laria through any pressure again.

CHAPTER 23

It had been a week since the bonfire and there was no sign of Edward. Laria remained in her sunken position in her bed, quietly waiting for answers. The mansion was quiet for the first time since she'd arrived.

Haroni never said where he was going and Tracy was at the school which left Laria alone to think about the week before. Edward knew that she had used the bloodlust, which was why he probably let them go.

Was killing someone else really something that she wanted? She swore to Chris that she would kill Edward, but Laria hesitated. Brodie was right; in the end she had to seriously consider fighting Edward. But did Laria really want to take someone's life from them?

Then there was the million dollar question, why were the shifters so desperate in taking her to their side? What did the sacred stones have to do with any of it?

After moping around her room, Laria knew she needed to clear her thoughts. She wore some athletic clothing and tied back her hair. If there was only one way to clear her head, Laria knew that it was to simply exercise her problems away. Writing a note to inform someone of her location, Laria walked out of the mansion to follow a path.

Laria began her jogging pace through the streets. Knowing the familiar route, she decided to let her mind wander. A week ago, Edward was talking about Azu – the Rosa stone that

Tahani ordered her to protect.

Then there was the problem with Tahani. When Laria visited her a few days ago, the dux looked like she was losing her confidence and Laria didn't blame her. They weren't any closer to finding out about the Beast. Laria had to make sure she got down to the truth, but they were probably being careful now that Tahani was behind bars.

But first she would have to-

A brute force slammed into her, knocking her off her feet. Her back connected with the concrete and she groaned at the sudden rush of air escaping her lungs. As she recovered, Laria looked up to see that Jason was in front of her, coughing for air himself.

'I swear, the universe truly wants us to crash into each other,' Jason swore as he offered a hand for her to take. 'But... no matter what the universe says, I will always offer to help you back to your feet.' Without hesitation, Laria took his offered hand and he pulled her up.

'So,' Laria began with a faint smile. She ignored the embarrassing moment and played with a strand of her hair. 'Are you jogging to get your mind elsewhere too?'

'How did you know?' Jason retorted with his boyish grin, wiping the sweat from his forehead and letting out a chuckle. 'It was weird, I was just thinking about you how you haven't been at school at all, lately; sometimes I wonder if you still go.'

A laugh escaped Laria's lips as she realised it as well. 'Oh, you're funny. I'm probably going to end up repeating a year.' If Lesley had been alive, Laria knew that her mother would be scolding her for ditching school.

'That isn't good,' Jason remarked before he offered a smirk. 'Maybe we could tutor each other – I know that me missing school isn't the greatest plan either...'

'But you have an excuse; you have to take care of Seth

while his leg heals,' Laria reminded him. 'Speaking of which how is he?'

'Seth's recovering,' Jason answered, his eyes serious. 'He's been worried about Maya nonstop; she's been a bit distant with Seth ever since she found out. Do you know why?'

'I know no more than you do. I don't even think she went to school – not that I would know.'

Laria felt her mood drop as she stared at Jason, recalling the news that she learnt from Brodie. Jason wasn't just another guy that she met at school – he was Brodie's brother. The first time she met him, Laria kept trying to figure out where she'd seen Jason in the past but now that she knew, it was hard not to see Leon.

It wasn't the main features that got her attention though. His brows were thicker than Brodie's, matching Leon's and the shape of his face was too. His chin was slightly different from Leon but he had the hints of stubble growing.

Laria realised she was staring and she shook her head out of the daze. Of all people, why did he have to be Brodie's brother?

'Hey.' Jason's brow furrowed in concern and Laria almost felt flustered at the attention. 'You did a one eighty on me.' He grabbed her shoulders and stared into her eyes, they didn't match Leon's but they held the tenderness that Brodie's had. 'Is something else bothering you?'

He always had that look of concern in his eyes and now it was up close and personal. In some cases, Laria found it to be incredibly sweet. Jason was a good friend, and he had shown countless times that he cared about her. In a way, it was like Brodie all over again but with different features.

Laria found herself lost between deciding if she should she tell Jason the truth? He had every right in knowing about his heritage. His dad was Leon and his brother was Brodie. But this wasn't her story to tell; it was Brodie's.

She spared a glance towards Jason nervously. 'Brodie told me something last week and it's been driving me nuts.' Jason's eyes narrowed but he remained silent and nodded, allowing her to continue, 'Jason - on the day you got Rel, it was reacting like it would with an extra Forte's presence.'

Jason suddenly stopped, as if he just figured out every secret to the universe. 'What... did you say?'

'Jason, Brodie is your twin brother...' It looked like Jason had a hard time believing her. Her eyes filled with determination to persuade him. 'I'll prove it... Your birthday is on the twenty-third of October, right? Well that happens to be Brodie's birthday – you can even use Rel as proof, it would glow if you touched it.'

When she saw his reaction, Laria knew that he believed her. 'I never even suspected it was me and that means Leon Forte was my father... What about my mother then? Did Mae fake her death all those years ago?'

'I still don't know,' Laria replied honestly before she noticed Jason's tensed body. It was her turn to firmly grab his shoulders and look into his eyes. 'Will you be alright Jason?'

His eyes briefly went to her, but he looked away as soon as he made eye contact. 'Yeah,' he grunted before clearing his throat. 'It was nice talking to you Laria, but I've got to go back home.' Jason gave a small wave before he went back to jogging the way he came from.

***

He still hadn't visited.

Haroni waited outside of his car, looking bored. At first, Haroni hadn't realised he was driving here until he recognised the building.

He wasn't sure if he should believe that Tahani wasn't the

Beast but then again... she didn't show concern for others. From what Zanobi told him, Haroni guessed that it was traumatising enough for her to make her give the humans a cold shoulder.

Then his mind went to Laria. When Laria came out of the station for the first time, she had determination in her eyes. It held no doubt and he knew that she was going to find the Beast's identity. It was a look that Haroni himself had not seen since Abeytu. He realised that Laria trusted Tahani and would do anything to set the woman free.

Finally, Haroni pushed himself from his spot and strolled into the station, recognising Nadia. It seemed that she recognised him as well, making a bee-line towards him with a glare.

'What are you doing here?' Nadia asked sternly.

'I wish to see my dear friend, Tahani,' Haroni replied smugly. Keeping his eyes firmly on the other woman, Haroni saw that she wasn't amused at his request. 'Surely you wouldn't refuse someone of my status?' At first, Nadia kept quiet before she quietly snorted at his behaviour.

'You have a lot of guts to threaten me in front of people, Fallen – my people can lock you up just as quickly,' Nadia stated as she took her keys out from her belt with a scowl. 'I don't fear you, but rather the safety of the shifters and humans alike.' She walked briskly to the next room, allowing Haroni to follow quietly

They made their way to the holding room. Nadia shook her head in disbelief and stormed up to the single cell. 'What's this?' she snapped as Haroni saw nothing in the cell except for an open door.

'Was she meant to be here?' Haroni wondered innocently, just as Nadia turned with a ferocious look.

'I will find that traitor!' Nadia declared, darting out of the room with a scowl to announce Tahani's escape. As Haroni suddenly stood alone in the room, he observed the door and noticed ice. It was frosted over the spot where the keyhole was.

'It looks like she could've escaped whenever she wanted to.' He looked around the cell with a serious gaze. 'However, where would she be now?'

Something – no... Someone nudged his arm from behind, surprising the fallen. That was the first time that someone managed to sneak up behind him and he didn't detect it.

He turned with a raised eyebrow to apologise for being in the way of the officer, but instantly his eyes went wide. 'Tahani?'

Tahani scowled at Haroni as his eyes roamed her body. She was in a police uniform along with the hat. The dux sent a nod. 'Angeli.'

'Are you mad, my dear?' Haroni demanded in a hushed tone. He grabbed her arm and pulled her out of plain sight. 'If I wasn't on your side about this investigation...'

'Yeah, *if.*' A smirk played on Tahani's face, and she looked around warily. 'I need a favour Angeli, which was why I broke out the moment I sensed ya getting in here.'

For a moment, Haroni was surprised that Tahani planned this out carefully. 'What do you wish for me to do?' The response that he got was a simple smirk.

***

Brodie cursed silently when he felt the pain in his shoulder. Being stuck in his father's office was driving him insane; it was a miracle that his father didn't end up going crazy.

After taking a drink from his glass of scotch, Brodie snapped. 'That's it – I can't take it anymore.' He grumbled as he laid his head on the desk. He couldn't care less about the fact he was sleeping on his father's desk. Soon enough the pain from his shoulder faded Brodie realised that he was dreaming.

'Brodie...'

He lifted his head and he felt his breath escape his lungs when he saw Leon in front of the desk with a serious look on his face. Brodie knew that it was a dream; it was impossible that his father would be in his dream unless...

'Rel is close – its presence is drawing near as we speak. Since my death, I have been a part of Rel that can contact you within your spirit,' Leon confirmed.

'Dad...'

'Your behaviour Brodie... The more you act with it... the more likely your bloodlust will erupt.' His eyes hardened at the word. 'You haven't told Jason either...'

'I can't stand him – there's this anger I can't control,' Brodie admitted with a scowl. 'You really went out of your way to hide him, didn't you? No hospital records? Making me resort to using your code and relying on Rel?'

Leon's eyes turned harsh at the thought. 'I figured that it would be something that only you would figure out. But I did not come here to talk to you about Jason, but rather what you've been searching for.'

'You should've told me about the Beast the night that you died,' Brodie growled. Every night since Leon's death, Brodie had searched for his sibling but it only turned out to be a waste of time.

'Tahani Rosa did kill the Laurences, Brodie,' Leon stated truthfully. Brodie suddenly halted and stared at his father's ghost with alarm. 'However,' he added, 'she was under the influence of another presence, so she wasn't aware that it was her.'

'Then how do I find out who took her over?'

'Go to my basement,' Leon ordered. It was enough to make Brodie realise he was serious. 'You know the code for entering. Everything is down there. This is for if you don't believe in what I'm about to tell you.'

'Dad... What are you talking about?' It was Brodie's responsibility to finish off Leon's final job – not as his son but as a Forte that guarded Rel.

Brodie felt the need for the answers. Leon's eyes made contact with him before saying, 'The mole is –'

The door from the office swung open and Brodie woke up on the chair with a heavy breath. His reaction was instant. 'Jason! What the hell are you doing here?' Brodie snapped as Jason's eyes turned into a glare. 'Get out of my house!'

Jason's scowl only deepened as he stormed up to Brodie who noticed that he had never seen Jason so angry before. 'You damn bastard!' Jason screamed. His blue eyes bored into Brodie's. He slammed his hands on the table and Brodie realised that the glowing Rel was next to Jason's hands. 'When were you planning to tell me about this?'

The only way that Jason knew the truth was if Laria told him. 'Does it matter?' Brodie asked, taking the stone away from his brother. 'You know now, though I have a feeling that this hasn't got to do with me sending you and Seth to look for my missing twin.'

'Do you have any idea of what I've been through since I moved here?' Jason asked. 'I was raised up thinking that my own dad hated me! Now I can't even be sure if Mae – the woman I considered to be my mother – is dead because your father just had to give me up!'

'Don't talk about my father that way!' Brodie growled fiercely. 'I lost him because of them wanting my bloodlust as well, so it's not all about you!' He soon calmed himself at the presence of Rel, placing it in the safe next to Verm. 'I don't have time for this,' Brodie realised when he remembered the final source to finding out the traitor. Without another word, Brodie left the office and went to the door of his basement.

Jason followed Brodie silently, still filled with irritation before he stopped at the door. 'What are you doing?'

'Finding the real person who wants to stab us in the back,' Brodie answered gruffly, pressing the key code to the door. 'The Ungue Dux isn't the one we're looking for. Someone else is pulling the strings. This stuff doesn't concern you, so you can get lost.'

The door clicked open and before Brodie could open it, Jason shot out to grab his arm. It stopped Brodie from moving but he glared at Jason.

'It does concern me if it's Tahani. Seth and I are the reason why she was locked up – if it isn't her then I would like to help,' Jason stated with a responding glare. 'Look, I know we hate each other... but as much as you hate to admit it, I've been a part of this mess ever since Edward killed my mother.'

'Alright then,' Brodie grumbled and opened the door, revealing an old wooden staircase into a dark room. He could smell something off. 'Listen to me and shut up – it's bad enough you're in my life.'

Brodie was the first to enter the dark room, relying on his other senses to keep quiet. They hit the concrete floor at the bottom of the steps. As they did, Brodie searched around for a light and flicked the nearest switch. The room was filled with a dim glow, revealing a rotting body on top of an examination table.

'Did you know about this?' Jason asked as he looked at the flesh. 'This is really bad for hygiene.'

'I haven't been in here in a while,' Brodie answered in annoyance, taking in the scent even though it was nauseating. 'He's the same victim that Laria found on the day that you spilt soda on her. It was rumoured that he knew about the Beast and gave a clue... a clue that Father saw.' He turned to see that Jason had his attention on a piece of paper, one that Brodie had to see.

'It looks like some sort of report,' Jason explained as Brodie came closer. He tried squinting his eyes but cursed. 'It's too dark,' he said. Brodie almost rolled his eyes, snatching up the paper.

'Stop complaining about everything,' Brodie scolded and read the first few words of the report... or if he was to be more precise, the letter. His eyes darkened as he remembered the night of his father's death. 'It's for me... like my dad knew I was going to be in here one day.'

'How can you read that?'

'Shifters that can transform into felines have better night vision than others– save for bats or owls. Now shut up and let me read this.' He scanned through the pages, worried of what it was going to say.

'Dear Brodie, if you are reading this letter... then it means that you are in the basement and I am dead... Also, that you want to figure out who the Beast is...'

Brodie read quietly. He continued reading the words that his father had left him, explaining everything from the start.

'Brodie?' Jason walked closer to Brodie. 'What are you reading?'

Brodie's hand tightened on the paper, and he clenched his jaw tightly with fury. 'It can't be...' He slammed the paper on its original spot, storming up the stairs.

'What?' Jason pursued after his twin. Brodie went

through the kitchen and picked up a set of keys. There was no time to find Nadia.

He quickly returned to Jason's side with keys in hand and shot a glare towards Jason. 'I know who the Beast is. Laria's in danger; get in the car.'

CHAPTER 24

Laria jogged her way through the forest path, distracting herself by forcing the mental bars on her bloodlust.

A wave of nausea hit her, making her halt her tracks to lean on a tree. Her breath was raspy from exhaustion, as she looked warily at her surroundings.

Suddenly Laria could smell him. She recognised his scent, different from other shifters, and it triggered the fear that Laria desperately tried locking up. He was different. Now Laria could stand against him and not worry about her fear.

It was time to finish this fight once and for all. If not for Lesley, then it would be for Tahani and Maya – who lost loved ones due to this man.

'You're not being stealthy,' Laria noted as she raised her gaze to see Edward standing on a tree branch above her. His stare was one filled with amusement, making Laria scowl. 'So, it's either that you're overconfident that I will lose myself right now or you're losing your touch.'

'Ah, I don't see fear in your eyes anymore, Laria,' Edward stated as he leapt down from his spot and landed in front of her. 'It's a shame really; it means that I will have to hurt you in order to bring it out.' A familiar pistol appeared from his holster and he pointed it towards Laria. 'I'm in no mood to play games – let's do this quickly.'

'I'm prepared Edward,' Laria stated as her eyes glowed amber. With a cry escaping her lips, Edward hesitated in his shot and Laria took that chance to race towards him.

She tackled him to the ground, pinning his arms down his sides with her knees. Edward's gun flew out of his hand, cursing as Laria felt her fist connect with his cheek. As soon as the shifter groaned, Laria felt the satisfaction bloom in her chest.

Just as she prepared to do it again, Laria wailed at the heat that filled the air. The flames from Edward's hands were small, but it still didn't change the fact that Laria hated fire. She pushed herself away from him, releasing Edward before he used this to his advantage and returned the punch to her face.

She felt a sharp pain in her jaw and fell back. Edward took this time to recover. Before he managed to get to his feet, Laria used her own feet to push him into the ground again. It wasn't much, but Laria regained herself and stood back up to search for the gun.

A silver glint on the ground gained her attention, but she lost it when Edward let out a growl and charged at her. His hand grabbed the collar of her shirt and he lifted her up with a hint of excitement in his eyes.

'Why...?' Laria finally asked and she felt something connect with her gut. The air escaped her lungs as Edward slammed his fist against her body. 'What made you want to take the path of a murderer?'

'You really are naive,' Edward sneered and threw her into the ground. 'I am a Rosa! I like to kill because it's fun.' He retrieved his gun from the ground and strolled his way to Laria She managed to prop herself up on her elbows. 'Our bloodlust was a result of a horrifying experience.' Edward lifted his gun and Laria felt the fear flicker back to life. 'My experience was back in the dark times – when humans thought nothing about us except that we were rejected creatures of nature.'

A loud gun shot went off and Laria let out a scream of

agony. He had missed her vital organs on purpose; Laria knew that he still needed her alive. Blood seeped from her left shoulder and Laria automatically raised her uninjured arm to nurse the wound.

'Do you know what they did to people like us seventy years ago?' the shifter questioned with a sneer, approaching her before he kicked her in the face. Her skull smacked into the ground and Laria found herself staring up at Edward's scowl. 'They either killed us or locked us up in tiny cells. Like animals!'

Laria's anguished screams echoed in the forest from the pain when he stomped his foot against her wounded shoulder. The bullet was only making it worse.

'We had no food – barely any water,' Edward snarled at the memories. 'And do you know what happened to the ones with powers? We were tied down with chains, doctors took our blood, injected us with agonising things I still do not know of! When my bloodlust was unleashed – I took control of it and I burned them!' Hearing the shot, Laria flinched and expected pain, but it looked as if he missed on purpose. 'Burned every single one of them! Now you want to stop me? Don't hold back on your bloodlust, Laria Alfero.'

'I won't... do it... I am going to keep fighting.'

Edward scoffed as he raised his hand directly near her face, 'I see that physical pain is not very persuasive... but maybe mental pain is.' His hand instinctively snapped up and grabbed the arrow that would've pierced his heart. He looked at it in his hands. 'Ungue Dux – you know that you shouldn't be shooting arrows at a dear, old cousin like me.'

Laria's eyes suddenly widened and she tilted her head back to see Tahani holding a bow with a quiver of arrows strapped to her back.

'Tahani...' Laria whispered in shock as she saw the cold

expression from the other woman.

'I owe ya a favour then Edward.' Tahani pulled another arrow from her quiver and prepared to fire. 'I think it would be fair if I killed the bastard that murdered Kaeylin!' Laria's eyebrows furrowed as she focused on the dux, before she found her chance to strike at Edward while he was distracted. She kicked her leg out from under his knees, forcing him to buckle.

Edward cursed as he caught himself, but an arrow punctured itself through his arm. A growl escaped from the shifter as he dropped his gun and Laria crawled to it. She forced the pain into the back of her mind and her hands clasped around the cool metal.

'Laria!'

She didn't notice that Edward recovered so fast until he grabbed her neck to shove her into the ground. She released the weapon to claw at his hand, fighting to breathe as her nose and mouth filled with dirt. He raised his injured hand towards Tahani who drew out her next arrow to shoot.

'Drop your bow, Ungue Dux, or Laria loses her life.'

Tahani hesitated. Eventually the dux chuckled and kept her position.

'Yer bluffing,' Tahani observed as a smirk. 'Yer know that Laria is the last Alfero shifter that we need... and ya need her to reunite the Corvena...' It made sense to her; Edward was after Azu and the remainder of the stones. Four deaths, four lives and the Uniter. Of course, Laria being an Alfero, needed to use her stone to reunite the Corvena.

Edward let out a chuckle in response. 'There is more than one Alfero that fits the bill.' Laria felt the pressure tighten her neck, pushing her face further into the dirt and she coughed. She had never felt the lack of air before, but it felt just like flames.

Fire. Edward's powers.

Her power was the only way she was going to get out alive. It was the only shot she had, even if she knew nothing about her abilities. Maybe this time she would be lucky, since her death was forcing her inner instinct to react.

Raising her hands to wrap her fingers around Edward's arm, Laria tried to focus on her darker counterpart. Her heart started picking up pace, triggering Lux. The bloodlust began to stir from its slumber again.

Lux...

Hatred. Laria hated to be connected to her dark counterpart. It was like fire, destroying everything in its path to cause misery. But at the same time, fire led the ones who were lost like leaders.

Whatever her bloodlust was, she didn't want to have any connection to it. It was the reason why so many problems happened throughout the previous weeks – throughout the centuries of the shifters! As the back of her mind darkened in unconsciousness, she found the renewed strength the second she saw a pair of amber eyes flash in the back of her head.

Laria pulled free of Edward's grip with renewed strength. His snarl widened when his grip on her neck weakened. 'Life drainer,' Edward growled weakly as he realised. 'Just like your father...'

'Tahani, now would be a good time to shoot that thing!'

Laria's loud voice got Tahani into action, she fired into Edward's shoulder and he let out another grunt. As he crashed to the ground in defeat, Laria slowly pushed herself to her feet and saw that Tahani drew another arrow. Her animalistic eyes narrowed in hatred as she pointed the arrow in the direction of the injured shifter.

'I missed that shot – a pity,' the dux muttered. Edward didn't react but amusement flashed in his eyes, angering the dux. 'Yer the reason why Kaeylin's dead,' Tahani hissed in fury as she held her shot. Laria went up to the woman and heard Tahani mutter. 'I have waited ten years to finally finish ya and I have to say that it is quite fun!'

'Come on dux,' Edward taunted. Tahani's eyes remained locked on him. 'Kill me right now... Shoot me in the heart.'

'Tahani.' Laria grabbed the dux's shoulder. Tahani didn't move as Laria continued. 'I know that you want to avenge your sister... but it won't do her justice. Think about Maya; you can protect her to honour your sister. I know a Rosa likes to take another's life but don't stoop to his level.'

The tension was weighing on Laria. Tahani once told her that she wasn't to be ordered, but hopefully things had changed.

Finally, Tahani let out a cool sigh and her eyes returned to their original colour. She lowered the bow and shot a familiar smirk to Laria. 'Yer pretty brave for standing up against me while I was about to shoot an arrow.'

Laria was glad to see the smirk. 'Hey – I trust you and you're my friend. I'm not going to give up on you just because you like to kill a bit more than I do.'

'Alright,' Tahani said as she returned her arrow in its quiver and smirked. 'Yer can stay here and watch Mister Hot Pants over here while I head out to Cheyenne. It's time to find the bastard that sent me to –!'

A gunshot interrupted them and Laria felt like the world stopped around her. Her movements were sluggish as she turned to see that Tahani's eyes were wide with alarm. Crimson slowly blossomed in the centre of Tahani's chest. She reached up to touch the blood. She choked out the remaining air and spared a glance towards Laria who felt like her own heart was torn to pieces.

Laria finally found her voice and she whispered one name,

'Tahani...' The dux fell to the ground, her body dropping like a rock. Laria regained her senses and panicked, 'Tahani!' She crouched down next to Tahani, who cursed at the pain. 'Tahani, stay with me!'

'Laria – thank yer for trusting me,' Tahani whispered back but her eyes slowly closed as she lost consciousness.

Laria let it out a scream in pure rage. Her magister was dying in front of her. Edward was going to be miserable before she ended him. She felt the anger bubble up to the surface as her eyes flashed amber and they darted towards Edward.

Edward was leaning on a tree; his hand dropped the pistol that Laria had forgotten. 'It looks like she serves a good purpose after all.' He laughed at Laria's hateful gaze. 'You finally let your bloodlust go, good job...'

Tahani was dying and Laria couldn't control herself. Her own limbs shook in rage as she got back to her feet; the pain in her arm forgotten. The tips of her fingernails sharpened into vicious clawed hands. That was when Laria knew that it wasn't her anymore – Lux had gained full control of her once again.

'I will rip out your heart.' It didn't even sound like her as she stalked her way to Edward. He looked satisfied as her clawed hands grasped the collar of his shirt, picking him up with newfound strength. 'I think your heart will make an excellent trophy.'

Without another word, Edward let out a cry as her hand went through his chest. Lux smiled at the feeling of his bones snapping. His heart was beating frantically underneath her palm, like it was truly afraid of its fate. It felt exhilarating to literally have his life in the palm of her hand; it was unfortunate that it was only going to last a moment.

Edward stared back at her and his lips formed a sneer.

'You lost Laria. It will come to life.'

As she tore out his heart, she heard a voice in the back of her mind screaming at her to stop. The heart remained beating in her hand, warm like the fire he manipulated. Laria finally regained herself but it was already too late. Edward's lifeless body dropped beside her.

See? Lux reminded with a snide chuckle of amusement. *It turns out that you need me more than you realise, Laria.*

It took her a second to comprehend what happened. Laria felt disgusted and dropped the heart, starring at her blood-soaked hands. She hated this – how could she want to murder someone like a cruel creature. This is not what Lesley would've wanted.

'No,' Laria's eyes began to sting as she went back to Tahani. In a panic, Laria screamed out Tahani's name and cradled the dux, who remained unmoving. 'Tahani help me, please!' she cried out, holding her friend close but Laria stopped when she felt a heartbeat. It was faint. 'I promise that you aren't going to die Tahani!' Laria lifted the dux's body and groaned at her own injures as she carried the woman.

The thoughts of the bloodlust still remained in her mind. No matter how hard she tried, the inner demon was always going to fight against its mental cage. Whether it was her friends or her enemies, Laria knew that it wouldn't hold back on its kills.

Laria tripped over a root and felt the pain burn in her arm as she landed on it. 'I'm not going to let you die Tahani; I promise you that you will survive this! You're a Rosa, you will get through this.'

'Laria.'

A familiar voice made Laria stop and she turned to see Zanobi with panic. He would help. His expression remained hard as he looked towards her and Tahani's unconscious body.

It took him a moment to realise that she was bleeding. 'What happened?' His shock showed in his face when he saw that Tahani was unconscious.

Once she heard his question, the tears reformed in her eyes and Laria broke down. 'I was stupid,' Laria sobbed as he approached them. 'I told Tahani not to kill him and she paid the price... It's my fault she's like this... I want to save her...'

'But Laria.' Zanobi frowned and left her body as it remained. 'Don't you know? Tahani really killed those people! She's the Beast that was willing to send you to the enemies.'

'I don't believe it for a second,' Laria retorted fiercely as she stood by her friend's slumped body. 'Tahani saved my life – if it wasn't for her, I would've been dead.' She ignored the stare from Zanobi as the tears streamed down her face. 'We've got to save her. You of all people should be up for saving her life.'

'We can't,' Zanobi admitted and Laria immediately looked up to see his serious gaze. 'As we speak, each of the duxes are on their way to chase after her – if we're caught here then we would be considered traitors as well. If we leave her here, then we can start harnessing your power... and we can get Azu from your friend Maya to protect it as Tahani wanted.'

'I refuse to leave her a second time,' Laria protested desperately before she repeated the sentence in her head. 'Wait a minute...' Zanobi turned back to frown at her. 'How did you know about Maya? Tahani said that she only recently found out when we were both in Cheyenne... I was the only one that knew.'

'*It's because he possessed her body and gained all of the knowledge while you were there. He's the Beast.*'

'Brodie!' Laria cried out when she heard the second familiar voice. Brodie and Jason both rushed into the scene. Jason looked determined, keeping a hard stare and Brodie looked like he was ready to kill something.

'Get away from him Laria,' Jason called out before he joined his brother in glowering at Zanobi.

Brodie's face formed a dark snarl. 'Zanobi is the one!' he snapped and growled in fury. 'Zanobi has been the one responsible for the other murders and he used his ability to possess Tahani when you guys went to Cheyenne.'

'Ah, the Forte brothers finally united at last,' Zanobi scoffed. For a moment, he remained silent with a sinister smile grew across his face. 'But I have a feeling that you aren't the only ones that have arrived.'

Before Laria could ask, she saw Seth enter from the other side. His brown eyes stern as he directed his glare towards the Beast. 'Zanobi. When Jason didn't come back right away I thought the worst. I'm glad that I wasn't wrong – we will stop you together.'

Laria was surprised that he arrived with his injuries still recovering.

'You bastard Zanobi!' Brodie snapped furiously and clenched his fist. His hazel eyes were filled with rage. 'You're the reason why my father's dead! How dare you stand here and act like you're on our side!'

'It's pity really. You don't have a chance – not like this,' Zanobi muttered as his eyes went towards Jason. He stiffened as Zanobi's expression darkened. 'I never killed Leon Forte – he knew that I was the killer though and I needed to cover my tracks. The man that killed your father is a man I envy more than anything.'

'Who is the man that killed Leon?' Laria felt her stomach churn at the grin Zanobi sent her way. 'Is he an Alfero?!'

'That's right Laria, but he's just not any Alfero,' Zanobi sneered. All four adolescents widened their eyes in fear and Laria trembled as Zanobi pointed a finger towards her. 'He is your flesh and blood… your father!'

It felt like a bucket of icy cold water had been poured on top of her. Her father was the one who killed, Leon? Memories flashed in the back of her mind when she was discussing her father's illness. Bloodlust killed the shifters from the inside as it escaped its shell.

'Just as I assumed,' Seth said coldly and brought out a hunting knife. Laria was frozen in shock, unable to move. 'We will stop you whatever it takes.'

Judging from Brodie's angry look, it seemed that he didn't notice her presence anymore. That was when Brodie snapped, his eyes turning bright with rage as he charged towards Zanobi.

'Brodie, wait!' Laria screamed in distress, not seeing that Zanobi had pulled out a blade to attack. As soon as the blade made contact with Brodie; Laria's gut flipped in horror. His blood seemed to float in the air as the knife pulled free, Brodie's features now filled with surprise as his body dropped to the ground in defeat.

'Brodie!' Jason tried rushing towards him but Zanobi was faster. Jason let out a groan as Zanobi stabbed at him and Laria screamed as she saw Jason look her way. 'Run… Laria…' He dropped to the ground and Laria felt the rage bubble up again.

It was Seth who struck next, preparing his blade but Zanobi was faster. With a swift, flat palmed strike to the chest, Seth was flying into the tree. He smacked into the ground and growled at the new wound he received.

'Pitiful,' Zanobi commented as he turned to Laria. 'Let's go then – I can drag you kicking and screaming if you wish.'

'Screw you – I'll never forgive you for hurting my friends,' Laria snarled as her eyes turned amber.

Then it happened.

She felt a wave of dizziness hit her and a sharp pain throughout her body. It was like her bones were snapping and Laria let out another cry of agony when her body dropped to the ground.

Judging from the look from Zanobi's face, Laria could easily figure out what was happening. She was told a shifter transformed into their animal form due to their needs. Her need was to stop him.

Zanobi appeared somewhat smug when he looked down to see Laria wailing in agony. Another bone snapped with a sickening crunch and Laria clenched her jaw together to shut out the pain.

I can do it... She told herself. *I don't need Lux to help me!* As Zanobi tried to approach her, Laria tried to stand back up, but she felt a similar presence. Zanobi's expression dropped to one of irritation as he glared at the new figures.

'Just my luck,' Zanobi muttered dryly when Laria felt the presence of more than one. The duxes arrived just when they were needed.

'I should've seen it coming,' Takon stated as he stood in front of Laria. 'The fact that Tahani didn't remember her kills was rather suspicious.' The Mandati Dux turned back an offered a look to the remaining duxes. 'Hugh and Tara –take the injured and attend to their wounds immediately. Jyle, Nadia and myself will deal with this traitor.'

'Yes, Mandati Dux.' Their response was immediate, and the two duxes went to work. Laria couldn't fight the pain anymore and slowly her consciousness faded to black.

CHAPTER 25

Haroni fumbled with his phone, a scowl on his face. After having enough of the device, Haroni's eyes went over to the unconscious figure on the bed.

He had no idea why he was sitting here, waiting for Tahani to regain her consciousness. It had only been a few days ago when Takon came to visit him and told him the dire news. Zanobi defected against them, Tahani was recovering but in a critical condition and Laria had finally transformed.

Finally, Haroni realised that he appreciated Tahani. Then Haroni's mind couldn't help but wander to Zanobi who had pretended that he was on their side.

Anger stirred when he allowed Laria to get close to the traitor. In the back of his mind, his past self whispered taunts about him being stuck in his position because he didn't kill Abeytu right away.

Sometimes Haroni wondered what would've happened if he had killed Abeytu without hesitation that day. Would Tracy have ever forgiven him? No – that wasn't the case; Tracy still hadn't accepted the fact that he killed the man she loved.

Haroni didn't personally know Abeytu. But his choices did lead Haroni to his life. During his years on this earth, Haroni had made many friends and had the privilege of having a goddaughter.

Also, if Haroni hadn't protested, he never would've met Tahani Rosa.

'Urgh... I'm gonna get drunk as soon as I recover.'

Haroni's brow furrowed when the Tahani slowly opened her eyes. He flashed a warm smile in her direction and brushed her hair from her face. The action looked somewhat tender. 'Hey there, dear.'

'Haroni,' Tahani whispered in confusion. Haroni's smile slowly dropped to a look of alarm as Tahani winced and felt her chest. Normally she would've called him by his nickname. This was probably the first time he had heard his name from her lips. It sounded foreign. 'How long has it been?'

'Three days,' Haroni replied before he straightened up. 'How much do you remember? From what I gather, being shot in the chest isn't pleasant.' According to the doctors, the bullet had been centimetres from her heart.

Maybe her strength was a Rosa thing. Her stubborn attitude was probably the reason why she managed to survive.

'Yer right,' Tahani grumbled. 'It bloody hurts alright – I can't remember much... except for being shot and Laria screaming.' She spared a gaze around the room as she sat up. 'Speaking of which... where is that kiddo?'

'Laria's in the forest, training her animal transformation.'

Tahani's eyes widened. 'Wait! What exactly did I miss out on?!' She noticed that Haroni's expression dropped. She tilted her head in confusion. 'Haroni?'

It definitely sounded weird. 'Tahani... Zanobi possessed you on the night you killed Seth's parents.' Her expression copied his and Haroni gave her a firm look. 'He was the traitor that set you up.'

'No...' Tahani whispered and she stared at her hands. 'That's impossible...' Haroni couldn't see her face and he couldn't tell what she was thinking. 'Is he dead?'

'No,' Haroni explained and he would've sworn that he saw Tahani relax. 'Zanobi managed to escape – Nadia has not slept.'

'I'm gonna drag him back to our side then,' Tahani announced with a smirk. 'I'm gonna go through hell and back just to save him from the darkness.'

'Tahani...'

'Yeah, I know what ya thinking.' Tahani's face formed into a scowl. 'I shouldn't go save someone who put me through so much, right?' When Haroni lacked an answer, Tahani spared Haroni a grin. 'But he saved *us* from going to the darkness. I owe him that much...' Haroni was unable to respond at first and Tahani jumped to conclusions. 'Look – I ain't normally that cheesy and lame but I have to do this for him!'

'I understand,' Haroni admitted. Tahani was filled with surprise at Haroni's confession. 'In that case, let me be with you to help him.'

'Thanks, Haroni! And no backing out of it! I'm a woman that punches hard if yer back out.'

He sighed as he heard his name the third time. It definitely didn't sound right when it came from her. With a chuckle, he added, 'Just call me Angeli.'

***

Jason yawned as he went through the television channels. His fingers automatically pressed the button on the remote and the television stopped on the news. The reporter was going on about a story that had to do with Edward.

It looked like they made it to the news again. It turned out Laria wasn't exactly gentle when she delivered punishments.

Jason winced and switched off the television and pushed himself to his feet. Seth's wound had slowly recovered and he'd already headed back to school to catch up on work.

But Jason had a new problem– how was he going to get through this? Was he supposed to get over the fact that Brodie was his twin brother? Knowing him, Brodie would probably pretend that they'd never spoke and expected their lives would go back to normal.

But Jason knew that no one's life could go back to normal after what they'd gone through. He had literally been cut with some blade like a medieval battle victim.

A sigh escaped his lips as he settled back into the couch and allowed his eyes to rest. Well, it could've been worse: Edward was dead, Brodie found out who his brother was, Laria managed to turn and he was seeing Heather.

He was still forgetting something. Slowly he walked towards his room and found the single envelope on the table. His fingers shook as he opened the letter. He may be unable to find Leon Forte, but Jason could do her final wish of reading it.

Jason only feared the worse as his eyes scanned the paper. When he recognised his mother's writing he felt like something was cutting into his heart at the memory. Finally, he sat down.

> *Dear Jason,*
>
> *If you're reading this, then I'm gone. I know now would be better than any other time for the truth. I'm not sure if I can say everything that you need to know on this piece of paper... but I promise I'll get down to the most important things.*
>
> *You see, I feel like a coward. I felt that if you didn't know, then you would be safer from this world but in the end, I really am making up excuses.*
>
> *So here it is.*
>
> *We left Cheyenne because you were destined for more than being just a normal boy. Our world is filled with the supernatural, but in this town there are shape shifters. They want to fight for peace. The reason I am telling you this is because of my next confession.*

Jason, you're not my son. Your father still lives. His name is Leon Forte. You were a second child to my sister, who passed on the day you were born. Her death shattered her husband, and we knew that you would never be safe so he passed you to me. Even though he loved you, Leon Forte was stuck with the curse of the shifter and the desire for vengeance was one of the reasons why he had to give you up. While his instincts blamed you for his wife's death, he would never want to.

Your father gave you up in order to give you the best chance. Goodbye Jason, I wish that you have the best future.

Love Mae.

Jason didn't realise that he was actually crying until he felt the tear trail down his face. Mae wasn't his mother but a woman that Jason never knew. His hand tightened the hold on the letter, before he placed his face into his palms.

'I'm so sorry, Mum.' It was his fault. Jason was going to do at least one thing that his mother wished. Jason was going to have the best future possible.

***

In the forest, a flash of grey revealed itself from the trees. As soon as the figure came into the clearing, a large, grey canine let out a soft growl. The top half of its body was a silvery grey and it blended in with the white legs and underbelly. It kept its amber eyes on its surroundings, trying to pinpoint any movement. Its large head sniffed the air, catching the scent of the creatures of the forest.

Slowly the canine let out pained yelps and it slowly morphed into the form of a naked Laria. She groaned as her human form took over and soon enough, she was panting for air. The lack of clothes made Laria shiver, she hated her new condition of having to take off clothes whenever she was about to shift. Wearing no clothes around a forest made her feel uncomfortable.

This transformation control was not as easy as Tahani said it was. First the pain as the bones snapped into place made Laria wish that she didn't have to turn into a wolf. She would then practise her new form, sprinting through the trees, focusing on her other senses as her inner animal took over.

So far Laria trained her transformation solo; hopefully Tahani would recover soon. In a way, Laria was desperate to start her training once again; solo training was a lot harder than people let on. As Laria went to throw on her clothes, she cursed lightly at the healing bullet wounds in her shoulder and arm.

As soon as Laria was dressed, she exited the forest and headed to Silver Roots. She hadn't been to a social place in a while and Laria was hungry. Without another thought, she entered the building and looked around for a familiar face. Disappointment flashed in her features when Laria didn't recognise anyone and took her own seat.

The waitress didn't bother her for long, giving her a small plate of fries and a drink of lemonade. Laria kept to herself, chewing on her lunch thoughtfully as she stared into space. Ever since she had transformed, Lux had been more involved with Laria. There were constant whispers, reminding Laria that she had to be on her guard.

Then there was the issue of her father being the man that led the rebellious shifters that lost control of themselves.

Why did it have to be her father? It irritated her. Edward was one guy – and the only reason why he ended up dying was because Laria lost control of herself when he shot Tahani. Would she be able to take out the man that she had to call her father?

Laria didn't know him well... but in the past, she had gotten into fights because Sara deliberately wanted to rile her up. Yet the thoughts of killing her own flesh and blood made her feel sick to the stomach. She let out a sigh of frustration and slammed her head on the table, ignoring the sharp pain.

You're weak, Mistress.

Laria froze at the sound of Lux as the bloodlust chuckled. Silently, Laria pulled herself up but she didn't comment.

You think you're strong enough? Lux taunted from Laria's mind. The flash of amber eyes haunted her to her bones. *I've been living in the same blood as your ancestors, you will fall victim just like your father.*

'No!' Laria yelled out angrily, startling the rest of Silver Roots. As the bloodlust fell silent, Laria silently cursed, paying the bill for the food and storming out. She couldn't fall victim to Lux.

***

Brodie noticed the look that his aunt was giving him.

'Leon never trusted Zanobi,' Tara said angrily as she shook her head. 'Yet, I dismissed it due to Zanobi's actions. He was a deputy and the sheriff had a good eye when it came down to recruits. In the end, he ended up being the reason for Leon's death and he managed to hurt you.'

Brodie felt the pain across his abdomen, reminding him that Zanobi had cut them down. It still felt strange to think Zanobi as an enemy. Finally Brodie saw that Tara flashed him a smile.

'Leon would be proud.'

He believed his aunt. Zanobi had declared that it was Laria's father who killed Leon. Now it made sense to why he looked familiar at the wake.

Before Brodie could speak up, a loud knock came from the

front door. Tara offered another smile and went to open the door. As she opened it, Brodie heard the sharp gasp from his aunt before raising his head.

'You...'

'Hey Miss Forte.' Jason's familiar voice stopped Brodie from having pleasant thoughts. Brodie scowled and approached the door, noticing that Jason was standing outside still. 'I'm sorry but I must speak with your nephew.'

'I don't want to talk.' Brodie's response was flat and determined.

Jason's eyes hardened. 'It won't be long.' A promise. It didn't take Tara long to piece the information together.

'I heard you found out about your heritage,' Tara spoke up before she let out a sigh. 'I'm sorry for keeping it from you when we met.'

'You knew about it?' Brodie wondered, gazing at his aunt who nodded. He kept himself from demanding answers from his aunt and turned away. Of course she knew; she was his father's sister. But it would've helped if she had told him. 'Alright, it doesn't matter right now. What the hell are you doing here?'

'I'll give you two a minute,' Tara decided heading to the kitchen to raid the fridge.

'I came here for a favour,' Jason proposed, sounding as nervous as he appeared to be. Brodie raised an eyebrow. 'We have the same father and mother. That makes us both shifters... correct?'

'Yes, but I was the one who got the shifter gift.' Brodie answered seriously.

'We don't know when the shifters will return,' Jason reminded him, his eyes still kept low and nervous for his next few words. 'I think it's a good idea if I train with you.'

'What?!' Brodie spat.

'Look, I know that we don't get along at all,' Jason said. 'But... I think we should at least try to get along – who knows what could happen and, whether you like it or not, I'm the only person that you can talk to.'

'Wrong, there's Aunt Tara,' Brodie corrected, folding his arms with pride. For a moment Jason's eyes went over to the spot that his aunt previously stood in. A frown deepened on his features as he thought about Brodie's words.

'This is my first time seeing her outside of school,' Jason pointed out. 'I have a feeling that she doesn't come here often – so there's no use lying to me about that one.' Brodie cursed under his breath, wishing that Jason hadn't seen through his lie that easily.

Brodie sighed with defeat. 'Alright, fine... you can train with me. Just one condition.' Jason looked back at Brodie, confused. 'We do this my way. So there's no whining and nothing changes between us. If you want to survive then you'll have to do everything I say. Are we clear?'

It appeared as if Jason was seriously considering this deal. Good. Brodie didn't want him to back out like a coward in the last minute. Finally Jason smirked and for a moment, Brodie though he saw his deceased father. 'You are crystal clear.'

***

David Embers, Golden Cliff's resident history teacher, clicked his tongue in boredom as a woman in a black suit spoke. Mayor Susan Cana, public figure towards the town and head of the hunting organisation that targeted unknown shifters.

'Mayor we have to do something,' said a fellow hunter and David frowned. Yes, they did have to do something.

'And we will,' the mayor said with a serious frown. 'We can't let history repeat – Kaeylin Rosa's intentions weren't to let us turn into monsters. But, I believe it's time to start ending the bloodlines.'

'Wait a minute Mayor Cana.' David said, repeating the words in his head. 'I teach history. I have students that are shifters – they wouldn't dare hurt an innocent life.'

'I know,' Susan replied sadly but her features quickly turned to a grave expression. 'However, we need to start making sacrifices. People have died; we can't afford to let them roam!'

'But we can't just kill innocents!' David argued, standing against the mayor. As the leader of the town, she was meant to be being careful. Attacking the supernatural was not a wise choice.

Immediately the mayor sent him a cold look. 'At what part did I not say we're making sacrifices? Keep quiet, David.'

David found himself speechless and he growled lowly under his breath. This wasn't a good plan; the mayor was a naturally wise woman but she had been acting rather foolish with her choices. Killing the shifters wasn't going to solve anything.

'So that's why, from next month I will start recruiting more people to join our cause,' Susan announced with a serious gaze. 'We will conduct an interview with everyone and see who has the potential. Who is with me?'

The audience cheered in agreement, but David remained silent.

What was running through her mind?

***

'I hear that Charmi wants to plot vengeance,' Zanobi admitted to another figure, who had his back to Zanobi, staring out of the window at the city below them.

'It won't end well for her to say the least.' Slowly the man turned and his eyes met Zanobi's. 'She's just a distraction – we don't want them knowing our intentions.'

'Of course not,' Zanobi said and noticed the glowing green stone. 'How long do you think it will be until your daughter realises that Viri is with us?'

Lucien's eyes remained stern and his gaze went to the glowing stone. 'I can sense her right now – she has no idea where to start searching. You know how the sacred stone works – it gives us a feeling of every Alfero out there. There are only few of us in the world so it's easier locating her. Once she finds Azu along with Tahani– we will take it from them.'

'And what of Rel and Verm?'

'Don't worry Zanobi... I believe that Charmi will cause enough disturbances for the Forte and Laurence boys to reveal their stones' location.' Placing Viri back in his pocket, Lucien stared out of the window with determination in his eyes. 'We will unite the Corvena once again with Viri, Rel, Azu and Verm.'

Zanobi nodded in agreement as his eyes darkened. Everything was beginning to fall into place, the four families' bloodlust was only step one. 'Yes,' he replied. 'They are indeed ready to awaken from their slumber.'

Four deaths, four lives and the Uniter.

It was time to take everything back.

A message from the author...

For the strangers that wished me luck, to the family that encouraged me and to my biggest inspiration which brought life to my stories. Thank you for everything.